THE BREAKING POINT

TAYLOR DELONG

ALSO BY TAYLOR DELONG

Creek Valley Creamery Series

Rocky Road

After Eight

Tin Roof Sunday

Cold Brew

Forever in Laketon Series

Waiting on Forever

Forever Squared

Forever and a Day

Laketon 2.0

Love Unscripted

Life Unscripted

Brew Play Love

Rocky Water Series

Defining Us

The Breaking Point

Murrtham's Tree Farm Series

The Magic of Us

The Magic of Her

The Magic of Baseball

Love on the Tree Farm (Box Set)

Standalones

The Highway Ride

Loving Rebel

Whiskey Tears

Can't Buy My Love (Girl Power Romance)

Where Forever Leads (Falls Village)

The Lawn Boy (All American Boy)

Up to Fate part of the Steamy Shorts anthology

Cathie,
You knew there was more to Natalie than what she shared with others almost before I did. Thank you for your encouragement. Here's to friendship, support, and to closing down Panera too many times to count.

THE BREAKING POINT PLAYLIST

Mercy Shawn Mendes
One Call Away Charlie Puth
Where the Boat Leaves From Zac Brown Band
Crash My Party Luke Bryan
The Good Stuff Kenny Chesney
Need You Now Lady Antebellum
Buy Me a Boat Chris Janson
Head Over Boots Jon Pardi
Hurricane Luke Combs
Bad at Love Halsey
Ask Me How I Know Garth Brooks
Hard to Love Lee Brice
What Ifs Kane Brown
Waiting for Superman Daughtry
Love Me Anyway P!nk ft. Chris Stapleton
True Colors Cyndi Lauper

PROLOGUE

NATALIE

FOURTH GRADE

The kids are making fun of me again. It's only day one, but it's started already. The teachers don't say anything because even they don't pay me enough attention to notice. Or care. I'm not sure which at this point. I'll just be over here, swinging by myself on the swings, kicking up the dirt as my hand-me-down sneakers trail through it as I drag them along. Back and forth. Back and forth. My big toe is about to pop through on the right sneaker, but Mom told me it will be at least another few weeks until I can get a new pair. In fact, her exact words were, "Natalie, you know we can't afford luxuries right now. Try to make those last a few more weeks." As if sneakers—the one of two pairs of shoes I have to my name—are a luxury, especially when you buy them at Goodwill. Remembering my conversation with Mom has me picking up my sneakers so they don't drag too much.

Recess is almost over. I see the teachers looking at their watches, getting ready to blow their whistles. And then the other fourth graders will take off for the door, needing to be first in line. Every day. They have to be first. To get back into a place where the teachers lecture at us for *hours on end. Yeah kids, let's race to be first in line so we can be told where to sit, when to stand, and need permission to use the bathroom. I sometimes wish I knew why the kids were so ready and willing to get back to class. Recess is where we had some freedom. The time when as long as no one notices me, I can hide out and just pretend I'm somewhere else.* Someone *else.*

When I hear the first whistle blow, I stop pumping my legs. I know I've got a good three-four minutes before I have to be at the end of the line and can slide in under the teachers' radar. The second whistle blows about one minute later. I know; I counted the seconds in my head. It was exactly fifty-eight seconds. The third, and final whistle, will come soon, but I have to get off my swing before that one sounds.

Even though the swing is going extremely slow, I stumble on the landing when I jump off. It's subtle, and I catch myself pretty quickly, but apparently not quickly enough.

"Have a good trip, Splatalie?" I hear from behind me.

Just what I need. *Janice Brixton. The meanest "mean girl" if ever there was one. I used to think I should fight back, but I've gotten wiser over the years. Now, I don't let her see how she affects me. I've grown a thicker skin the last three years, not just because of Janice, but she's definitely added to it.*

Suddenly, I'm being pushed from behind, and still a little unsteady from getting off the swing, I topple forward, landing face-first in the dirt. My stupid arms forget to brace my fall, so I face-plant hard. Before I can get up, I hear Janice's cackle and her sarcastic, "Be sure to wipe the dirt off your face. We wouldn't want anyone mistaking you for a mud person."

Forcing back my tears, I slowly push my way up to sitting. Gazing around as I wipe my face with my palms, I notice someone walking toward me. Wow, a teacher actually out to help the poor girl.

As he makes his way closer to me, I realize it's not a teacher at all. It's a boy, about my age, whom I've never seen before. He isn't wearing mesh shorts like all the other boys wear; instead, his khaki cargo shorts come to about his knee. The brown shirt he wears enhances the choco-

late in his eyes. When he kneels next to me, I can see his left knee is all scraped up, a Band-Aid covering most of the scratches.

Reaching out his hand to help me up, he asks, "Are you okay?" His expression is somber, but there's kindness to it. In his voice, I hear an accent from a different place. It's not necessarily distinct, but it doesn't exactly match the ones heard around here either.

Happily, I reach out for his hand and allow him to help me up. I wipe the dirt off my legs as best I can and notice a tiny bleed on my left knee. At about the same time, my new friend notices it too.

"Your knee is bleeding. Come on, I'll take you to the nurse." And just like that, I know we will be friends.

I don't let go of his hand, and he doesn't seem to release mine either. "I'm Natalie," I whisper as we walk past the kids lining up.

"Grayson." It's the matter of fact way he says it that somehow manages to make me smile even bigger.

Walking past the line, I see the kids staring. I hear them whispering to others standing around them. As we pass by Janice, I stick out my tongue.

Ha ha, Janice, you won't get me down with my new friend here.

Her eyes bug out of her head and she turns around to whisper to the others around her, except there's no one there to listen. The line has already started moving and she just stands there, gaping at me.

I don't even notice what Grayson mentions to the teacher; I'm too busy goading Janice. By the time she's out of sight, we are already inside and heading down to the Nurse's Office. He walks me inside, but then he lets go of my hand and turns around and walks out. I step cautiously up to the desk; the nurse and I don't have the best relationship.

"I need a Band-Aid, please." I somehow manage to get my mouth to form words. It takes Mrs. Bryer a full minute to acknowledge my presence and when she finally does, she doesn't hide the scowl on her face well. Nor the eye roll.

"Oh, Natalie, it's just you." Before she moves from behind her desk, she goes back to finishing something up on a form in front of her. "What's wrong this time?"

"*Um, I fell, and I um, just need a Band-Aid.*" I don't bother to look up at her.

"*And they sent you to me for a Band-Aid?*" She's clearly agitated but with a huff, she gets up out of her chair and waddles her plump body to grab a bandage and wipe from her stash. "*Sit,*" she commands, motioning to the hard chair next to her desk. Not the comfortable seat with the blue padding that reclines; no that's too good for Natalie Pressman. But like the good girl I've been trained to be, I sit in the wooden chair.

It takes her all of ten seconds to wipe down my knee, open the Band-Aid, and slap it haphazardly on my cut. "*Okay, you can go now,*" she dismisses me. As if her words aren't enough, she actually shoos me away with her arm.

"*Thanks,*" I mumble under my breath and head back to class, hoping this day doesn't get any worse.

The rest of the afternoon drags on, but at least the kids leave me alone. I really shouldn't have expected this year to be any different than any other year. I'm still the same broken girl who lives in the shack from the wrong side of town that won't ever fit in with the "rich" snobs here at the school. At least in two more years, I'll be in middle school and can make some new friends. Friends who are more like me.

Once the final bell rings for the walkers to be dismissed, I make my way to the front of the school. Outside in the sun, I notice Grayson waiting in the car line for his ride. A girl stands next to him. She's on the shorter side, especially compared to Grayson, and her hair is cut short. Like boy-length short. He's holding onto her hand as they wait for their ride.

"*Gray, there's a girl coming toward you. Who is she?*" I hear the little girl squeak out. I'm going to guess she's his sister the way he seems so protective of her.

Since I have to walk right by them to get to the street, I want to talk to Grayson, hoping to find out which class he's in.

He glances in my direction, and his expression softens as he gives me a small smile. "*That's Natalie. I met her today.*"

His sister slips out of his grasp and walks closer to me. She looks me up and down and claims, "Yeah, she'll do."

"Isabella!" he hisses. "What did Mom tell you about staring at people?"

"I wasn't staring. I was checking her out." Her eyes roam up and down me one more time. She doesn't seem to notice the tattered clothes, my worn hand-me-down sneakers, or my stringy hair. And considering I already got her stamp of approval, I walk up closer to her.

"You're Grayson's sister?" She bobs her head up and down to confirm. "How old are you?"

"Six. You?"

"Nine."

Her face lights up a little more. "Same as Gray." She steps closer to me, but she turns around to look at him. "See, I told you she would do." Clearly embarrassed, Grayson shakes his head from side to side, then his gaze lands on the ground.

I like this girl's spunk. It's too bad she's so much younger than me.

Suddenly, there's a horn beeping in our direction. "That's our Mom," Isabella states. "We gotta go."

"Oh. Right." I hope she doesn't hear the way my voice falls. I knew they were leaving, but it's always nice to have someone to talk to.

A brand new van pulls up to the curb next to where they are waiting. The woman driving, who must be their mom, is smiling. She looks friendly, kind, and sweet, clearly where her kids get it from.

"I'll see you around," I start, walking past them on the sidewalk to continue on my way. "Bye." I walk away and then realize I never thanked him for earlier. When I get back to him, he's about to climb into the car. Not knowing why, I throw my arms around him for a hug. He's startled at first, his body stiff, and while he doesn't reciprocate the hug, at least by the end of it, his body is less rigid. "Thanks for helping me at recess," I tell him, pulling away.

As I walk away, I hear him call out, "You want a ride?"

I'm instantly ecstatic; I don't think anyone has ever offered me a ride home before, and it's not even raining. And then I remember where I live, and if I want to keep him as my friend, he can't know where I live. And so I turn down the ride, wishing things could be different in my life, hoping that the one person to finally show me kindness at this school, continues to be my friend. It must be because he's new here, I think as I wave and walk away. When the other kids get a hold of him, he'll change his mind about me. They all do; it's only a matter of time.

I follow the same route every day to get home, but today, I realize I'm not alone. When I turn off the main road, so does Grayson's van. I come to a stop, and the van pulls up next to me.

"We're going the same way. Are you sure we can't give you a ride?" Grayson's mom asks through the open window.

"No, I'm good. I promise. I'm used to it," I tell her. I've lied my way through enough adult conversations to know which smile to give. I know I've chosen well when she flashes me one in return.

"Okay, dear, but if you ever want a ride, just let Grayson know. I'll be picking them up every day from school."

I can only nod my head; the lump in my throat is too big to actually speak. Even if I did, I know I would start to cry.

That's seriously the nicest thing anyone has ever offered me. Ever. In my life. It's because they don't know where you come from, *the stupid voice inside my roars.*

From the backseat, I hear Isabella yell, "By the way, only call me Bella. We'll see you tomorrow."

I raise my hand to wave as they drive away. For today's walk home, my smile doesn't fade once.

The walk home takes about ten minutes or so. When I finally get home, I grab the mail from the mailbox and start the trek down the long, dirt driveway that leads "home." Still on a high from Grayson's family's kindness, I walk into the house a little louder than I should, letting the screen door slam behind me.

"Natalie!" I hear my name being yelled from the back of the house. "You're too loud."

"Sorry," I mutter knowing full well she can't hear me. I drop my bag on the kitchen table, hoping it doesn't get lost in the mound of papers and other crap that collects there.

In the fridge, I find one lonely apple and a half-full container of milk. This will do for now, I suppose, even though I'm starving. Finding one clean glass in the cabinet, I pour myself a hearty amount and place the milk back in the fridge. Collecting my bag from the disaster, I head back toward my bedroom.

From my mom's room, I can hear an unfamiliar man's voice grumbling. No surprise there. Mom doesn't often have guests with repeat appearances.

I push open my door, my "N" that hangs in the middle is slightly askew today. Reaching up to straighten it out, my mother's door opens. She walks out, dressed for her shift at the diner, followed by a short, roundish man with a bald head—and he's not bald by choice.

Seriously, Mom? You can do better.

Although my mom isn't young—she had me when she was thirty-five—she could be pretty, if she bothered to take care of herself. I get I was not planned for, and may be an inconvenience at times, but she could still find a nice, decent guy who wouldn't be put off by her having a kid, rather than the guys she chooses to bring home. I can't remember the last one who even acknowledged my existence. But then again, I'm not supposed to acknowledge them so why should they notice me?

I hear the door open and close and then my mother lets out a deep sigh.

"Natalie, Anita will be here in an hour. Stay in your room until then. There's mac and cheese in the cupboard for dinner. Be good. I'll see you in the morning." She's out the door after I hear her slipping into her shoes, not bothering to wait for my response.

"Bye," I call out, again knowing she can't hear me. "By the way, I love you too."

Making my way further into my room, I throw my bag on my bed and flop down next to it. My room is my sanctuary; I spend most of my hours and days in here, away from the chaos that is the rest of the shack. There's not much to my room, but what I do have, I keep neat and tidy. My bed is always made, the three items that sit on top of my dresser are always in their place, my clothes are folded and put away in the drawers or hanging in the "closet." It's not much, but it's mine, and that alone is enough. I'm thankful that my mom stays out of the room, except to vacuum and dust once in a while.

I dig out the papers they sent home and start to fill them out. I've perfected mom's signature over the last year, so now I don't even need her to sign the papers that the school requires every year.

Once done, I start on the one piece of homework my teacher assigned: "What are you most looking forward to in fourth grade?" I know she doesn't want my real answer, so I make up a story that will satisfy the requirement and allows me to start the year off under her radar.

When my assignment is safely tucked back into my bag, ready for tomorrow, I grab my book and cuddle in with my teddy bear to escape my reality and jump right into Narnia.

Today, I'm not only thankful for the escape but also the fact I've hopefully finally made a new friend at school. That thought alone makes me smile.

1

NATALIE

THE PRESENT

*T*he white sands of the beach stretch before me for miles, the ocean reaching many more. It's early morning so the beach is deserted. I left Caleb sleeping back in the room, with a note that I went for coffee. I'll get to that, eventually. Right now, I just need the peace and quiet of the beach; the only sound, the waves crashing against the shore. The aftereffects of last night's storm scatter along the shore. I can't help but remember it's not the only storm that hit last night.

I watch a few birds hunting, pecking for food from my perch on the lounge chair. A gentle breeze brings goose bumps to my skin making me wish I wore a few more articles of clothing. Deep down, I know it's not just the breeze, it's everything. My life, my job, my actions, Caleb.

"Natalie," Caleb whispers to the side of my chair, startling me.

Placing my hand over my chest, I turn to look up at the man towering over my chair. His arms are crossed over his chest, but he's not angry. No, Caleb doesn't do angry. His expression reeks of concern, worry, anxiousness. I could have predicted that reaction, yet it wouldn't change my decision.

Without another word, he scoops me up into his arms, not caring if I'm done with my alone time or not. I'd be stupid to protest; it would be a losing battle. The man's got inches and pounds on me, and I lack the emotional strength to fight back just as much as the physical.

We make it to the edge of the beach, our villa room just mere steps away, when he speaks again. "Did you get your coffee yet or can it wait?"

I hate sometimes how he knows me so well, sees through my lies. Yet, I couldn't love him more for it. I shake my head, then add, "It can wait. You can join me."

One nod of his head shows his agreement as he continues to carry me back to our room. He's got the door open before I can consider how he even pulled the key out. He walks into the room, shifting his body so that my legs draped over his arms don't knock into the doorway. Always thinking, always considerate, always protecting me. Can't say it's not warranted.

He stalks over to the bed and gently places me on it. The satiny sheets of the unmade bed feel cool against my back, my shoulders especially, the thin straps of my tank top doing nothing to guard against the cold. I attempt to drag the covers up, for warmth but also to cover myself from Caleb's intense glare.

"You can't hide from me, Nat," he says on an exhale, plopping down next to me on the bed. "Just let me love you. Why is that so difficult?" He lies on his back, staring up at the ceiling. I know he wishes things were different, that *I* was different.

The answer to his question should be simple, but for me, it's a struggle. One I'm losing lately with myself.

I told myself that's what this trip is for, to reconnect with the guy I love, to let go of the fights that have plagued my life in the past few weeks. It's easy to make these claims ahead of time, but in the actual moment, I'm left with just excuses. Even in my own head, they are pathetic. No way Caleb will let me get away with them.

I sigh, letting out a deep exhale, giving in. I prop myself up on my side, facing the man who, if I allowed it, would be my everything. Actually, that's a lie I tell myself. He IS my everything. My heart knows this; my head still needs to catch up.

My fingers reach out to touch him, sneaking under his shirt, trailing over the curves of his abs. I never tire of the feel of his skin and muscles, yet the sight of them is even more to behold.

"Natalie," he groans, dragging out the last syllable. "Don't start something you won't finish."

Ignoring his comment, I scoot closer to him, nudging the shirt higher. Caleb sucks in a breath, releasing it slowly, not wanting to relinquish control unless he knows I'll follow through. Except in the bedroom, I have a superb track record of follow-through; it's everywhere else I lack it.

I maneuver so I'm straddling him, seating myself on top of his glorious abs, knowing I won't hurt him. It's my best vantage point to tease him but also to watch him. Watch him as he takes in what I'm doing. Watch him as he tries to keep himself under control. Watch him as he tries to anticipate my next move.

I tug his T-shirt up higher, scrunching it up by his armpits. Placing my hands on his shoulders, I bring my face closer to his abdomen. Slowly, with as much grace as I can muster at the moment, I draw my tongue along his abs, licking each divot with extra attention but never resting in one spot too long. My eyes catch sight of the change in Caleb's breathing, how his chest rises a little bit faster than the last breath.

"Take off your shirt," I command in between caresses. Somehow, without making me move, he finagles his shirt over his head and tosses it to the side. Resourceful, this guy. Now that his entire chest is bare, I run my hands up and down, abandoning my kisses for the present time.

After a few more minutes of teasing, rubbing and quick kisses along his chest, I lower my mouth to his ear, his breaths coming even faster now. "Love me, Caleb. Make love to me," I demand.

I pull away to observe the significance of my words filtering into his brain, the meaning sinking in almost immediately. His face flashes with understanding, the look of concern long gone with my present actions. He doesn't question my words, but he's not propelled into instant action either.

Over the years, I've learned that Caleb takes cues from me in the bedroom. He intuitively knows exactly what I need in any given situation. Today is no different.

Cognizant that there's no urgency in our lovemaking, he sits himself up, holding me by my waist so I won't topple off completely. He brings his lips to mine and in the most tender way, starts to massage my lips until little moans escape me, and he pulls away. His kiss ignites something deep inside me, a longing for more, a promise of what's to come. And I do mean *come*. Multiple times if I'm lucky.

Despite the awakening inside me, I won't hurry him, won't push for him to go faster. No, I will revel in the way he worships my body. Every. Single. Inch.

Blinking myself back to the present, it's in just enough time for me to lift my arms above my head so Caleb can remove my tank top. He tosses it aside, his eyes never leaving mine.

"Fuck, girl," he growls as his gaze lowers to my now bare chest. His pointer finger traces lines up and down, all around both breasts, giving each equal attention. He dips the other hand into my shorts, a surprised yet pleased expression at finding I'm bare underneath. "Fuck," he echoes again, this time, drawing out the word as his fingers dig into my ass.

"I'm sorry for..." I start to apologize for my childish actions yesterday and last night, but he puts his hand over my mouth, silencing me.

"Shh. We're here now. The rest is in the past."

I'm not naive to believe he'll let it drop for good—we always have to discuss it—but I can certainly tuck it away while we're intimate. I really should get out of my head anyway. I spend too much wasted time there as it is.

"Knees," he commands, his tone of voice strong, confident, and I find myself obeying immediately.

Still straddling him, I push up to my knees. He slips my PJ

shorts down from my waist, then stops, confused as to how to continue. Before he can wonder how he'll get the shorts off, I push up a little more and shimmy my way out of them, kicking them off the foot they get stuck on. Caleb chuckles, his eyes lighting up with laughter.

"Hush," I chide with a playful giggle. "Let's see how you do, Big Guy." As soon as the words escape my mouth, I realize I shouldn't have issued the challenge.

I slide back into my original position, sitting on his abs, moving my ass slightly back toward where his sweatpants sit on his waist. However, my change in location doesn't deter him. With a wink in my direction, he lifts me with one arm, reaches for his pants with the other, and wiggles his hips back and forth, somehow working his sweats down to his ankles. Turning my head, I notice he's not wearing any underwear. Smugly, I face him again.

He shrugs. "Worked for you, didn't it?" I don't get a chance to ask how he knew I wasn't wearing any before minutes ago because I'm suddenly flipped over to my back, now lying underneath Caleb, the wicked gleam still twinkling in his eyes. "You. Are. Beautiful." He dotes a kiss to my nose and cheeks. When he finishes, his eyes bore into mine. I hold his gaze, his love for me emanating out of his dark eyes. The amount of love I see still amazes me after all these years.

As if confirming my thoughts, a hearty "I love you," barrels out of Caleb's mouth. His words, the same words I've heard thousands of times, make my heart elate.

"I love you, Caleb." Second nature now and not parroted back in any way.

He hovers over me, watching me, checking in with me. Some days, I wish he didn't need to, but other days, I'm so grateful that I found a man who protects me as fiercely as Caleb always has. I'm not really sure he knows any other way to be.

"Okay." It's our word, and with the one word and a nod of his head, he sets to work, loving me.

Lowering his lips to mine, he leaves a single kiss, a quick peck to initiate the start of more, of so much more. Because when Caleb does something, he does it right; he goes big. Kind of like everything about him. His size. His heart. His love for me. BIG.

It doesn't take him long to pull away from the kiss, to move on to bigger and better things. Because yeah, I love Caleb's kisses, but more than those, I love how he plays my body, how he knows how to light up every single sensation, starting with my lips.

As he settles his own body into a better position, I widen my thighs making room for him. Trust me, it's needed. His tongue then starts its assent down my body, hitting my neck, which sends goose bumps up and down my spine; my breasts, each one, but one at a time; and my abdomen. He spends a delicious amount of time licking around the entire area, igniting a fire within. I feel it— oh do I feel it—the master workings of his tongue.

My hands find themselves on his back, dragging my fingertips up and down, slowly, in rhythm to the way he trails licks up and down my front. The connection I feel for him, *to him,* renews every time we do this, growing stronger each time since that very first time so long ago.

My pulse quickens, his lavish tongue licks heightening my arousal for this man, for what he promises to do to me. And then, before I know it, he stops the sensual assault and sets to work on something else. For a few seconds, I dread the sense of loss of his touch, of mine on him, but the feeling is short-lived. He takes a few breaths, kneeling over me, peering down, love and fire emanating from him to me. This time when he starts, it begins an even deeper connection of our bodies.

He strokes himself three times, leans down, and pushes inside in one thrust, not hurried in any way. I still falter for a moment at his size, my body jolted at the intrusion. Even as accustomed as I am to how big he is, it takes a moment to settle, a moment Caleb always gives me. We've done this dance for so long, he doesn't even have to look for my approval; he simply senses when I'm ready. Maybe it's the little smile that forms on my lips or the little hitch in my breath, the small gasp that escapes my mouth. Whatever my tell is, once I've given it, he moves.

He starts slow, moving his hips in a wavelike motion, priming me up. That's when he finally meets my gaze. The wattage of his smile powers something inside me, the fire that flickered earlier now roaring to life.

Wrapping my arms around his neck, I bring him closer to me, not losing sight of his gaze, getting lost in those deep browns, lost in him. I don't realize when my body starts moving in accord with his, when we become one, when my breathing picks up. I only see him, feel him, deep, moving in and out, setting the pace for our lovemaking.

My legs open wider, my knees falling to the mattress, accepting him as he pushes deeper, still deeper, hitting that spot inside only Caleb is privy to. I climb higher and higher, chasing the release, the dousing of the fire that burns like an inferno now.

"Caleb." His name falls out of my mouth on a loving sigh.

"I've got you, Natalie."

That's when I fall. Not at the sound of my name, but at the other words: *I've got you.* In the moment, I don't even wonder about the truth of it; I just fall, toppling over the edge of bliss, a free fall to euphoria.

Closing my eyes as I ride out the waves of my orgasm, a deep moan releases from my mouth, one soon matched by Caleb's. Yet, it's less of a moan, more of a promise. Two words: My Nat. With those two words, he comes, his dick emptying inside me, pulsing over and over, filling me. An overwhelming sensation of satiety comes over me, not from the act itself, but from the love that pours out of this man into me. I feel it deep in my pores, in every vein, *everywhere*, as it transfers from Caleb to course through my body.

Today, this is just what I needed. Caleb knew, he *always* knows, reading me like a book even if I don't share all my secrets.

I come down from the high, Caleb still inside, his body hovering over mine. I pry my eyes open, met with a watchful look from Caleb.

"Hi," I whisper, a grin forming on my lips with it, my hand reaching up to touch his face.

It's what he says in return that makes me weaker than the love-making already left me. His gaze locked on mine, he rasps, "You're the beauty and calm of the storm."

The meaning of his words causes my heart to flutter, an ecstatic grin erupts onto my face. It may only make sense to us, but I'll forever be okay with that. And for the time being, I know the storm has passed.

Or so I thought.

2

NATALIE

A FEW MONTHS LATER

"*W*here are you going?" Caleb barks at me. "This discussion is not over."

I turn on my heels and march back into the living room. "Discussion? How is it a 'discussion' if I'm the only one doing the talking?"

I'm pissed, more so than I've ever been at the guy. And while maybe I don't have a "right" to be angry with him, my emotions are all over the place lately. Chalk that up to a visit from my mother last week, a hellish week at work, and well, Caleb telling me I "haven't been myself lately," pushing me over the edge I've been teetering on for a short while now. I'll be the first to admit I'm *not* myself, but truthfully I have no clue why. Except I'm lying to myself if I believe that.

"Natalie!" Caleb's scream brings me back to the present. "Your phone's been ringing nonstop."

I look down at the phone in my hands. It's him, and while I can't answer it with Caleb in the room, I have to make it stop ringing. Turning my back to Caleb, I answer, "Hello?"

"Are you coming or not?"

I hesitate a minute. I am coming, even though I should deal

with the mess at home first. "Yes. I'll be there in twenty." I hang up without waiting for a response.

Guess I wasn't quiet enough.

"You're really leaving? Like this?" He's irate, yet his expression bears something else too. Fear? Remorse? I don't know what exactly, but right now, I'm too pissed to even stay here and deal with the shit swirling around in my head. I know if I stay, it will only drive a further wedge in our relationship, yet if I go, it's bound to do the same. So, really, I'm in a lose-lose situation.

I'm leading with my head tonight, not my heart, so without another word, I turn around and walk to the front door.

Before I can make it out, Caleb's behind me, grabbing my arm.

"Nat," he starts but soon trails off.

I can't turn around and look at him. He's going to be a mess, I know it. And it's because of me, yet I suddenly feel like I have to leave before I completely lose it.

It's been a while since I've felt this way—trapped. Just when I thought I had overcome all the obstacles, gotten to a place I could trust myself again, old feelings have reemerged. As much as I wish I could blame Caleb for his part, ultimately, the fault all falls on my shoulders.

He tries once more. "NAT!"

As a single tear slips down my cheek, I walk out the door, away from the man I've loved for the past five years. A man who's prepared to give me everything I've ever dreamed of, and probably more. Yet, I'm still walking away tonight because I'm pissed, and that's what I do.

It's not the first time I've left, but it's the first time I've left to potentially be with someone else. As much as he likely knows it, he's letting me walk away. Which pisses me the hell off even more. I mean, fight, man! Fight for me to stay. Don't let me walk out on you. Again, no less. I may not keep coming back; I don't know if I have the strength. I *know* I don't have the strength tonight, which scares me a little. No, a lot. But my time with Caleb was always limited in my mind; truthfully, I'm surprised we lasted this long, got to *this* point in our relationship. *Because he loves you, Natalie. Why isn't that enough?* my inner bitch taunts me. Shut up; no one is talking to you.

Wiping the tear with my sleeve, I hold my head high and walk out to my car, start it up, and drive away like a bat out of hell.

Knowing Caleb, and I do *know* him, he'd follow me if he knew that's what I wanted. My stupid head can't decide if I want him to or not. Of course, my heart is begging for him to follow me, but since I've already decided it has no say tonight, I'm not concerned with what it wants. So I keep driving, away from the man who has it all to one who has nothing to offer me except sex. No-strings-attached sex which is exactly what I need right now. No commitments, no hang-ups, just raw, carnal sex.

I know what you're thinking; you agree with my conscience, the bitch. And you are right to agree with her; that bitch has some pretty good ideas. But not tonight. Tonight, despite my loving another man and despite him loving me back, it's not enough. Or it's too much. Again, I can't decide. Yep, I'm as confused as you are, trust me. So let's just let tonight play out, let the chips land where they may, and I'll deal with the repercussions.

See, the thing about Caleb loving me? He'll forgive me. He'll let me back in; it's what he does. Because I've fucked up before, and he took me back. Sure, it was on a smaller scale, but he still forgave me, and we stayed together. He'll do it again. Right? It's in his nature.

Shrugging off any feelings of why I shouldn't be here, I continue on my way. *I can do this,* I think to myself as I approach the bar. I can, but should I? The tug of war inside my head is making me more crazy than usual.

What if I push Caleb too far this time? What if I've run out of times to run? What if he's run out of forgiveness? It's these thoughts driving me to have one drink and see where that leads. I don't have to go through with it; I can always walk away whenever and go back home.

Home. With Caleb. Fuck! What the hell am I doing? I love the guy. Like, really *love* him. Like go the distance LOVE him. He drives me crazy almost every day, but I've never been happier in my life than when I'm with him.

I pound my head against the steering wheel. I can't do this to him. To us. I can't.

Letting out a long breath, I make my decision to turn back around. To run back to the only man who's ever loved me, who puts up with the shit I throw his way, realizing despite my actions, he's my *one.*

Before I can even get my car started again, he's there. And it's not Caleb who's knocking on my window, smiling that stupid crooked smile that does funny things to my heart. Thank goodness it's not in charge tonight.

He knocks on the window and motions for me to roll it down. And like a fool, I do. "You're coming in, right?" he asks, that damn smile still plastered on his face.

With one simple question, my decision to have one drink with him is made.

We're friends, my head rationalizes; it's no more than that. To which the bitch laughs. *If that's what you need to believe, Natalie.*

"Shut up," I mutter, hopefully inaudibly so he doesn't hear me. He's too involved with just staring at me to have heard my words.

"Okay, one drink, and I have to be on my way." My voice is confident, strong, like I've done this before and know what I'm doing.

If only.

I quickly put the window back up, he opens my car door for me, reaching his hand out. The kind gesture isn't lost on me; it's what's lacking from Caleb lately.

I smile up at him as I rest my hand in his, and when he gently tugs me up, he pulls a little too hard and I lose my balance momentarily. Of course, he takes it as an invitation to lean me in for a hug. And I don't stop myself; I allow his arms to wrap around mine and then find mine wrapping around him as well. Because he's my friend. Just like I would hug Grayson.

Ah, fuck. Damn Grayson. He's so going to kick my ass if he finds out about this. And he has every right to do it. He'd never understand what drove me here, especially now that he's found Ainsley. That girl is a fucking keeper, and he knows it. *Damn bastard.* They deserve each other, and everything great that comes their way. I've never seen him this happy with a girl. Ever. And that's saying something because the guy doesn't fool around, he's not a player, he's a fucking *nice* guy who never finds the right girls. Even I knew he'd never end up with Molly and was so glad how all that played out.

As much as it would never work between us, I secretly always hoped I could be *the* girl for Grayson. Maybe one day. Then I met Caleb, who used to look at me the way Grayson looks at Ainsley, until we got too comfortable with each other, and he stopped somewhere along the way. Which is why I'm here now with *him* and not at home with Caleb.

Damnit. There's that word again. *Home.*

Shaking off my thoughts, I pull myself out of the hug, grab his hand, and toss out, "Let's go inside." He couldn't be happier to oblige my wishes.

As we walk, I decide to live in the moment, to see where the one drink I've decided takes me. I'll focus on nothing else but having a good time with him and there will be no regrets about whatever happens.

One drink....

* * *

*I*f I know anything of what happened last night, it's that there was more than one drink. Way more than one drink. Hence the feeling of the Mack truck currently driving at NASCAR speeds around my head. I can barely open my eyes, my head pounds so much. And my stomach. Let's not even talk about the state of that.

Great decisions last night there, Natalie. Of course, the bitch is back.

It takes me a long while to wake up; I don't even know where I am.

This is bad. This is really bad.

No shit, Sherlock.

Sometimes, I wish I could reach out and slap the bitch. She needs a good bitch slapping one of these days.

When I'm finally able to pry my eyes open, blinking because of the light that's pouring into the room, I realize I'm in my own bed. *Hmm, that's interesting.* Wonder how I got here.

Turning just my head, I notice the bed beside me is empty and a glance over at the alarm clock reveals it's just past noon. Good thing I have nothing planned for today.

Staring up at the ceiling, I try to piece together anything from last night. Besides the alcohol, because clearly, there was alcohol.

Rubbing my forehead, I close my eyes again as I will the contents of my stomach to stay put. Knowing it's never going to happen, I try to remember the last time I was this plastered. Thank goodness for Caleb always being there to haul my ass off when I could barely stand, let alone walk. So, the question arises again—how did I get to my bed last night?

And then another thought crosses my mind: did I drive? Praying against all hope that I wasn't *that* stupid—because let's be honest, Grayson would probably stop talking to me if I pulled a stunt like that—I realize I'm going to be sick, and if I don't move fast enough to get to the bathroom, I'll be cleaning up more messes than just the one of my behavior last night.

Struggling to get myself out of bed quick enough, I take off for the bathroom that's unfortunately down the hall, and yep, just out of reach right now.

Vomit spews from my mouth, covering the floor of the hallway. *At least it's hardwood,* I think as I stand there, continuing to get sick.

Just when I think I'm done, my stomach rolls again, and every-thing that's possibly left now not only covers the floor, but me as well.

And then come the heavy footsteps. They aren't moving fast, but by the intensity of the steps, he's still pissed.

"Natalie, what the hell?" Caleb snarls loudly at me. "The floor is covered. *You're* covered in vomit."

Even in my current condition, it's not lost on me that he hasn't even asked if I'm okay. Swiping the back of my hand across my mouth, I look up at him. Yep, he's furious.

His eyes are wild, mean, as they dart back and forth between the mess on the floor and me. The guy's got dark eyes, yet currently, they are even darker. A storm brews there, one that's going to be nasty. One that I cannot seriously handle at this moment.

Stepping around the vomit, I continue down the hall to the bathroom to grab some towels. I get a drink from the sink and before I can grab the towels, I hear Caleb yelling. Slamming the door, I stupidly glance up at the mirror and catch a glimpse of my reflection. It's not flattering. At all.

Looking beyond the vomit, my face is pale, ashen. While I'm sure that has something to do with being hung over, there's more to it. And my hair. The blond locks are all stringy and lay flat on my head. The dark circles under my eyes make me look like I haven't slept for days; were they this bad yesterday? As if to match Caleb's, even my eyes are darker today than normal and lack the sparkle that's always there. It's like the light that has been slowly dimming the past few years has finally left. I don't like it.

"Are you coming out here to clean your mess?" Caleb shouts from the other side of the door.

"In a minute," I yell back. "Just give me a minute." I hear him sigh, loudly, and then he stomps away.

I wonder if I can ever really fix the mess I've clearly made for myself. And I'm not just talking about last night. As if that thought isn't enough, flashes ripple through my mind. Laughing with *him,* stumbling out to his car (oh thank goodness for that), being in the back seat. Wait, *what?* Hold up. What's that about being in his backseat? But for the life of me, no other memories come.

Putting down the lid to the toilet, I thump down, throwing my head into my hands and trying to massage my eyes with the back of my hands, like I'm trying to wipe the past twenty-four hours away. In my inebriated state, even I know that's not possible.

I hear Caleb's footsteps again and as quick as I can, with a hangover and a queasy stomach, I hop off the toilet, grab the towel, and march out to the hallway to start cleaning up one mess. Caleb stands there, off to the side of the vomit, hands shoved into his pockets, broad shoulders slumped, watching me. I have a hard time reading his expression beyond the fury wafting off him.

"Not now, Caleb." I walk past him and try to make headway of all the vomit. It's everywhere! Damn, what the hell did I drink last night?

Trying not to breathe in the stench so I don't vomit again, I manage to clean it mostly with one towel. When the towel's soaked through, I deposit it on top of the washing machine in the bathroom and grab another one. This time, before I can bend down, Caleb tugs it from my hand and starts to wipe down the walls and the rest of the mess.

"Change your clothes," he commands.

I would have expected his voice to be sharper, with more of an edge to it, but it's missing. I decide it's best to obey his orders; not for him, but because I stink and need to change my clothes.

I head back to the bathroom and wrestle myself out of my clothes as best I can so as not to make more of a mess. Turning the shirt and pants inside out, they go next to the towel. My underwear are next, and once I'm naked, I jump in the shower.

Standing underneath the hot water as it rains down, I take stock of my life: where I am right now, where I want it to go, where this behavior is coming from. Knowing it's not an excuse to grow up poor and with throngs of men parading around me from the time I was little, it's the only explanation for my behavior I'm willing to admit and accept, not wanting to deal with emotions I've stuffed way down deep in the recesses of my mind.

The fact that all of my friends are gloriously happy and getting married doesn't help. Before Caleb, I would have said I never needed any of that; I was content playing the field, no strings attached sex. When I fell for the guy, things changed. And then things changed again when he got his new job and I got the promotion, and we got too comfortable where we were at: going to the pool hall, drinking at the bar four nights a week, him going fishing on the boat, me knowing that it was only a matter of time before what we had expired. But when it still seemed to be working, I began thinking of a future with him. Until two defining moments brought everything to a screeching halt.

Realizing the water is now ice-cold, I quickly rinse myself off and climb out, jumping when I see Caleb sitting with his back resting against the back of the bathroom door. He's staring off into space, a faraway yet concerned look on his face and hasn't realized I've stepped out of the shower yet.

"Still not ready to talk about it," I tell him forcefully. "But seeing as how you are the king of that, I know you'll understand."

He hands me a towel from beside him, and I accept it graciously. His eyes study my every move.

First, I wipe down my face, then dry the ends of my hair. I slowly wrap the towel around my upper body, tucking it in between my breasts. He blocks my exit, forcing me to inch closer to him.

"Move." His eyes narrow, the shock of my request evident on his face. "Please," I add. He sighs but then unfolds his over six-foot frame and stands up.

"Natalie," he starts after clearing his throat. "What the fuck are we doing?" His tone is rough, edgy. He's still pissed, but his emotions war with each other.

"What part of 'I don't want to talk about it' do you not understand?"

I try to push past him, my fury returning from last night's

unfinished argument. He grabs my arm tightly just above my elbow. I try to shake it off, but the guy's way stronger than me. He'd never hurt me, but his grip is tight. He pulls my arm leaving me no choice but to face him. I pull back slightly as he lowers his face into mine. His eyes move swiftly back and forth, his nostrils flaring slightly. Suddenly my stomach is queasy again, but it's not from the alcohol. In fact, between Caleb's look and my shower, I seem to have sobered up quite a bit.

Before I know it, he's spun me around and has me shoved up against the still closed door. I brace myself with my hands, wondering what the hell he's thinking. Sure, we've had angry sex before, but this brings it to a whole other level.

I don't have too much time to react. His arm comes around my front and unhooks the towel. It floats down to the ground, pooling around my feet.

Standing naked in front of him, I don't dare turn around. I keep my focus on a spot on the door in between my palms. My breathing kicks up a notch, and I can feel the wetness amassing inside my thighs, hoping Caleb makes a move soon.

I'm not sure what he's waiting for, but soon, his arm is back around my front. His fingers start massaging my breasts, taking his time, kneading each one until the nipples are hard and perky. And the ache between my legs grows needier.

"Caleb," I warn, although I have no idea what I'm warning about.

The hand that massages my breasts now covers my mouth. He steps up closer behind me, snaking the other arm down between my legs. When he finds my clit, he mumbles, "Fuck, Nat," and immediately starts to make circles with his thumb.

My eyes close as he drives me higher and higher. He removes his hand from my mouth to rest it on my ass, his other hand continuing to work me up into a frenzy. My breathing kicks up into high gear as he brings his mouth to my neck. Instead of kissing it, he starts biting, gently at first, but harder as he feels me ascending. He comes a little closer so he can shift his arm around to a more comfortable position, and soon one finger enters me. Before I can protest and tell him I want his dick, he adds another finger as his thumb still circles my clit.

My legs go stiff as I push onto my toes, trying to hold onto the feeling a tad longer. He thrusts his fingers in and out, knowing what I like and what it takes to make me come. And that's when I explode.

Throwing my head back, I give in to the orgasm and let it wash over me, letting go of some tension in my body. In doing so, I scream out his name. It's only when Caleb's hand stills inside me I realize my mistake.

I yelled Scott as I came.

Ah, fuck.

3

CALEB

*A*s soon as the other guy's name barrels out of her mouth, I pull my hand out quickly. I push her to the side and speed out of the bathroom, down the stairs, to the kitchen. A moment or two later, I hear her footsteps on the stairs. When she scrambles into the kitchen, she's managed to secure her towel back in place.

I can't even look at her right now. My body radiates with anger, a feeling I've managed to keep at bay recently.

When she left last night, I knew she was running away; all the usual signs were there: the depressed mood, the anger, her lack of communication. Things had been brewing for weeks. She's run before, a few times actually, when life gets too hard for her. I don't get it; I never will, but I promised myself the first time she ran, I'd be here when she got back. She always comes back. It's never about me; it's about her: the way she views herself, the fact that she can't overcome her childhood, the fact that she "isn't cut out for a life like this." When I asked her what that meant, she simply stated: "being an us."

But last night? She fucking ran to someone else. Her saying his name confirmed my suspicions. And that I won't tolerate, and she fucking knows it.

She starts to speak, but I cut her off. "Save your bullshit, Natalie. I don't want to hear it." I run my fingers through my hair and begin to pace the kitchen, not exactly sure how to handle the situation.

She has my heart, has pretty much since I met the girl, and despite her faults and insecurities, we've managed to navigate this "us" thing pretty well. Or so I thought. I'm not sure where we go from here.

She stands there, looking miserable. Not sure if it's because she's sorry for what she did or because she got caught or a combination of everything that's been going on lately that's taken its toll on her. Whatever the reason, she deserves it.

I'm the only person she allows to see this side of her, and ironically, this is the side of her that I fell in love with first. Sure, the bubbly persona she portrays to the rest of the world has my heart too, but when she's bare and stripped down, that's the girl who's only mine. That's the girl who will forever hold my heart, no matter what happens from here on out.

At first, I wanted to protect her, play the hero; I thought I could save her. Now, I realize there isn't anything to her that ever needed saving—loving the essence of Natalie is knowing all parts of her and being able to love them all, broken and not. Kinda like my favorite kind of storms I've loved since I was a kid.

I angrily swipe my keys off the table and grab my jacket from the back of the chair. "I have to get out of here; I can't be with you right now."

"Caleb. Wait," she calls out. She doesn't make any motion to come closer so I bide her out. Not that I want to hear what she has to say right now. She sighs deeply. "Look, I'm not going to apologize; let's just agree that I screwed up. But you have to know something."

My mind chooses to ignore the "I'm not going to apologize" for the time being. She's clearly beating herself up enough for the both of us. Biting my tongue, I hold my thoughts, "protecting" her.

When she doesn't continue right away, I look over to her. Her head is down, and she's picking at her fingers. When she finally looks up, there's a tear in her eye. It takes all my strength to stay where I am and not run to her to wipe it away, to make it better. Not everything can be fixed.

"I love you," she whispers, "but lately I don't know if that's enough."

That one sentence about rips my heart to pieces, and I have to fight off the urge to comfort her. Adrenaline zips through me, my emotions almost getting the best of me, but somehow I manage to stand my ground and not cave.

"The girls invited us to Grayson's tonight for dinner. I told them we'd be there." As soon as the words leave my mouth, I wonder if I should retract our acceptance of the invite. Neither one of us are in a position to be around other people.

I watch as what I've just told her sinks in; she can't hide the worried look of how she's going to hide what's going on, a trait she does so well.

"Um, okay," she stammers out. "So you'll be back before that?"

"Yeah," I grunt. I head to the door and just as I'm opening it, she speaks again.

"How did I get home last night?"

"Check your phone." I don't bother turning around to answer her, just step out the door and slam it behind me.

Outside in my truck, I don't start it right away. I look over to her seat, where she sat less than ten hours ago, inebriated out of her mind. Because somehow she managed to text me with her code: "Need you." And like I always do, I tracked her down and picked her drunken ass up. I didn't realize at the time the fact that she had been with someone else.

When I got to the parking lot of the bar, I could see her slumped over on the bench by the entrance. One of the bartenders was sitting next to her, to make sure she got home okay.

I got out of my truck, walked over, and shook hands with the bartender. "Thanks, dude. I appreciate it."

He shook my hand and handed me her keys. "Yeah, sure. The other guy couldn't wait around."

At the time, I didn't think much of it; I scooped her up and carried her to the truck. She didn't really stir too much; she was too drunk to even realize it was me. Or she was used to me picking her ass up, she assumed it was me. Who the hell knew.

Like always, I took her home and put her to bed. Nothing seemed out of the ordinary. I mean, she was drunk and angry, but surprisingly, she's not an angry drunk. A long time ago, I learned —the hard way—to curb my anger when it comes to a drunk Natalie. So that's what I did last night. I tucked her into bed and climbed in next to her.

I couldn't shut my mind off. I kept playing back the fact that she got a phone call, no several phone calls, in the middle of our argument, the bartender's comment about the other guy not waiting around. And then I just knew: she went out with someone else. And as much as I wanted to say "fuck you, Natalie," something stopped me from getting out of bed. Not that I slept much at all; I tossed and turned all night as she slept peacefully. *Stupid alcohol.* In the end, she did pay the price for her drinking.

Starting up my truck, I turn up the radio loud and let the music drown out everything: my thoughts of Natalie, the fight we're in the middle of, what I want to do about said fight. I just drive.

Right about now, I wish that Grayson was home instead of on a flight from wherever he went. Or it was boating weather. That boat can clear almost anything from my head. I don't even care too much about the fishing anymore; just being on the water, with or without my friend, can make a bad day better. Hell, it can turn an entire week around.

Instead, I find myself pulling into the bar. But something stops me from actually going inside. Getting drunk and wasted isn't going to solve any problems right now. So I start up the truck again and drive some more.

I grab some food on my drive and then head home. When I get

there, Natalie sits at the table, staring at her phone. She's dressed now but still looks fucking miserable. When she hears me come in, she gazes up at me. Her eyes are sad, the blue in them reflective of the color of her shirt.

"You came to pick me up?" she asks hesitantly. All I can do is nod. "I don't remember texting you, or much of anything last night. I know I was mad when I left, but that's about it."

"And the other guy?"

"I was meeting him for a drink, as a friend. There may have been kissing." Her eyes drop to her lap, and she begins to pick at her fingers again.

"You fucking kissed him?" I seethe. Now it's her turn to nod. "Is that all?" I abandon my food and start pacing having lost my appetite.

The vehemence returns with a vengeance. Having my worst fear confirmed hardens me.

With the smallest shake of her head, she continues. "I remember I was in the back seat of his car."

"Stop. I don't want to hear anymore. You realize you cheated?" I don't know why it's adamant to ask the obvious question, but the words tumble out of me without thought.

She's quiet for several minutes. She tries to speak several times, but each time she stops herself. I can only imagine the war she's having in her head right now.

"It went too far last night, is that what you want me to say?"

"That's your response?" I growl at her. "Are you even sorry?"

"I've told you before. I don't know how to do this." She's yelling now. She's still sitting, but give her some time; she'll be standing.

"You say a lot of things, Natalie. It's been five years. Why now?" She shrugs. "We got too comfortable."

"Are you fucking serious right now? That's why you left last night to have sex with someone else? Because we are 'too comfortable'?"

"That's one of the reasons, yes."

Her tone spurs me on; she's quite infuriating when she wants to be. "Do you want to share the other reasons too?" When she shrugs again, my pacing resumes, but this time I walk out of the kitchen to the living room.

And like I figured she would, she follows me. "You didn't even fight me last night. You just let me walk out of here."

"Because I knew you needed space! No matter if I had fought for you, you'd still be pissed at me. I couldn't win." The words come fast and hard, something we're both used to, spurred on by the strain in the air, the stress of the last day or so.

She takes a deep breath. "You once told me you couldn't tolerate cheating. "Did I totally screw this up? Did I totally screw us up?" I sense the tiniest bit of remorse on her features, but it's not enough.

"I don't know," I reply honestly after a few tense minutes.

We are at a standoff; there's about ten feet between us, but when I answer her, she takes a hesitant step in my direction. And fuck if I don't see her soul bared for me. All of the other Natalies fade away and I'm left with *my* Nat. And I don't know how to process that, especially since she's coming closer. "Stop," I tell her. She obeys, for about a second and then comes closer. "Natalie, don't." Her expression has changed and fuck me if my walls don't start to crumble. One last time, I try to stop her advances. "Please, Nat. I'm begging here."

That stops her movements. But not her mouth. "For what it's worth, I'm sorry, okay? I didn't intend to cheat on you. Yes, I was pissed beyond belief yesterday, but that wasn't my intention. I love you, Caleb. But I don't know how much more I can do. I want to, but I don't know if I have the strength to keep this up anymore. I don't know how much longer until I completely break." She pauses, and just when I think she's done, she adds this. "Maybe it's best if we go separate ways for a while, take a break from being us."

I almost trip at her admission. *A fucking break*? She wants to take a fucking break? So what, she has "permission" to have sex with whoever she wants? Fuck that.

"Is that what you really want?"

She doesn't react. She stands there, five feet away from me, stock-still. I realize I've stopped breathing waiting for her answer. Slowly, she begins to shake her head. "I don't fucking know what I want," she whispers. "How pathetic is that? I'm a fucking mess. And I don't deserve your sympathy or forgiveness right now. I get that. I screwed up; I broke us. But god damn it, if I don't need you right now."

This girl is shredding what's left of my broken heart. Every word out of her mouth right then is genuine; I can tell by the look on her face—she's fucking wrecked and conflicted. And I know I should walk away right now—hell, *run* even—but I can't. But I can't go to her either.

"You're not going to say anything, are you?" she asks, with a glance in my direction. "God, why do you always go silent in times like this? You drive me crazy." Her tone is edgier now, her eyes are back to their darker blue color.

"No way. No way are you throwing this one on me, Nat. You want me to answer you? I can promise you that you aren't going to like it, but I'll say what's on my mind." I take a deep breath and wait for her response.

"Say it," she whispers, goading me.

Without thinking of what to say, I begin.

"Every time you leave, a piece of my heart goes with you. And every time you come back, that piece gets glued back together, just in a different spot. I promised myself that you could always come back, that when you worked out your shit, I would be here waiting for you. But cheating is my hard limit, which you knew from day one. And you fucking crossed that line last night anyway; I won't even excuse it because you were drunk. But the inner war I'm waging with myself is nothing compared to what I see on your face. And that breaks me more, Nat.

"You're my fucking *life*, but not like this. You can't keep doing this. You have to decide what the hell it is you want. From me. For yourself. For us. And if that means time apart, then so be it. But not without some sort of rules put in place. If all you are going to do is fuck around with other people, I'm out. This won't ever work if you aren't committed to me, and only me.

"But if you need time to work shit out for yourself, by yourself, then by all means, take it. I'll be here waiting, still pissed, but waiting. But don't think I'll wait forever. Not happening. And don't think you can keep running away either. Deal with your shit. I've allowed you to escape it for too long now. You want me? You deal with your shit. And if you decide I'm not who you want, then so be it. I'll let you go without a fight. Because I'm not going to fight something bigger than me, and right now, this is bigger than me. So, ball's in your court."

When I finish, I suck in the air that I missed out on during my speech. Once I started speaking, the words wouldn't stop. I poured it all on the line, everything I should have been saying all along.

She takes one more step closer to me. "Yeah that was tough to hear," she whispers. "Okay."

"Okay what?" I ask.

"I need time to decide what I want, what I need."

"By yourself?"

The words hang in the air as she hesitates a minute, chewing on her thumb. I hold my breath awaiting her answer.

"By myself," she whispers. I watch her face, looking for clues that she's lying. Not seeing any, I take a step toward her.

"I'm still mad as hell, you have to understand that. You fucking cheated."

"I heard you, Caleb. And I get your message. Loud and clear. You should be pissed; I'm pissed too. Mostly at myself."

"Mostly?" I ask incredulously. "Unbelievable, Nat." And just like that, the anger is back and this time, I have to walk away. I leave her standing there, mouth open.

Grabbing a beer from the fridge, I call out to her, "We are leaving here in thirty minutes for dinner with our friends. See what you can do about hiding away your anger for the evening."

"It's a little ironic that when you chose to finally speak your mind, that's what you choose to say," she retorts angrily from the other room.

I offer her no response, just slam the door behind me.

* * *

*A*greeing to dinner with our friends was a huge mistake. Every little thing Natalie says or does just irks me. I can't help snipping at her. Now, she's off with Ainsley, spewing nonsense no doubt about the situation because no way would she give up her secrets tonight. Although he's tired, Grayson's ecstatic mood he's been in since he met his woman sickens me with what I'm going through. That's on me, though, because that guy deserves to be happy. The firecracker that is Ainsley is *the* perfect girl for him. Ironically, he says the same about Natalie, but I'm highly certain, he doesn't know all of her issues. I've never told him about the times she's left, the reasons why. While Natalie's never mentioned it to me whether he knows or not, I'm doubtful she's let him in about her issues, even if they have been friends since elementary school.

I somehow manage to make it through dinner, although not unscathed. Ainsley, Bella, and Kylie—Bella's wife—seem to know about Natalie's night of drunkenness, but again, I'm sure it's not the whole truth. Heck, it sounds like Nat doesn't even know the whole truth of what she did last night. That irks me even more.

When I can't stand it any longer and have to get out of there, I grumble that we need to leave. I get a quick hug from Bella and Kylie, but Ainsley lingers a little longer than usual. In her eyes, I see that she knows, that Nat came clean, although how clean is yet to be determined. "Call me if you ever need to talk," she whispers in my ear before pecking my cheek.

I wasn't expecting that comment, and I'm sure the shock is written all over my face. This girl really is something else.

"Thanks," I mumble.

After a handshake to Grayson, I drag Natalie out the door. I'll give the girl that she managed to pull her shit together for the most part. But she's always been good at hiding her secrets, the deepest parts of her.

Once we are in the truck, I throw her keys at her. "I'll drop you off to get your car."

"Oh, thanks." Her tone is clipped and her face resembles someone who's had a few too many shots, even though I know she's sobered up some from last night, and she didn't have anything to drink at dinner.

The ride to the bar is silent; she even turns off the radio. After I pull into the lot and she's about to hop out, I ask, "Are you coming home?"

With a sad shake of her head, I have my answer. "Don't wait up."

"By yourself, Nat. That's all I'm saying." My tone is harsh, but it's what I'm feeling, what she needs to hear from me. I'm not going to play games with her now; her leaving has never been about playing a game.

When she turns back around to face me, her expression has changed, and only my "broken" girl is left. "Duly noted, Caleb. And for what it's worth, I love you."

I'm not sure what makes me say it, but just as the door closes, I toss out, "Text me if you need me." She doesn't even acknowledge I've spoken.

On the ride home, I'm at war with myself again. I'm furious, but she needs to be safe. And if that means, having to go pick her drunk ass up somewhere later, then that's what I need to do. It's me hanging on by a thread to the one piece of string that tethers me to her.

4

NATALIE

*A*fter Caleb dropped me off to get my car, I drove around for a while trying to collect my thoughts and figure things out. I've had more clarity about last night.

Earlier, I lied to Ainsley because I did in fact sleep with Scott in the back seat of his car. Like I was a horny teenager.

Caleb's right to not excuse my behavior because I was drunk; it would have happened even if I wasn't drunk. And I don't even have a good enough reason why I did it. I know it's pathetic. *I'm* pathetic. At least I didn't act on it right away. Scott had been flirting with me for a few weeks, yet it took a fight with Caleb to push me into his arms.

So, that's where I'm at. Sitting in my car at one a.m. contemplating the big decisions in my life.

The biggest question I need to answer is why. Why did I cheat on Caleb? When I strip away my excuses (we were too comfortable, jealousy toward Grayson and Ainsley, feeling good about the fact that Scott *looked* at me), I'm not left with much. Except deep down, I know why I did it. And it's all on me, yet I'm not ready to admit it aloud, if even to myself.

Once I finally admit it to myself, I can tackle the question of where does that leave my relationship with Caleb. Again, another hard question to answer but I think I know how to answer this one. It requires my "big girl" panties to fully commit either way.

I walk around to the back door, not necessarily sneaking in, but not announcing myself through the front door either. Closing the door behind me, I jump when I hear Caleb sigh, because the kitchen is completely dark and I'm not expecting him to be there.

"Shit, Caleb, you scared me."

"Sorry." He sighs again then I hear his chair scrape across the kitchen floor. In a voice barely above a whisper, he states, "Night. Just needed to know you were home safe." I hear him start to pad away from the table and know if I don't get this out now, I will be too chicken shit later today.

"Wait." I put down my purse and keys on the counter. He stops but doesn't turn around. It's probably better this way, him not looking at me for what I have to say. "In many ways, I don't deserve you, Caleb. I never have and maybe I never will. I fuck up constantly, and while you say it's me taking the time and space I need, it's more than that, and you know it. I told you from the beginning that I don't know how to be an us, and while I appreciate and even love the fact that you get that about me, it's not fair to you. You deserve someone better than me, someone who doesn't question who she is at every turn, someone who can love you the way you deserve to be loved. And I'm not that girl."

I pause for a minute, and he fucking turns around. And his face guts me: the devastation, the lack of trust, the heartbreak, all things I've put there. I can barely manage to get out the rest of what I need to say.

"But in so many ways, I want to be. Not just for you, but for me too. And while I don't fucking deserve your sympathy right now, you allowing me to have the time and space I need, on my own, gives me a tiny glimmer of hope that maybe I can be that girl. The one we both deserve for this to work."

I don't feel the tear in my eye until it's running down my cheek. And at the same moment, I notice the one that's slipped from

Caleb's eye. Struggling to stay strong and not lose it, we stand there just staring, neither one of us knowing exactly what to do.

After a few minutes, he turns and walks out. And that's when I crumble. I catch myself before I completely fall to the floor, and then I just lay down. I expect the tears to come, but they don't. It sucks to feel this way: that you've not only broken yourself beyond repair, but you've broken the man you love. Because I do. I love the guy, as much love as I'm capable of. So I lay there on the kitchen floor, broken and feeling like I'm bleeding from the inside out, my heart torn into tiny pieces, and my thoughts all over the place. But I don't allow myself to feel sorry for *me*. Sure, regrets and doubts creep in, but I can't allow myself to feel sorry. I. Did. This. To. Us.

Staring up at the ceiling takes its toll on me, and apparently I eventually fall asleep. When I wake up, it's five a.m. Getting up because I have to pee, I decide I need to change my clothes too.

In the bedroom, the bed is empty, which means Caleb must have slept in the guest bedroom. I'll deal with that later because right now, I need to get out of here. I change my clothes, throw my hair back in a braid, and then hit the road.

Realizing I haven't eaten anything since dinner last night, I'm reminded that Ainsley said she would be up early so I head in the direction of her house. When I pull up next to the curb, I shoot her a text so that I don't wake up Grayson.

> I'm outside your house. If you're up, I need to come in. Please.

The phone is silent for a few minutes but then I see the front door opening and she waves me over. Wiping the tears that slipped out on the drive over, I make my way to the door. Ainsley ushers me inside with a hug. "Are you okay?" she asks, a look of concern on her face. "Follow me to the kitchen. I have to make Grayson breakfast." And so I do.

As I watch her make her man breakfast, it hits me that I don't do that for Caleb. I used to, in the beginning, but somewhere along the way, I stopped. The rational side of me knows that she and Grayson are still in that "honeymoon" phase of their relationship, but one look at the two of them, you can see it; they have a love that will last. I knew it the day I met her at the pool hall. They make it look so easy.

Despite what we portray on the outside, my relationship with Caleb hasn't always been "easy." Again, that's on me. And the tears start coming, harder this time. Although they are silent, Ainsley notices and sits down beside me, putting her hand over mine and squeezing. And when her hand moves to my back, I know she deserves the truth.

When I start to speak, I notice Grayson appear. His confused look says it all, as he looks between Ainsley and me. It doesn't take long for his confusion to morph into something more along the lines of anger. And then when Ainsley shakes her head at him and says, "Your shake is in your mug. What time will you be home later?", I can read the anger loud and clear on his face.

He mutters, "Noonish. Thanks for the shake." He grabs the shake from the counter, tosses a "Hey Nat" in my direction and then literally grabs Ainsley from her chair and drags her into the living room. I can't make out their muffled conversation, so I just sit and take in the view. I've sat in this kitchen many times, since I was a kid. Grayson definitely made some great updates when he inherited the house. And well, Ainsley's touch makes it that much homier.

Ainsley comes back into the kitchen first and sits back down, followed closely by Grayson. "You want to hang out today?" she asks me.

Looking over to her, I nod. I need some girl time and well, there's nothing else on my agenda for today.

Ainsley kept my secret from Grayson, not that I thought she'd tell him. I didn't mean to put her in the middle of anything or to keep a secret from Grayson, but somehow that's what happened. Despite not having many girl friends, Ainsley knows how to be a great one.

Looking up at him, I start, "Grayson." Hell if I know why his

whole name comes flying out of my mouth. Pretty sure I haven't
called him by his real name in years. "Ainsley says you don't know
what's going on."

"Nat, I have no clue, no clue what to think about you being
here so early in the morning, crying no less. You're not hurt?"
I lower my gaze to the floor and shake my head.

"Look, Nat," he starts but he doesn't keep talking until I give
him my attention. "Whatever is going on, you know you can talk to
me. We've been friends practically forever. And while I'm glad you
have Ainsley to confide in now, it's a little unnerving that you're
shutting me out. You've never shut me out. And I'm pretty sure that
you were the one who was going to kick my ass if I shut you out
when all that shit went down with Molly. Is that how you want to
play this?"

I don't know how to respond. On one hand, he's correct; I
confide in him, just not everything. He really has no idea what I've
kept from him over the years. I became really good at hiding what
was going on with me when I was young, and while Grayson has
always been my closest friend, he's too good to deal with my
baggage. So I never shared everything with him. And I'm not
about to start right now, so I give him the only thing I'll allow for
the time being: "I'm sorry." I stammer the words out, biting back
everything else and then take off running down the hall to the
bathroom.

When I get there, I close the door behind me and sink to the
ground. It's never bothered me that I didn't let Grayson in on every
aspect of my life. I decided years ago that he didn't need to know it
all; this way, I could keep his friendship because if he truly knew
the real me, he'd walk away, just like everyone else. But now, I'm
adding it to my list of questions I need to find answers to. Am I
wrong for hiding all parts of me from Grayson?

Taking a few more minutes to compose myself, I wipe the
stupid tears that keep falling and walk back to the kitchen. Ainsley
is just coming in from the garage. She's got a smirk on her face,

and I know that whatever shit they were dealing with because of me, they've worked out.

Oh, I wish it were only that easy.

She holds up something in her hand. "Grayson gave me his credit card. Let's go wild!" She laughs, and I can't help but crack a smile too. It's the first one in a rough few days. "Let me go get dressed."

As she walks away, I whisper, "Thanks," not loud enough for her to hear.

Ainsley and I spend the day shopping, which actually makes me feel a little better. She's so not a shopper, but if anything, she's a good sport about it all. She treats me to lunch on Grayson at a tiny little café. Despite knowing I should be upfront with her, I can't quite find the words to tell her the truth. And so I don't.

After our shopping spree, we head back to Ainsley's house. I've managed to avoid thinking about my actions of the past few days and all things regarding Caleb as we shopped. When she decides we need to watch a movie, I don't argue with her, just settle down on the couch.

I don't pay much attention to the movie, and within twenty minutes, Ainsley's sleeping soundly. It's about that time Grayson comes home. He takes in the scene, his brows furrowed and a hard edge to his face and his tone. "I have to shower but when I get back down, we are talking. Don't you dare think about leaving." He kisses Ainsley on the forehead and goes upstairs.

I have a good idea of what he's going to say to me, and as much as I know he's right, I don't want to hear it. He doesn't know the whole story, and while that's on me yet again, I don't deserve the lecture he's bound to give me. Oh, who am I kidding? Yes I do.

"Kitchen. Now," he indicates when he comes back downstairs freshly showered. Slowly, I follow him into the kitchen. He sits down at the table and motions for me to do the same. And then he lets me have it. "What the fuck, Natalie? Are you seriously cheating on him?"

"Calm down, Gray." My tone comes out harsher than I expected, but once it's out there, I realize I'm okay with it.

"That's your comeback?"

"What do you want me to say?"

"I want you to tell me the truth."

His response is totally genuine; he needs to know why I've cheated on Caleb. I have no idea what Caleb's told him about my past and even about most of our relationship, but I can bet it's not much. First of all, they are guys. Second, Caleb and Grayson are private people and men of few words. Third, I know in my heart Caleb wouldn't ever share my secrets. Obviously he told him that I cheated, but I'm going to bet that's because cheating is so hard for him to get past.

In a voice barely above a whisper, I mutter, "Yes."

"Wow." That's all he says. And stunned isn't even the right word to describe his expression. "You want to explain why?"

Deciding not to hold everything back, I start. "You can hold your judgment and your lectures. I don't want to hear what you have to say. I've already given myself the lecture multiple times and yet, I can't stop myself. And I fucking love Caleb. I do. I love him, and I know he's so fucking hurt right now, and it's all on me, but I don't know how to fix it. Or even if I want to fix it at this point. You should have seen the look on his face last night when we got home. And I get it. I did this to him, to us. And I have no excuses so I'll at least spare you that." It all comes out in one breath, so when I stop speaking, I have to catch my breath. And the way he's looking at me tells me that I was right to tell him this much so far.

"Why? What made you do it?" he asks hesitantly but like he's expecting and waiting for my answer.

"I don't fucking know!" I practically shout, finally looking back up at him. He seems taken aback slightly, and I get it. This isn't the Natalie he knows, but I'm too far past the point of caring right now. And if the earnest look on his face is any indication of whether or not I should continue, I know I have to. Like everything else in my life, I'll deal with the repercussions at a later time. And so I continue, not even sure what's going to come out of my mouth at this point.

"No wait, that's not true. I do know. I see the way you look at Ainsley, the way Caleb used to look at me, and I was fucking jealous. Jealous of her and jealous that you finally found someone who makes you ridiculously happy. And you deserve it, Gray. You fucking do. You deserve everything Ainsley offers you and then some. You truly are the best guy I know, and she's freaking perfect for you. And I fucking want that. I thought I had it with Caleb, but I started questioning it. And there was this guy, and he made me feel special. And I fucking slept with him. I'm a horrible person because I was so fucking jealous of my best friend." So I guess I'm going with that. And while it's not exactly a lie, I know it's an excuse, but at least it's one of the same excuses I gave Caleb.

His expression changes to one of pure shock. And then as if things couldn't get worse, Ainsley walks in. She looks from Grayson to me and then heads closer to me.

"You lied to me?" she asks, her voice unsure, quaky, her face bearing an expression of confusion. And I know she's heard it all.

So I deflect; it's what I'm best at anyway. Getting up in her face, I yell, "I couldn't tell you the truth. I saw the judgment on your face; I saw how you thought what I did was so horrible. I couldn't risk you hating me any more. So yeah, I lied."

"Wow" slips out of Grayson's mouth yet again. When I look over to him, his eyes are wide, but then he looks over to Ainsley and his look automatically softens. Because she looks like she's going to start crying. And heck, I can't blame her for that. I did just admit to lying to her and using her love for Grayson as a reason why *I* cheated.

You don't have to say it; I'm a horrible person.

I sink a little lower in my chair.

"Wow." Ainsley echoes Grayson's sentiment. Taking a deep breath, she continues. "You cheating on Caleb has nothing to do with me, or Grayson. That's all on you. And until you figure out why you not only felt the need to cheat on that man but deflect the responsibility onto one of your oldest friends, you aren't welcome here. I'm sorry if you have nowhere else to go, but I really think you should leave."

Whoa. I wasn't expecting those words to come out of her mouth. I've seen her stand her ground, but wow. Good for her for standing up to me. And her words hit me hard. Like really hard. Harder than Caleb's words even.

Dropping my head into my hands, I mumble, "Oh my god. What have I done?" Because for the first time since this whole mess began, I realize the true severity of what I've done.

Tears spill from my eyes as I look back and forth between Ainsley and Grayson. "What the hell am I doing? I have got to get my life in control. Ugh," I mutter louder than I mean to, but it pulls Grayson's attention back to me.

Wiping my eyes with my sleeves, I finally admit something to myself: I'd be lost without Caleb. I'm not ready to admit everything else right now, to myself or him, and I will take the time he suggested I take to figure my shit out. But fuck, I can't lose him.

Grayson speaks again, bringing me out of my head. "Darling, go upstairs and I'll be up in a few minutes. I need to talk with Nat alone. Say goodbye, or don't; that's up to you."

Ainsley looks back at Grayson, her face plastered with confusion. "Yeah, okay." Tentatively she throws her arms around me and whispers, "I'll be here for you when you need me, but you've got a lot of work to do on you." All I can manage is a nod. No wonder Grayson loves this girl. I don't deserve her kindness, yet here she is giving it to me.

Before I let her go, I say, "You're right, for what it's worth. It's all about me. I'm so sorry that I not only lied to you, but I dragged you and Grayson into my mess. And I'm sorry that I put you in a position where you had to choose to keep my secret from him. I'll give you a few days, but if you decide you can't forgive me, I will be crushed but will understand." I know I owe her more, but it's all I can give her at the moment. I just hope I haven't screwed up my friendship with her because I'm such a coward.

Ainsley chooses not to say anything more and instead walks away.

Once she's gone, I face Grayson. I don't know what I need from him at this point. I guess I just need him to be the friend he's always been to me, even if I've never completely reciprocated that friendship.

"He's pissed, Nat, and rightly so. And he's hurt. Truthfully, I don't know what I would do in his situation except to say that if it were Ainsley, I would demand the truth, demand to know why she didn't come talk to me before acting impulsively. And I'd want to know what I could have done differently, but this is all on you. If there's any hope of getting him back, you fucking take all the blame."

"I know. It's all on me. I just wish sometimes he was a little more forthcoming with his feelings and would talk to me more."

Guess I'm not completely done being an ass or a coward.

"Natalie," he warns. "That's a cop out, and you know it. You know who he is; he's not going to change. You can't use his personality against him; that's not fair."

And there's the Grayson I know and love.

"Damn you, Gray, for being so smart. And sentimental. When did you get this sentimental?"

He shrugs. "It may have something to do with the girl you tried to tear to shreds."

"Ah, fuck. I screwed up with her too. You going to have to do damage control?"

I know I don't know everything about their history or their relationship, but I know that beneath Ainsley's confidant façade she portrays to the world, there's also a piece of her that has been beaten down. Thankfully Grayson knows how to keep that confident girl afloat.

"Nah, not too much. But if you ever blame her for something you've done again, I won't be so nice." All I can do is giggle at the truth in that statement. He covers my hand with his, not unlike the gesture that Ainsley shared earlier today. Looking back up at him, I know the shock I'm feeling, the shock at his kindness, is shown on my face. "Fix it. Fix it soon, or I will fucking sic Bella on your ass. And she will not be nice to you." And that gets a full out laugh.

Fuck, Bella, I think as my face falls a bit.

So I say the only words I can: "I love you, Gray."

"Yeah, yeah. You sure have a funny way of showing it lately. First you kiss my girlfriend, then you go and cheat on your boyfriend, *for real,* and then you take your problems out on Ainsley and me. You're damn lucky I love you." He stands up and catches me off guard when he drags me up to standing and yanks me into him. And he hugs the shit out of me, letting me know it's all going to be okay.

"You going home?" he asks, pulling back just slightly.

"I have nowhere else to go and well, Caleb and I have a lot to discuss."

"You okay to drive?" Leave it to Grayson to always be concerned about everyone.

"Yeah, I'm good, but thanks for checking." I squeeze him one more time and pull out of his embrace. "You're going to go have makeup sex now, aren't you?"

"You better believe it. That girl upstairs deserves it and then some. I'm sure she'll call you in the morning and fill you in if you want the details." He walks me to the front door.

"I'm perfectly fine without knowing," I giggle, "but tell her to feel free to call me. I'm pretty sure I owe her a better apology."

"Yeah, you do. Bye, Nat. Stay safe."

Walking out of the door, I glance his way one more time. In good faith, I throw a kiss in his direction. "I'm damn lucky I have you for a friend, Gray, but Ainsley's even luckier." With that, I dash to my car and quickly hop in. As soon as I'm in, the tears start again, but these tears are different than before. These tears are because I know I have some soul searching to do, some big questions I need the answers to; I just have to be big enough to answer them.

I don't drive home right away but decide I need more time to figure out what the hell I'm going to say to Caleb when I get home. On the way, my phone pings with a text. Pulling over into the gas station for gas, I check the phone.

SCOTT
Hey, can you meet me tonight?

To procrastinate my answer, I put some gas in my car first. Once it's done, I grab my phone in my hands and shakily type my one-word answer.

NO

Shoving the phone into my purse, I decide it's time to face the music and drive home. When I get there, Caleb's lounging on the couch, the TV on but he's unfocused. Not sure how to start, I just stand there, shifting my weight from one foot to another. I take a tentative step closer to the couch, not wanting to startle him. I sigh, and his eyes fly over to me. "Hey," I begin.

I can tell he's been drinking today, even if I hadn't noticed the beer bottle in his hand. I didn't notice it last night, but he hasn't shaved in a couple of days. His dark hair is evident that he's run his fingers through it a bunch of times and his clothes are wrinkled. He doesn't respond, just keeps staring at me.

"Are you sober?" My voice is hesitant as I wait patiently for his response. I hope there's not a hint of judgment in my tone because I hadn't asked the question to judge him. It's more to gauge his awareness because I'm not about to discuss anything of importance if he's too drunk.

Instead of speaking, he nods his head.

"Can we talk?"

He pushes himself up to sitting on the couch, making room for me if I want it. I choose the other one, just to be on the safe side.

As soon as I sit down, I take a deep breath and start speaking, needing to get it all out.

"I need time, time for myself to get my shit together, and all I can promise you is that I will try my best to work through my shit. I want to put the work in. I want to get back to a place that involves us, together, as a couple, for the long haul. And I know it's not going to be easy, but I'm willing to work on it. But I'm scared, Caleb." Deep down, I knew most of my issues stem from being scared. I'm fucking terrified that if I go through with this, that somehow it will still get all screwed up. "I'm scared that I'm not enough. For me. For you. And I can't put in the work and then not be enough. And I get that it's not fair for me to ask you to promise me that I will be enough, no matter what. So that's where I'm at."

The entire time I spoke, he didn't move an inch; he blinked, that was about it. While I couldn't focus on him the entire time, whenever I stole a glance in his direction, he was staring right at me, watching my every move, hanging on to every word. I'll give him that; the man doesn't say much, but he's a fantastic listener.

An awkward silence hangs in the air. I've said what I needed to say; I need him to respond.

"You are always enough," he whispers. "No matter what. You will always be enough."

The truth of his words exudes off him. All I can do is hope he's right.

"You mentioned ground rules for this 'break.' Name them."

He's quiet for a minute. Taking a deep breath, he says, "Three rules. One—no sex with anyone else." (Okay, I can handle that). "Two—no sex with each other." (I gasp at that one). "Three—every day, you check in with me to let me know where your head is at."

"That's it?" He nods as he rubs his fingers down the scruff on his chin. "Okay," I whisper.

"Nat, one question." His voice is hesitant, his face set in almost a deep scowl. It's not one of anger, but frustration.

"Yeah?"

"I think I need to know why. Why you cheated." When he sees

my face contort, he adds, "On your time. It doesn't have to be tonight. But you owe me that much."

"Okay," I whisper again. "Okay, I can do that." Once I am willing to admit that answer for myself, he will be the next one to know.

I get up from my spot on the couch, intending to head up to bed. Even though it's not late, the day has been draining, to say the least.

As I walk past him on the couch, he reaches out and grabs me, pulling me into his chest, his strong arms enveloping me in a giant bear hug. He's quiet, his breathing even, and when he just seems to want to hold me, I melt into him. And he just holds me, for what seems like hours. Every once in a while, his grasp on me tightens and then as he works through whatever he needs to, he lets go slightly.

He finally speaks, after who knows how long. His voice is low, steady, but there's an edge to it. "I fucking love you, Nat. Don't lose sight of that. It's still going to take some time to forgive you, but I'll get there. You just focus on you." With his words, he pulls me in for one last tight hug. With a kiss to the top of my head, he lets me go. "Bed. You're exhausted. I'll sleep in the guest room." When I start to protest, he adds, "It's not forever, but at least for tonight. We both need that."

I can't argue with him; it would be futile at this point, so I march myself upstairs to get ready for bed. Pretty sure that even though that was a heavy conversation, I won't have a hard time falling asleep tonight.

Little did I know the real reason why.

5

CALEB

$\mathcal{I}$ have a hard time falling asleep that night; my head just won't quit, and well, it's not a good thing when my head is going nonstop. Once I finally fall asleep, I sleep restlessly. My mind wanders to Natalie, to our tormented past, our unsteady future and everything in between. At five, I finally say fuck it and get dressed for the gym.

Before heading downstairs, I sneak a peek into our bedroom. Natalie's asleep, but I know by the tangled sheets and her position that she's had a restless night too. There's an almost scowl on her face even while she sleeps. Reminding myself that she cheated, I'm able to draw myself away from her before I make any moves, stupid or otherwise.

On the drive to the gym, my mind wanders to the first time she left. We had only been dating two months.

I told Nat I'd pick her up at six for our dinner. I was finally getting to treat her to my favorite restaurant, The Land Lubber. I knew she wasn't a huge fan of seafood, but the burgers they served were pretty kick-ass. Although I still can't understand how the girl grew up in Maine and didn't like seafood. She always had some excuse of why she didn't like it. I was learning the girl could not only find an excuse for anything, but she could charm her way out of any situation she ended up in. *This included me out of my pants on our first date.*

I pulled up to her apartment at ten minutes before. Knowing full well she wouldn't be ready, I always showed up early. Call me crazy but I liked watching her get all dolled up. For me. And sometimes if we weren't in a rush, there was always time for a quickie of the sexual variety. Such was the case tonight. I would have been here earlier but I couldn't sneak out of the office quick enough and the traffic on the highway was heavier than normal.

Walking up the three steps to her apartment, she didn't give me a chance to even knock before she's throwing the door open. Shocked didn't even begin to explain my face as I took in her appearance.

"Nat?" I asked, because there's no way this girl was the bubbly girl I've been seeing for the last two months. The girl who has an answer for everything. The girl who's always put together.

The girl who stood in front of me was completely disheveled, right down to her mismatched socks. Her blond hair was piled atop her head, not in the messy bun I'm used to, but just piled there haphazardly. Her sweatpants—didn't even know she owned sweatpants—were not only baggy but were on backward. She wore a button-down but none of the buttons were lined up with the right holes. Her cheeks were covered in mascara-stained streaks and her lips were bare. That in and of itself wouldn't have gotten any notice but coupled with everything else, I didn't know what the hell to think. And I found myself in protective mode.

"Natalie, are you hurt?" She shook her head. "Sick?" Again with the head shake. "Are you okay?" She was more hesitant this time, but she finally shook it. "What's wrong?" Instead of answering, she started crying, sobbing so hard she couldn't catch her breath. She threw herself into me and immediately my arms wrapped around her. I hoisted her up into my arms, she burrowed her head into my shoulder, and I carried her over to the couch.

I don't know how long we sat there, her sitting in my lap, crying. I tried to wipe her tears, but they were coming so fast, I couldn't keep up. I was barely able to keep wiping her hair out of her face.

At one point, she finally stopped crying long enough, and I thought she had fallen asleep. But when she started speaking, I realized she was just quiet.

"I can't do this tonight," she started, her voice quavering.

"Go out for dinner?"

She nodded and then explained more. Her answer, the first of many things I would learn about her that night, was not what I was expecting.

"I told you from the beginning that I've never been in a real relationship. I don't know how to do relationships. I barely know how to do a friendship, let alone be with a guy. So this," she motioned to the space in between us, "is doomed."

I placed a kiss on the top of her head, not understanding where any of this was coming from. So I asked her. "Nat, did something happen to make you feel this way?" I kept my tone as even-keeled as I could.

She shook her head. "Not specifically. It's just a feeling I have. Like what we have isn't working anymore."

This was news to me. While I was new to the whole relationship thing, and our relationship itself was new, I didn't feel like it wasn't working, like we weren't working. And this was the first I've heard her say anything.

"What's not working?"

"It's hard to explain. You won't understand," she said exasperated.

"Try me." No clue if that's what one would say in this situation, but it seemed like it made sense.

She climbed out of my arms and started pacing her living room. The room was tiny so by the time she took five steps, she had to spin on her heels.

"Like tonight."

I waited for her to continue but when she didn't, I asked, "What about tonight?"

"Like what if I don't want to go out for dinner, especially at that restaurant? You didn't give me a choice in the matter." She huffed and continued to pace.

She can't be serious. This girl knew how to communicate. Of course, there were many things still to learn about her. It was only a short time we had been seeing each other, but I felt like I'd known her forever. Probably because of the way Grayson talked about her, I felt like I knew her. I'm pretty certain Grayson had never met the girl I was seeing right now.

I tried to get her attention. "Natalie." She briefly stopped the pacing but soon continued as if I hadn't even spoken. As she paced, she muttered shit under her breath. "Natalie," I called even louder. This time when she stopped, her eyes flew over to mine, the wildness in them making the blue an even darker hue.

"Huh?" she asked, confused.

I got up from the couch and gently walked over to her. Putting my hands on her shoulders, I forced her to not only stop moving but to look at me. Behind the wildness, there was fear in her eyes. Having little experience in situations similar to this, hell if I could even begin to gamble what that was about.

"If you don't want to go out tonight, we don't have to. We can order in. All you had to do was say something."

Her gaze dropped as she muttered, "But then you would be mad and we would fight."

Treading extremely carefully, I shook my head. "I promise I wouldn't be mad, but we probably will fight over things in the future. It's human nature and can't be avoided."

"What if you decided that you really wanted to go to dinner and I didn't want to and then you decided to just call it quits?" The look on her face said it all: the girl had been burned in the past.

Well, that stopped now.

"Hey, I'm not going anywhere, okay? Just talk to me when you have something you need to say or when you feel like something's off or whatever. I can promise you I won't go anywhere."

I could see in her face she didn't believe me. It would take actions to make sure she understood what I meant. I could certainly do that; all I had to figure out was what those actions were, starting with dinner tonight.

"Do you want me to order a pizza for dinner?"

Hesitantly, she nodded yes. It was a start at least.

"I really like bacon pizza." *She cracked a smile in an attempt to alleviate the heaviness between us. I watched as it slowly slid from her face as if she even knew it didn't help.*

"Bacon it is," *I told her.* "I'll call it in and go pick it up."

"That would be great, thanks." *She looked like she had more to say, but when she went quiet, I didn't push her.*

While I waited for the pizza to be ready, she busied herself with stupid chores around the kitchen, almost as if she didn't even know how to communicate anymore.

"I'll be right back," *I called out to her as I threw my jacket on.* "Need anything to drink?"

"No, all set," *came her reply.*

I couldn't put my finger on it, but something more was at play.

We ate in silence. When we were done, she cleaned up our plates and sat back down at the table.

"Thanks for the pizza. I'm sorry about the dinner you had planned." *Her hands fidgeted under the table, her gaze focused downward.*

"No worries. Another time."

She looked up. "Sure," *she responded, and while she tried to be convincing, her face said it all: there might not be a next time. Which was not okay with me.*

"You still want to go on the boat tomorrow?"

"Oh shit, that was tomorrow?" *At my nod, she quickly continued,* "I totally forgot I have plans with one of my coworkers. Rain check?"

She had me so off my game tonight that I couldn't tell if she was lying or not. The statement fell off of her lips like it could have been possible that she had plans, but I also knew she was good at thinking on her feet when she needed to be. And as far as I knew, she hadn't lied to me yet.

"Sure thing. You know Grayson and his boat."

That garnered a chuckle. She looked like she wanted to say something else but was holding back for some reason or another.

"Nat, what is it?"

Hesitantly, she started, "I think I need to be alone tonight." *She cautiously floated her gaze up to mine, her eyes pleading with me to be okay with this. That's the moment I first met "my Nat." And for her, I had to be okay with it.*

"Okay. Text me if you need me." The beginning of that as well.

Despite whether she wanted me to or not, I drew her into me. Her body stiffened right away and she didn't bother to even hug back. But she let me hold her and that was enough for tonight.

When I let her go, she whispered, "Goodbye, Caleb." It was the way she said it that told me it wasn't just for tonight.

"Night."

When she closed the door behind me, I swore I heard her heave a sigh of relief.

I drove home, not knowing what to make of the night. All I did know was I wasn't going anywhere and would be there for whatever Natalie needed. And I'd prove it with my actions.

Making sure Natalie knew I wasn't going anywhere proved to be harder than I expected. The next morning, there was a text from her.

I can't do this. Don't hate me.

Noting the time stamp was 3:45 a.m., I texted back when I woke up. I never heard back from her.

I texted her every day for a couple of days. I kept telling myself it was to make sure she was okay, but I knew there was more to it.

From the first day I met her, I could tell that there was something different about her, something I needed in my life. She wasn't like any other girl I had ever been with. The fact we had lasted two months was saying something for me, and I wasn't about to let a simple miscommunication be the end of us. I just had to find a way to get to her, to get through to her.

I thought Grayson would be a help, but he looked at me like I had five heads when I had only just mentioned she wasn't texting me. Either they weren't as close as he claimed them to be, or she hid this side of her from him. My suspicions told me it was the latter.

I found myself driving by her house, again under the guise that I was making sure she was okay, but I secretly needed to just see her, even from the distance.

After two weeks of her radio silence, I showed up at the coffee shop where she worked. She was busy and didn't see me come in. I didn't want to scare her nor have her think I was spying on her, but I also needed the element of surprise.

I watched her from a corner table for about fifteen minutes. If I hadn't witnessed her meltdown, I would have thought she was her usual bubbly self. But upon closer inspection, I could see the sadness behind her eyes, the exhaustion in her face, the fact that she was not okay. At first I thought I was imagining it, but when I finally stepped up to the head of the line and came face-to-face with her, it was even more evident. I watched the smile slip from her lips as she registered my presence.

"Hey," I said quietly.

She stumbled back a step, and as she caught herself, she plastered the smile back on her face, but it wasn't genuine. I didn't have time to process what that meant before she was asking me what I wanted to order.

"Large black coffee."

I smiled back at her as I watched her grab a cup and write my order and name. When I handed over my cash, I was forced to touch her hand. I took it as a good sign when she didn't pull hers away immediately. When she handed me my change, her hand hovered over mine longer than necessary to just dump the change.

Looking around, taking in the people around her, she whispered, "Don't go just yet. Stay. Please."

My heart flipped at her request, but my gut told me not to let her know that. "Yeah, I've got some time. I'll be in the back."

She cracked one more smile before taking the next customer in line.

While I waited for my name to be called, I watched her. She was a hard worker and precise in her movements that included running many different machines to prep a variety of drinks.

When I finally heard "Caleb," I grabbed my coffee from the barista and made my way back to my table. I powered up my laptop and pretended to get some work done, but I was distracted the entire time. I wondered why she wanted me to stay but my brain wouldn't allow itself to wander to any conclusions.

When I was done with my coffee, I realized I probably needed to make an appearance at the office sooner rather than later today. The coffee cup flipped on its side as I pushed back from the table, and I noticed the black scribble on the bottom. On further inspection, it was a note from Natalie.

Two words. MISS YOU.

Pretty sure my heart skipped a few beats. These words, coupled with the fact that she asked me to stay, had to mean something right?

I had to sit back down for a moment, overcome with emotion. When I looked up again, she was standing there, shifting from one foot to the other, like she either didn't know why she stood there or whether she should sit down.

"Do you have time to sit?" She glanced nervously around for a clock or her boss, I guessed, but then shuffled into the seat. "How are you?"

Taking a closer look at her, she seemed to be as put together as the Natalie I knew. The earlier sadness in her eyes had faded slightly. I couldn't help but wonder if that was because of me. Sure, I could hope.

"I only have a few minutes," she replied in response, avoiding my question.

"Yeah, I have to get back to work too. But, how are you?"

She hemmed and hawed, looking every which way but at me. It wasn't until I "Natted" her, that I finally got my answer.

"Somewhat miserable," she muttered, mostly under her breath. I couldn't help but crack a smile since she wasn't looking at me. As soon as her gaze traveled my way, I wiped it away. There'd be more time for smiles later, once she saw things my way.

"Look, Caleb, I owe you an apology. I was wrong..."

I cut her off. "Not here. Meet me at Trephines tonight. Seven-ish?"

I held my breath. I was in uncharted territory. In my mind, I pleaded with her to say she'd meet me. Begged, actually. Two weeks without talking to her, texting her, really seeing her, hell being inside her, was my own version of some kind of hell.

With a quick nod of her head, she hopped up out of her seat. "Seven," she replied as she walked away.

I sat back in my chair and watched her walk away. She walked a little taller, and her hips swung from side to side. Her tight jeans under her apron hugged every one of her curves, but I was getting ahead of myself. Way ahead of myself. It was just dessert, but I had learned Trephines' cheesecake was her kryptonite. Point one to Caleb.

The day dragged on. Work was pitiful because I had no focus but thankfully no one seemed to notice. After hitting the gym, I went home and showered.

I showed up to Trephines at a quarter till seven, surprised to see Natalie's car already parked there. She was still sitting in it, and I debated whether or not to knock on the window.

After five minutes, that part of me won out and there I stood, knocking on the window. If she was surprised to see me there, she didn't show it. She just put down her Kindle and got out of the car.

"Hey," she said, wiping her palms on her jeans.

"Hey. Come on. There's a cheesecake with your name on it." She walked a few paces behind me, but when I insisted on holding the door for her, she finally stepped in front of me.

We ordered our slices and sat down at a round table toward the back of the shop. It was a small shop, with only a few tables, but luckily it was quiet tonight.

As soon as we sat down, she appeared even more nervous, but I could tell she needed to talk.

"I don't want this to be awkward, so I'm going to just come out and say it." She paused for a moment to gather the courage to go on. Her hands were in her lap and even though I couldn't see them, I knew they were fidgeting.

"I owe you an apology. I freaked out, like really freaked out, and now that I've had time to digest it all, I see how much I overreacted. I wasn't lying when I said I don't know how to do relationships. The Abbotts are the only positive relationships I've had in my life, for myself and as models, ever. Without going into major details, suffice it to say I'm worse than a teenager when it comes to relationships. Sex I can do,

but when it comes to committed sex, I might as well be back in high school. I can also do single, and I'm okay with being single. Or I thought I would be. But I fucking missed the hell out of you these last few weeks, Caleb. Like going out of my mind, missed you. But I couldn't call or text you and come crawling back to admit that. Not because I'm too proud, but because I'm too scared. I'm scared that I will screw this up. Hell, I'm scared I've already screwed it up."

At that, I shook my head, earning me a small smile. *"That's good to know, because..."* She paused again. Pulling her hands out from her lap, she placed them next to mine. I watched as her pinky finger crept closer to my thumb, but I needed her to make the first move. *"Because I want to try again. I want to go back to being your Natalie."* She stopped, her pinky finger finally made its way to my thumb.

"I want you to be my Natalie again, too," I confirmed for her. *"On one condition though."*

I waited until her eyes met mine, not wanting her to misunderstand what I had to say. *"If you feel like it's not working, for any reason, let's talk about it. And I get that coming from me, that's not saying much, but I'm crazy about you and want this to work."*

"I can do that," she answered, moving her entire hand on top of mine.

After our cheesecakes were delivered, she dug right in, and I assumed our conversation was over. I didn't want to push her for more information or even *"where do we go from here?"* just to have her pull away again. Our relationship was still new, so I had to tread lightly, almost on thin ice if I wanted to see where this was going. And I could do that because hell, if I'd been on the other side, I'd be the first one to shut down. I'd earned the "silent type" moniker honestly. However, Natalie brought out a different side of me when we were together, at least when we were alone.

"I don't know who my father is," she began in a whisper.

If I hadn't been looking at her, I would have missed what she said. I put down my fork so she knew I was listening, but she didn't continue. I resumed my eating until she finally racked up the courage to speak again.

"And I won't pretend that my mom played the roles of Mom and Dad; she was barely Mom. Sometimes I think it's why I'm so screwed up." Her voice caught at the end, her face almost expressionless, as if she'd just accepted this fact about her life.

I threw my fork down. Before just blurting out she's not screwed up, I took a minute to gather my thoughts. And when I came up somewhat empty, all I could do was nod. And think about the situation I'm getting myself into with her. And for one hot minute, I contemplated that maybe it's not worth it, but then as quick as it came, I dismissed it entirely because she was worth it. And hell, I knew how to play the protective role.

Yep, if that was what she needed, I was her man.

"You're not screwed up," I told her.

"Well I screw up all the time," she retorted.

While I don't necessarily agree with her, I'm not about to argue with her in the middle of Trephines or allow her to feel like she should pull away again. Almost as if she sensed this, she changed the subject.

"Is it too presumptuous of me to ask your place or mine tonight?"

And just like that, our conversation was over, she was back to being the Natalie I knew, and she hid away *"my Nat"* for the time being. I was naive to think that things would ever be that easy with her.

"I'll meet you at your place in twenty. Need to run home for a few things," I said, starting to clean up our mess.

"I'll be waiting," she told me earnestly, a twinkle in those blue eyes.

Yeah, she was definitely an enigma, but I couldn't stay away.

As I finish up ten miles on the treadmill after my workout, I think about how I got her back for a while after that, and she opened up a little more about her past, especially about her mother. I never pushed her for information; I didn't need her disappearing on me again.

We settled nicely into a routine, and even when things got a little rocky, she pushed through and we were able to talk it out. I found myself opening up to her, but her alone, and we both let the world believe what they wanted to see about us; we were alike in that way.

Grayson comes over as I hit the STOP button. The thing I admire about the guy is that we don't need words to communicate, and since neither one of us is a huge talker nor into sharing our feelings, we know when to leave well enough alone. So his, "Hey, how's it going?" didn't have the same connotation as anyone else who may have asked the same question.

"I'm here at the crack of dawn," I offer as my way of answering him.

"Touché." He looks like he wants to ask more, which is strange for him. But well, Ainsley has done odd things to his personality, in the best possible ways.

To ease his mind a little, because I know he truly does care for Natalie, but not wanting to give away her secrets, I say, "She's okay."

He nods, glad I answered his unasked question. "She going through something?"

Without going into details nor wanting to elicit more questions, I answer, "Guess work has been rough." I can see in his eyes that he doesn't believe that's the reason, but he won't push for more.

"Here if you need to talk," he tosses my way and walks away.

My inner war continues to wage, and it's to the point where I'm not sure which side will be the victor at this point.

6

NATALIE

ONE WEEK LATER

*S*hit! SHIIIIIITTTT! No, make that fuuuuckkkkk! Like truly, I'm fucked. Like karma hates me or something. And the entire universe too. I mean, maybe one test could be a false positive, but five? Nope. I'm thinking that not all of them could be wrong.

The third positive is when I officially flipped out. Thank goodness Caleb wasn't home. By the fourth, I was hyperventilating. Now, with the fifth, I'm just a shit show. I can't make myself get off the bathroom floor. The tile is so cold that instead of getting up, I grab the nearest towel and lay it down for a pillow. Just my luck that it's Caleb's towel, and it smells like him. It would be better if it could be like old gym sweat, but no; it's the fucking Axe body spray that the man douses himself in. Because he needs to be more manly. *As if.*

What the hell am I going to do now? I've spent the last week already reassessing my life, taking stock of how I feel about Caleb, me, our relationship. Saying an unplanned pregnancy throws a monkey wrench into things is the understatement of the year. I haven't even figured out where I stand with Caleb, let alone having a BABY with him. Sure, we discussed the potential of kids, in the future, the distant future, not the we-are-on-a-break-and-I-need-to-sort-my-shit-out future.

For about ten seconds I contemplated if it was even Caleb's baby, but then I dredged up memories of tenth-grade biology class and realized it was nearly impossible for me to be pregnant a week after having sex. And I was at least three days late, if I calculated everything correctly. So, there's that.

I need someone to discuss this with. Someone who isn't Caleb. We're talking, which is good, but I know there's still some resentment on his part, which I totally get and understand. He even slept in our bedroom last night, even if he did stay completely on his side.

Again, I get it. I fucked up. But this isn't something I can even bring up right now anyway. How would that conversation even go? Yeah, can't go down that path right now.

Grayson is out because there's too much history I would need to dish out for him to even understand all of it, and the same goes for Bella. Which leaves me with Ainsley and/or Kylie. Ainsley, god love that woman, forgave me for lying to her and all it took was me promising not to do it again and a pedicure. I feel like I don't want to burden her with my problems again. She's got enough to deal with planning her wedding and her cupcake-business thing.

So that leaves me with Kylie. I'd have to catch her up to speed with a few things, but I wouldn't have to go into every detail, and she's like a vault, that one. She tells Bella almost everything, but I know she can keep a secret as long as it doesn't affect Bella or their relationship in any way. Let's be honest: this does not. While I love Bella, she can be too much to handle sometimes.

With my decision made of whom to talk to, it means getting up off the floor to go and get my phone. Slowly, like I'm an old woman or something, I push up to sitting. Drawing my knees into my chest, I sit for a little while longer, allowing my heartbeat to return to normal.

When I've waited it out a few more minutes, I push up to standing, eyeing the damn tests I so neatly lined up on the sink. I don't know what to do about them: keep them and hide them? Throw them away? Not in the mood to make the decision right then, I leave them there and go down the hallway to my bedroom to grab my phone, a text from Caleb waiting for me.

> Hey, I'll be home a little after 6. Can I take you out to dinner?

His text brings a smile to my face. It's what I love about the man; asking to take me on a date. In a lot of ways, he's stepping up his game during this break so I know what he wants life to be like. He's also showing me how much he loves me, and in other ways, what I would be missing if I don't choose him and can't work out my shit.

> Sure. How about the diner?

It's cheesy, I get that, but it's our spot. Stupidly enough, it's where he took me on our first date but only because there was nothing else open after our original plans for bowling ended. Now, it had become our place.

While I wait for his response, I text Kylie.

> So, I need an ear. Doesn't have to be today, just sometime in the near future. Please. So I don't freak out more than I'm already freaking.

I flop down on the bed as I wait for both responses. As if taunting me, I'm suddenly reminded of the night last week in which I had way too much to drink. Great, one more thing to add to the list of "how much can life suck right now?"

I'll tell you: infinitely. Life sucks infinitely.

When I hear the ping of the text message, I see who has responded.

> With or without the Mrs.?

> Definitely without. Will explain why.

No explanation needed. One hour?

I look over at the clock. It's 2:30. I love friends who work from home.

Perfect. You want to come over to my place?

Sure. See you then.

I have one hour to decide exactly what I'm going to say to her. I kinda know what I need to say, but I have to figure it the exact words.

I spend the hour lying in bed, looking at the ceiling for answers to life's greatest mysteries. I get nothing, so when I hear the front door open, I make the wise decision to just head downstairs to meet Kylie.

"Hey, where you at?" I hear from downstairs. Meandering down the stairs, when she comes in to view, I notice not only cups of coffee from Joe's Café, but a plain white bag that I know has to contain some sort of delicious, sugary concoction. If it's from Ainsley's kitchen, all the better.

"Hey," I call out coming into her view. "Can I just tell you how much it means that one, you are here? Two, you have coffee? And three, you brought treats?"

"Not just any treats: cupcakes. Not sure if they are Grayson's or Ainsley's but does it really matter?" She gives me a smile and a wink.

"It does not. Most of the time I can't tell the difference anyway. I'm not sure if they secretly love or hate it."

"Right?"

While Ainsley may be the one pursuing a business venture in cupcakes, Grayson is more than just her financial backer. As if he's not perfect enough, the guy can cook and bake like nobody's business.

I make my way into the kitchen, Kylie following me. Setting

the coffee and our treats on the table, she pulls me into a hug. "You looked like we should start with that."

"Thanks. I most certainly did." I let her embrace me and fight like crazy to keep my emotions in check. Not wanting to let go, my desire for the cupcakes finally wins out, and I pull myself out of her arms.

Sitting down at the table, she hands me my coffee and the bag. I peek in to find four cupcakes, each one a different flavor. "Do I even want to know why you have these? Or am I just going to be jealous that you have them but were at least kind enough to bring some for me?"

"I stopped over there on my way here. They were both there, baking away, so I just swiped a few. I figured they didn't need to know they weren't for Bella."

"I hoped you knocked before you went in." I watch her expression as she answers.

"With those two? Always! I've heard enough; I don't need to see it too." She shudders.

I can't help but laugh. I take the red velvet one and pass the bag over to her. She chooses one that looks like it may be chocolate and peanut butter. Taking a hearty bite, I can't help but moan. It's simply not fair how delicious the cupcake is. It's also not fair that they both can whip them up from scratch and make them taste this delicious. I'm pretty decent in the kitchen, but the two of them? They take the cake, pun intended.

We eat our cupcakes in silence, but I know it's because Kylie is waiting for me to talk. I slow down the eating of my cupcake both as a stall tactic and as a way to savor the deliciousness.

"Shit, that's good. I needed that right about now. Thanks." I look over to Kylie. She's eaten about half of her cupcake and sits there waiting on me to speak. Her hands are folded on the table in front of her, eyes watching my every move. "Long story short, Caleb and I had a fight last week and I got wasted."

"Yes, I'm well aware of that fact. You texted Bella and then we saw the aftermath of your fight at Grayson's."

I nod in affirmation. "Right. I can't tell you what the fight was about, but what you don't know is that I slept with a coworker that same night." I study her face for cues of judgment. Her expression remains stoic. Either she's not here to judge or she already knows, but it's beside the point right now.

When she stays quiet, I continue. "Caleb decided, or maybe it was me, I don't remember at this point, that we needed a break. More like I needed time to figure my shit out and what I wanted, blah blah blah." I don't mean to minimize it, but this isn't why I asked her here. "So that's what we've been doing for the past week, kind of like our relationship is on pause while I figure out what I want. Great man that he is, he's going to be there until I decide. He's still mad, but at least he's letting his anger ebb for now."

I pause there for a moment, needing to take a sip of my coffee. Not like it's alcohol, but I need some sort of liquid courage. The dark roast flavor hits the spot, especially after the red velvet cupcake.

All of a sudden, it hits me that in my condition, I may not be able to even drink coffee. And I literally spit it out. While she isn't sitting directly in front of me, some of the spray hits her. "Shit! Sorry."

I hop up and grab some paper towels, handing her a few so she can clean up the spew that landed on her arms.

"What's that about?" she questions. "Are you pregnant or something?" She chuckles, but when I still, the laugh dies on her lips. "Oh shit." As she wipes down her arm, her expression changes. While it's a look of concern, it's clouded by worry.

"Yeah. So that's why I needed someone's ear. I don't fucking know what to do!" I thought it might feel a little better to get it off my chest, but I can feel the panic starting to rise again, threatening to drown me. I rest my arms on the table and then lay my head on top. I feel Kylie's arm rubbing my back.

"It's going to be okay," she starts.

My brain wants to yell at her: "Don't say that; you don't know that!" but since she came here when I asked, I hold those thoughts in. Instead, I say, "I fucking hope so. I can barely keep my head above water with other things in my life, but this? I don't even know how to process it."

Kylie's quiet, but she doesn't quit rubbing my back. After a few minutes, I sit up and grab another cupcake, rip a piece off and shove it in my mouth. Swallowing, I mumble, "Oh my god! I think I'm just going to eat these for the rest of my life. I can exist on cupcakes, right?"

"Good thing you have an in with the bakers," she responds with a giggle, as she takes a seat back in her chair. "So where do you go from here?"

I get it's a logical question, but I don't have an answer for her and really can't even think about where I go from here.

"I'm not entirely sure. Figure out a way to tell Caleb without it ruining anything that I'm working on for myself. Guess I'm glad it happened now so at least he knows it's his and not someone else's." I laugh but know it's not funny. It's pure irony is what it is.

Kylie nods in agreement. "You want my advice?" Her voice is hesitant.

"Yep. Please." I look over to her, awaiting her advice. I trust and value her opinion.

"As much as you can, put the baby aside for a moment and focus on what you want. If this wasn't a factor, what decision would you make? Once you've given that some thought, see how a baby fits in with that decision. Maybe it does, maybe it doesn't. Only you can decide that once you've evaluated other aspects of your life."

Her advice makes sense. I haven't fully made my decision of where I stand yet, about how to even get my shit together because regardless if I end up with Caleb or not, I still need to do some work on myself. I have a good idea of where I want to be, but I just have to figure out how to get to a place where I'm committed enough to it. And this new wrinkle complicates the hell out of things.

"So wise. That's why I chose you to confide in."

"And I owe you a secret," she agrees. "You going to be okay?"

Slowly, I nod. I force myself to give her a little smile, not just for her benefit, but for mine too.

"Thank you. Not sure what you had going on today but really glad you came to listen. And you brought kick-ass cupcakes. And the coffee. I'll have to Google if I can drink that." I get up to grab my phone and realize I left it upstairs. "Be right back."

I find it on the bed and as I'm making my way back down to the kitchen, it pings with a text from Caleb.

Yeah sure. Hopefully our booth will be available.

I can't help the smile that seems to overtake my face. I'm still smiling when I get back to the kitchen.

"Caleb?" Kylie guesses. I nod. When she adds, "I see," I get it. With a simple text, my smile is automatic; it means something, like even my inexperienced heart knows what it wants. Now to just get my stupid head there too.

"On that note, I'm going to go. Keep the other cupcake. I'm sure you will enjoy it more than I will." Kylie stands up and draws me in for another hug.

"This stays between you and me for now, right?" I know I don't need to ask, but it would help to just confirm it.

"Always. But Sunday night is dinner at Grayson's, yeah?"

I shrug. "Not that I know of."

"Oh. Shit, sorry. I thought Bella said something about all of us going over there, but I could be wrong. Sometimes she talks so much I only half listen and nod when needed."

I laugh. The woman has her wife pegged so well, and as overwhelming as Bella is, when you need someone to have your back, she's your girl. I've known that since the day I met her.

"No worries. I've got enough of my own shit to worry about now anyway, none of which involves our friends."

"Yeah, you do, girl. Let me know if you need to talk anymore. Getting out of the house breaks up the monotony of my day."

"Glad I could help." She smiles at my comment, and we both laugh. "See you soon."

I walk her to the front door and with a quick wave in my direction, she's gone. I go back upstairs and hide away the evidence of my current situation, knowing that sometime in the near future, I will have to tell Caleb. But I'm not focused on that right now. I text him back.

> Sounds like a plan. See you soon. Going to take a nap.

And so I do, but sleep doesn't come easy. I eventually fall asleep because later, I'm woken up when the bed dips with Caleb's weight. When he hears my groan, he whispers, "Sorry, didn't mean to wake you."

I sit up in bed and glance at the clock.

"You're home early. Give me a few minutes to wake up and then I'll get ready for dinner."

"No rush. I had a late lunch." He kicks off his shoes and lays down next to me in the bed, his large body taking up more than his share. I want to snuggle into him, but I know that I shouldn't. But the temptation is so strong. "Did Ainsley stop by today?" he asks, out of the blue. Looking over at him, I shake my head.

"Kylie did, but she brought the cupcakes. I've already had two; feel free to eat the last one. It's damn delicious."

He laughs. "I'll save it for dessert."

He looks over at me, like he's got more to say. His eyes narrow as he sweeps them up and down my body. I would love to know what's going on in his mind. When his tongue darts out of his mouth and licks his bottom lip slowly, I have a pretty good idea of what he's thinking. And then I feel bad for him because since we are on a break, he instituted the no-sex rule.

Although it's only been like ten days, some days it feels way longer. I can only imagine how he must be feeling. The man is a machine some days, but I've never struggled to keep up with him, too much at least. Our sex life has never been an issue for us; hell, angry sex between Caleb and me is fucking hot. Like, scorching hot. I realize I'm not helping my own situation by thinking of past sexual experiences, so I hop out of bed to get ready for dinner.

"I can't handle a dress tonight, Nat. Or cleavage." When I turn to look at him as he utters those words, his eyes are closed, but he's adjusting himself.

Since the guy pretty much worships my body daily, I oblige him. And tell my mind that it needs to figure shit out sooner rather than later.

7

CALEB

$\mathcal{I}$'d be lying if I said that this break was easy. Every day it gets harder, everything gets harder, including my dick. Especially my dick. I can't even remember the last time we went this long without sex. The answer to that question may be never. I'm just thankful that she's respectful of the "no sex" rule and not trying to get me all worked up. It's not her fault I do that to myself. I can't seem to help it because she's damn sexy and because knowing I can't have it, makes me want it more. I know I said I'd wait her out and let her have her time to work on her shit, but damn. This. Is. Hard. Puns intended.

I've lost track of how many days it's been. I don't ask her where she's at with everything either. She checks in with me once a day, but I don't push her. Whatever she wants to give me is enough. I can only be hopeful that one of these days she'll tell me she knows what she wants, and that it will be me. Not sure how life will go on if she doesn't choose us, so I avoid thinking about it at all costs. I've definitely seen the inside of the gym way more than ever before, and I may need new sneakers soon with all the miles I've put on them running out my stress.

I eventually told Grayson that we were taking some time to

work out some things; he didn't need to know it was Natalie who was working shit out. I didn't really have to tell him anyway; he could see it from our interactions at dinners, and I'm sure Natalie had to tell Ainsley some of what was going on.

About three weeks into our break, Natalie starts acting weirder. I curse myself for not being able to ask her what's going on, for being the stand-up kind of guy who will let her come to me. I almost lose it one night at dinner.

I'm home later than usual. One of my clients had a crisis at their shop, so of course I had to go and fix it. I can tell she's not happy when I walk in, the table set, and dinner already laid out. She sits at the table, hands clasped together, a rigid look on her face. Without thinking, I kiss the top of her head.

"I'm sorry. There was an emergency at Sal's I had to take care of. Dinner smells amazing." I put my stuff on the counter but need to wash my hands.

"You could have sent a text to let me know you were going to be late," she chides.

"By the time I realized I was going to be so late, I was on my way already and didn't think it mattered at that point."

After washing my hands, I sit down across from her. I take a bite, and it's cold, which is my fault.

Standing to warm it up in the microwave, she asks, "What are you doing?"

"Warming it up. It's cold."

"Yeah well, you said you were going to be home by five so it was ready for 5:15." Her tone is not only edgy, but it gets louder as she finishes speaking.

"I said I'm sorry. What more do you want?"

"Never mind." She huffs but begins to eat her meal.

"Do you need me to warm yours up?" I ask hopeful I can find a way to make this up to her.

She shakes her head.

Well, okay then. This is how we are going to play it.

Once mine is warm, I sit back down and dig in. It's good, not great, but I wouldn't ever let Natalie know, especially with her annoyance tonight.

I try to lighten the mood a little. "How was your day?"

"I spoke to my mother," is her response.

Suddenly things fall into place. Natalie and her mother have an odd relationship. Since it was only the two of them for all of Natalie's life, I would have expected them to be closer. However, Natalie's made it very clear that they were never close and will never be close. In five years, I've only met her mother twice. She moved out of state when Natalie graduated college and doesn't come back to visit much. She's never been to our house, not that we have lived here long.

The only time I questioned her about her mother, Natalie shut me down so fast that I've never asked again. She's told me bits and pieces about her mother growing up and even now, she doesn't share much about her life. I've learned not to ask, and I'm especially not asking under tonight's circumstances. She'll volunteer information when she feels necessary.

Natalie's quiet, so I try another tactic. "You want to go bowling tomorrow? I think the gang will be there."

She looks at me. "Yeah, that could be fun. At least it's not pool."

When she smiles, it's all the crack in her armor that I need.

"No shit." Ainsley's a bit of a pool shark, and even though she's a damn good bowler too, she's not as good as she is at pool. "I'll let Grayson know. I think it's like some sort of specials night, including two-dollar pitchers of beer. Should be fun."

She chokes on her food. Once she's swallowed, she looks back at me. "It will be." She puts her fork down. With no hesitation in her voice, she questions, "Have you forgiven me yet? For cheating?"

Well, that's out of left field.

I put down my fork and take in her appearance. Her face gives nothing away; she's hiding what she's feeling from me, which can never be a good thing.

"Do you know why you did it?" I ask instead of answer her. I've forgiven her, mostly. It still hurts a little that she chose to do it, but she's berating herself as it is so I figure I need to let it go as much as I can.

Her eyes gaze down toward her food. She pushes the meatballs around the plate with her fork.

"I was overwhelmed. We were fighting, and I was pissed. I knew the ultimate revenge was to sleep with someone else because I knew your feelings on the matter. And while those all sound like excuses, I'm not trying to make excuses. I just needed to feel good about myself for the night, and I thought he did that for me."

"Because I don't make you feel good about yourself?" I hesitate even asking the question, but fuck that. I deserve to know.

"You used to, but I feel like lately you don't. And he did, so rather than talk to you about it, I stupidly thought he could give me what I needed."

"He fucked you in the back of his car, Natalie. How special did that make you feel?"

Her eyes fly up to mine, shock quickly registering on her face. And maybe that was harsh, but it's what she needs to hear. I push up out of my seat to grab a beer and chug more than half before I sit back down.

"You want to know what I was thinking while he was fucking me in the back seat of his car? Because I remember it now. All too clear."

As much as I don't, the words, "Tell me," escape my lips.

She hesitates and then appears to be working up the nerve to tell me.

"I don't know if it was the backseat of the car or if it was him, but I remember thinking that it all felt wrong. That I shouldn't be there, that the sex was mediocre. Sex with you is never mediocre. And once I started thinking about you, I knew how pissed you were going to be. And that I should stop what I was doing. But I couldn't stop. Until he called me sweetie. And it was all wrong."

She's got tears at the corners of her eyes, and it takes all of my strength not to wipe them away, not to comfort her. "I just had to let him finish, but I couldn't. I couldn't finish because he wasn't you. And he was stupid enough to believe me when I told him I was good. So how's that for irony? Even when I cheat, it sucks."

I don't know how to react. I don't know whether I should be glad she was thinking of me or disgusted. And let's not forget she shouted his name the next time when she came on my fingers. What the hell was that about? Not thinking I should ask her, right now at least. So I don't say anything.

When she starts talking again, her voice is small. "I was wrong, Caleb. I was so wrong for cheating on you. I know what I want, but I'm not there yet. But I want you. I just need a little more time to sort a few more things out. I need to make sure if I feel this way again, that I handle it better. That I talk to you about it; that we work it out together. Because I didn't feel special in the back of his car, but earlier, when you kissed the top of my head, that simple gesture made me feel special, and I'd be damn stupid to throw this all away."

I want to hug her. I want to kiss her. I want to fuck the shit out of her. I just want to hold her, to make her see that she IS special.

I'm not stupid enough to know that none of this is about me; it's about how she feels about herself, how she deals with love, but it can't hurt to make sure she knows I think she's pretty damn special too, and that I'm not going anywhere.

"Storm," I start, using the nickname I gave her on our second date because even then, she'd had a storm brewing in her eyes, and her personality is nothing if it isn't stormy. As expected, it softens her expression, breaking through to her a little more.

"I told you, I'm not going anywhere. Take all the time you need. Although I will say that I'm glad you are leaning toward us."

She wipes the tears from her eyes. "How can you be so sure all the time? Why do you keep waiting for me? I fuck up all the time, Caleb, and you are always here."

"Because I love you, Natalie, and that's what you do when you love someone."

"I love you, too. It's not that I don't feel that for you; it's just that I need that extra push to take that leap of faith."

Once again, I get myself out of my chair. Pulling her chair away from the table, I kneel in front of her. Her hands in mine, I look deep into those baby blue eyes of hers.

I whisper, "Jump, Nat. I'll be here to catch you."

And because I know I've gotten most of my girl back, I lean in for a kiss. I intend for it to be sweet, but she unlatches her hands from mine, throws her arms around my neck and launches at me, all the while kissing me back.

There's nothing gentle about her kiss; it's needy, raw, and enough to make me want to take her upstairs and fuck her until the morning. But I won't; I'll just continue kissing her until she pulls away. Or until I can't breathe any longer, whichever comes first.

After what seems like hours, but is probably only minutes, she pulls away, having thoroughly attacked my lips.

"Caleb." My name falls from her lips in a murmur. She keeps her eyes closed and her breathing is ragged, which matches my own. I unlatch her arms from my neck and stand up.

"I'll clean up dinner in a bit. Going to go take a shower."

Her eyes dart to my erection, straining to break free. She covers her mouth to try and hide the giggles.

"Sorry, not sorry," she calls after me when I've walked away.

I have no comeback.

* * *

I'm glad to see that bubbly Nat is pretty much back, especially when we go bowling the next night. After another restless night of sleep next to her, I decide to finally forgive her for her transgressions. It's not because of what she told me, how she felt in the back seat of the car; it's because I love her.

In some ways, we will always have a tumultuous relationship; it's all we've ever known, but it works for us. I just hope she can finally take the leap of faith and trust my love for her is enough, and what she feels for me—that she loves me—isn't something to be scared of. No matter what happens, we will work through it all.

After the second game, the two-dollar pitchers of beer are starting to take effect. Poor Ainsley's the worst, which is usually not the case; it's usually Bella or Natalie. Nat's pretty much sober, and as for Bella and Kylie, they are holding their own.

After knocking down nine pins, Natalie sidles up to me. "Grayson wants your keys." Knowing the drill, without arguing, I hand them over to her. Before I let her walk back to him, I grab her into me.

"How's he going to drive us all home?"

"I'm fine," she tells me. Taking her all in, even in my inebriated state, I can tell she's not lying. "The cheap beer isn't doing it for me tonight," she adds with a shrug. "But Ainsley's taking a hit, huh?" She giggles as she looks over at her friend who's practically asleep on the chairs.

"Gray," I call out to him. He's taking off her bowling shoes even though we are in the middle of a game. When he looks over at me, I gesture to Ainsley. "She okay?"

He shakes his head. "We are out once this game is over. You give Natalie your keys?" Natalie holds them up to confirm. "Okay, I'll drive the girls home. Let's get this game done."

We finish out the game, and I down the pitchers of beer still left. When we are all finished and packing up, Grayson has to carry Ainsley out. Not sure she even woke up.

"Dude, how much did she have to drink?" I ask with a laugh. "I've never seen her so wasted."

Grayson eyes my girlfriend. "Natalie kept refilling her cup. I should send her home with you. She's going to be hurting tomorrow."

"Yeah, she is," Natalie agrees. "Sorry, Gray. Hope you didn't have any big plans for tonight." She laughs, but her face falls when he glares in her direction. "Tell her to call me when she's coherent."

Grayson grunts something in reply, tells the girls to get a move on, and continues outside.

"Well, that was fun." Natalie's got that look, the one that says I should pack up my shit now and let her drive me home. But I don't, and when she suggests, "Wanna bet the next game?" all of my rational instincts go out the window.

"Game on."

I don't even know what we are playing for, but with Natalie, it doesn't matter; it will be good. I erase our friends' names from the computer and get our game started.

"Since sex is clearly off the table, what are we wagering?" She stands in front of where I'm sitting and places her hands on my thighs. Her eyes are hungry, hungry for something I can't give her yet.

Taking a deep breath, I push her back and stand up. A man's only got so much control. She's taken aback at first, but then she shrugs.

"I'm leaving that up to you. This is your bet."

She takes her time deciding what to wager. She mutters things under her breath but I don't catch all of what she says. As if a light bulb goes off in her head, she declares proudly, "I've got it!" And then she stops, the huge grin never leaving her face.

I wait for her to continue but when she doesn't, I ask, "Are you just going to leave me hanging?" I wouldn't put it past her to make me guess.

She strides over to where I'm standing next to the ball rack. At first she just stands there, but I feel her heart pounding. Okay, maybe not physically *feel* it, but with Nat, I just know. She looks up at me, and since she's got flats on, the distance between our faces is a big one, at least eight inches.

She starts in a whisper. "For one week, the loser has to make coffee for the winner." I think she's done, but then she adds, "No, not make coffee. Buy coffee. From Joe's Cafe and have it piping hot and ready for the winner before he/she gets out of bed." She winks her left eye at me and the smile becomes a smirk.

Both of us are huge coffee drinkers, especially in the morning. I usually skip it on the mornings I head to the gym, but when I get home, I've either stopped on my way for my first cup, or I make it as soon as I walk in the door. For Natalie, the only thing she does in the morning before her first cup is pee.

The bet is actually ingenious, except for the fact that if she loses, she'll have a hard time getting my cup for me in the early morning. And that fact alone not only tips the scales in my direction, but also makes my grin mirror hers.

"Storm, that may be the best bet you've ever come up with, besides the sexual ones of course. May the best bowler win." I place a kiss on the top of her head and get ready to throw my first ball.

I may have underestimated a few factors in Nat's favor. One, I'm past tipsy and while I'm sobering up a bit, it's hard to get my ball to go straight down the lane. It's veered off into the gutter a few more times for my liking. Two, Natalie's stone-cold sober which gives her just enough of an edge to knock down a few more pins than I've been able to. Three, every time she walks up to the lane, her hips sway in an exaggerated motion and her ass is on full display. She's doing it on purpose but damn it if it isn't working to her advantage. The little smirks she tosses in my direction as she walks back after throwing her ball divulge she knows exactly what she's doing.

After five frames, she's winning by five. I figure I still have time to catch up; it's only five pins.

In the sixth frame, she manages a strike. She can't quite believe it herself and as she turns around after watching all ten pins fall, she's got a stunned look on her face. When she glances up at me, it quickly disappears as if she's trying to hide the fact that she's surprised.

"Let's see what you've got, BG."

I take my time deciding which ball to choose. I haven't quite found one that has worked for me yet tonight, so I keep selecting different ones.

Once I've settled on the one I'll start with, I make my way over to the lane. Just as I'm about to start my routine, she whistles at me. Needless to say, the ball ends up in the gutter. Again.

As I walk back, I shoot her a look.

Pointing behind her, she admits, "That guy over there got two strikes in a row. I was just sharing my congratulations with him." Try as she may, she can't hide the pleased expression on her face that has me scowling.

"Yeah, okay."

Taking a sip of the beer that remains, I use it as liquid courage. Courage to stay focused on my game and ignore the beauty that's trying to sabotage it.

When I'm ready to throw my second ball of the frame, I glance back at her. She's pretending to pick at her nails and ignoring me. Thinking I'm good, I quickly get into position and release the ball. It knocks down eight of the pins. A small victory.

After my turn, I take a seat in the chairs to watch her. She's got more pressure on her because she's got the strike to add on to. A part of me wants to catcall her, but I remain silent and watch what she does. She seems to have it all lined up, but when she lifts her arm, her wrist twists, causing the ball to ride the gutter. It does hit one pin right before it lands in the gutter at the end of the alley.

"Well that was stupid," she exclaims to herself. She glances in my direction, but I keep the stoic look plastered on my face. I won't let her know that I'm inwardly cheering her mistake.

Her second ball manages to hit three and they in turn knock down a few more. All in all, her frame wasn't too bad, but if I can get a strike or even a spare, I may be able to eke out the win.

Before I grab my ball, I sidle up to where she's sitting by the computer. I lean in and whisper in her ear, "Nothing good ever comes from cheating, Storm."

The double innuendo isn't lost on her as I hear her draw in a breath. I know the target hits its mark because she stays silent the rest of the time I'm bowling.

The game comes down to the tenth frame. She's leading, but

only by three pins. Unfortunately, I'm up first. I hit the spare with the first two balls but only manage to add five pins with the third. For her to win, she needs a spare or a strike, but at this point, nothing is an impossibility.

The first ball knocks down four. She stares up at the screen, doing the math in her head of how many pins she needs to win. I can tell she's slightly nervous from her body language and because she won't look at me. She bounces from foot to foot as she waits for her ball to be returned.

Once her "lucky" ball has come back to her, she hesitantly grabs it from the return rack, sticks her fingers in, and walks to the lane. She pauses for a moment, almost as if she's figuring out a way to knock down the last six pins she needs to claim her victory. I bet she has her eyes closed, willing the pins to be knocked down by the ball she'll throw.

When she finally steps back and releases the ball, it goes straight down the middle, knocks down the headpin, spins off to the side, and knocks down the rest of the pins that were still standing. She does a victory dance, swaying those hips from side to side, jumping in the air every so often while fist pumping.

"Nat, I hate to burst your bubble, but you haven't won yet."

Her eyes narrow and she scoffs in my direction. "Yeah, but I only need to hit three pins down to win. Piece of cake." She's quite sure of herself, and while there's a tiny part of me that will be happy if she wins, I'll be more ecstatic when I win and she's serving me hot coffee in bed every morning for a week.

"No time like the present," I tell her, motioning to the ball that's just come back from the return chute.

Instead of taking her last turn, she comes over to where I'm sitting. I can tell what she wants to do, but she just stands in front of me, her thumb in her mouth, her teeth nibbling on the nail. If she won't do it, I will. She's slightly taken aback when I grab her and pull her onto my lap. "One last ball, Nat. Make it count."

I try to push her up, but she won't have it. Instead, she settles herself more on my lap, facing me, her legs straddling mine. She's got a wicked gleam in her eyes, but what comes out of her mouth doesn't match the look.

"I've missed this, Caleb. Not just the fact that we are out on a date, but the fun times we have. When did we stop hanging out with just each other?"

While I'm glad she's opening up, I can't have this heavy conversation with her at the bowling alley, still tipsy. Teetering on a fine line between letting her say what's on her mind versus shooting her down until later, I give her my truth.

"I don't know. But now that we are both aware of it, let's change that fact." It seems to be the right answer based on the softening of her expression, but she doesn't move her body. "Finish your last frame, and we can discuss it at home."

She nods and hops off my lap, mumbling and repeating "home." She picks up her final ball, approaches the lane, sets up the shot, and releases the ball. It doesn't go exactly the way she wants, so she leans her entire body to the left, trying to coax the ball that way too. Right before it hits the pins, the ball seems to magically listen to her and at least four pins get knocked down. And that's when she really celebrates.

"Yes!" she shouts. "I win. Coffee every day for the next week. Just for shits and giggles, I may change my order every day for variety. Oh, I can taste that macchiato now."

She's jumping up and down in victory and starts to take off for a victory lap. Before she can do that, I grab her into me and hold her tight. Her back is to my front and I cross my arms over her chest, boxing her in.

"Stop with the sexy, Storm. You win fair and square. But just stop with the sexy."

She looks back up at me with a smirk. "Glad I know how to work you up, BG, even when I'm not trying." And then just because she's my Nat, she swipes her hand across the straining erection in my jeans. When she naughtily whispers, "Soon, my friend, soon," I hold on with every ounce of man strength I have not to come in my pants.

All I can do is release her and take a loser lap around the alley before I lose more than just a bowling game.

8

NATALIE

$\mathcal{C}$aleb's quiet on the drive home, and even though he convinced me he was okay to drive, I wasn't taking any chances. I didn't need Grayson mad at me again. He definitely loosened up after the fight about my situation with Caleb, but after I pretty much forced Ainsley to drink not only her share of beer, but mine as well, I don't think he's too happy with me right now. I don't need to add any more fuel to the fire.

I didn't tell Ainsley about my current situation, the one thing I'm holding back from Caleb too, but she has an inkling. I didn't even tell her Caleb and I were on a break, but she may have figured that out too. She's pretty perceptive that one. While I'm not trying to put her in the middle again between Grayson and me, we've come to an understanding that sometimes as friends, you don't share everything with your significant others. I owe him a lot after I talk with Caleb and we figure all our shit out. And by our, I mean mine. Well except for the baby. That we need to figure out together.

In some ways, the shock still hasn't worn off. I haven't truly accepted it yet, either, but I'm working on it. What I have decided is that I owe Caleb a discussion, tonight, about where I'm at. I'm glad he's more sober now after our little bet than he would have been had we left with the others.

Pulling the car into the driveway, he mutters, "Home."

He said it before, and it sent shivers down my back. It's never been so high on my radar to be calling the place I live "home." All of a sudden, in the past few weeks, it's like the word has taken on a new meaning, one in which has more significance than ever. And I think I've finally realized why.

Once inside, he kicks off his shoes and heads upstairs.

"Can we talk?" I call out to him, hoping he hears it before he's too far up the stairs.

"Make a pot of coffee, and I'll be down in a few."

As I get the coffee going, I hear the shower start. I can't help the smile that spreads over my face and how it warms my insides that I'm getting to him. It's not that I'm doing it on purpose; it just makes me realize what we have is stronger than I've given credit to lately. I guess I stopped paying attention to my effect on him. Secretly, I'm thrilled I still turn him on, without even trying. It makes my decision that much easier.

Once the coffee is ready, I pour us each a large mug, dump some creamer in mine, and take them into the living room. Since the water in the shower is still on, I quickly dart upstairs to change into sweats.

Coming out of the bedroom after changing, I hear Caleb's drawn-out "Fuckkkkkk." I kinda feel bad for the guy. It was his rule for no sex, but it's because of my stupid actions that put us here. But that will hopefully be remedied tonight. If I can just figure out a way to tell him about the baby.

He waltzes into the living room a little while later, freshly showered, in a shirt that he would wear to the gym. The T-shirt is stretched tightly over his biceps, and the way his sweats hang low on his hips, I have to will myself to contain my excitement. And then I remember what we need to do tonight. I try my best to tone down my emotions because I can't turn them off.

He takes a seat in his recliner but doesn't recline it back. His mug is on the table next to the chair so he takes a long sip and then looks in my direction. He's waiting for me to start, and if I could just work up the nerve to do so, I would.

Taking one last sip, I take a deep breath. I have to be strong and actually look at him when I speak; I know that it will be more meaningful that way, and I need him to know I'm serious this time. His expression is neutral, his eyes their usual brown. He's pretty much sobered up all the way so it's now or never.

I begin. "Okay, so here's where I'm at. I've already apologized for my indiscretions. I've done a lot of thinking the last few weeks. A lot. More so than I've probably ever done before. And the one thing I keep coming back to is *you*. You love me. And while I may think I'm undeserving of that love sometimes, it's an unwavering fact that you love me, more so that I've ever shown you I've deserved. Especially with my behavior of late.

"A part of me has always known what you feel for me is true love, a force so strong that has allowed you to forgive me when I've walked away because of my issues. And to say that feeling has overwhelmed me in the past is quite an understatement. I don't know how you can look past the fact that I've walked out multiple times to deal with my own stuff and you've still been here waiting for me. I didn't get it because I never understood where you were coming from."

I pause for a minute to let that sink in. Of course the guy doesn't react to my words because either he knows I'm not done, or he truly gets me. Maybe a combination of both.

I drop my voice to a whisper. "I get it now, Caleb. At least I think. Love isn't about making grand gestures every day to show the other one you care. It's about the small things, which you have always done for me. That I took for granted and also seemed to not appreciate. For that, I'm sorry. But I realized that I can't keep apologizing for doing stupid shit." Yep, *that* gets his attention. "I just have to stop doing stupid shit." He cracks a smile. "And I'm not saying that I won't ever do stupid shit again, except for the cheating. That I'm done with. But getting overwhelmed and realizing that what I'm feeling is bigger than me, yeah that's going to take some time for me to still work out all the kinks. And I may disappear from time to time, but just for a few hours." Deep breath in and out for the rest of my speech. "But I know what I want. I want you, Caleb. I want us. And if the offer is still on the table, I want nothing more than to marry you."

His eyes go wide at my admission. I kinda expected that. "You're sure?" He's barely able to get the question out in a whisper. I nod my head. "It's always been you, Caleb. It just takes me longer to get to places you seem to be comfortable with. There are some things we should still discuss about our relationship, things that I'm learning need to be communicated to you. It's kind of ironic how I always find myself not knowing how to communicate the big things in our lives, the things that mean the most, when I find ways to let myself be heard in every other aspect of my life. But I feel like it's always been that way with us. You never let me go."

He interrupts me, getting out of his chair, coming to sit next to me.

"I don't know how to, Storm. I couldn't imagine my life without you, ever. It's why I wait. From the beginning, I am the only person you've ever let into your life, fully and completely; you let your guard down with me. And while sometimes you put those damn walls up, you always come back. Whenever I see the slightest crack in your walls, I figure out ways to knock them down, without you even knowing what I'm doing. It's because deep down, I know you're just scared. But you don't have to be scared anymore. I'll always catch you."

"I was hoping you'd say that."

Taking him by complete surprise, I literally jump into his arms. He wobbles for a few seconds, but then his strong arms wrap around me, holding onto me for dear life. I realize I still have one confession left to make. And it just tumbles out of my mouth. "I'm pregnant."

I scrutinize his face. The smile that was there just moments ago falls, his eyes narrow, and anger takes over. His grasp on me starts to falter; I can feel myself slipping back down onto the couch. He seems to realize I'm falling but instead of picking me up, he drops me gently to the couch.

"How long?" he grunts out.

"Eight weeks." I can see his brain trying to figure out the timeline. To ease his thoughts, because I'm sure I know where they are going, I add, "It's yours."

He shakes his head from side to side and starts pacing. "You're sure?" His voice is edgy but quiet. Almost as if he didn't want to ask it but knew he had to. He stops momentarily, waiting on my answer. At my nod, he starts to breathe again and resumes his pacing.

"The timing sucks."

"You think, Nat?" comes his sarcastic reply.

Okay, wow, that was harsh.

I sink back deeper onto the couch and sigh. He stops his pacing.

"Oh shit. I didn't mean that. I'm just surprised." He comes over to me and sits next to me on the couch, pulling me onto his lap. "Shit, Storm. I wasn't expecting that to come out of your mouth." He looks into my eyes, and I can see the fear in his. I'm just not sure how I feel about the fear or what to make of it.

"I don't know how it happened," I start. And then it hits me that I actually do. "Crap. I do."

He looks at me questioningly. When I don't offer up a response right away, he asks, "You want to enlighten me?"

"Remember how we were supposed to go away last month, but we didn't end up going?" He nods. "I played around with my birth control so that I wouldn't have my period while we were gone. I bet it screwed it up, especially since we didn't end up going."

"Oh." It's just the one-word response, but there's so much conveyed in the word. And then as if something hits him, he asks, "Are you okay? Other than the fact that it's probably the worst timing, are you okay?"

I think about my answer for a minute. "It's horrible timing, that I get. But given my track record, I'm okay with it. And I know this because I didn't run. But I also don't know if I've accepted it fully yet. Does that make sense?"

He nods as he runs his fingers through his hair. "I know you need time to process it too, but now we can process it together. I'm sorry if you think I should have told you sooner. I just had too much on my plate and needed to work through some stuff first."

"I get it, Storm. We'll work through this piece together." I smile at him. "What's that for?" he questions.

"You called me Storm twice in the last five minutes. We'll be fine." He cracks a small smile.

I love when he calls me Storm. I think it started on like our second date. He knew then what havoc I could cause on his emotions, and well, I've proven him correct so many times. Sometimes, like today, he does it without even thinking about it; other times, it's deliberate to let me know where his head is at. I always know things will be okay when he uses it, no matter what the context. And when he "Natalie's" me, I know he's pissed.

He wraps his arms around me. "A baby, huh?"

"Yep."

He pushes me off his lap and jumps up off the couch. "Oh, I forgot."

He rushes out of the room and up the stairs. I've got no clue where he's going until he comes back with the black box. The black box that contains my ring. The one that got us into this mess a little over a month ago.

I came home late from work. I was kind of hoping that either Caleb had cooked or would be okay with takeout. It was a long day at the office, and I had no desire to have to not only think about what to make, but to actually cook dinner.

When I got into the kitchen, it's empty, but I could hear noises from the TV drifting from the living room. I dropped my stuff on the table and followed the sounds. In the living room, I found Caleb snoozing on the couch. Guess he hadn't made dinner yet.

Not wanting to wake him, I headed upstairs to shed my work clothes. On the bed, I found one of my dresses with a note on top.

Storm,

Wake me if I fall asleep. I want to take you out for dinner.

Caleb

I hated when he did this on days when I just wanted to come home and veg. Of course, I should be thrilled he took the time to pick out a dress for me to wear and decided to take me out. But it was a long week, and I'm exhausted. The last thing I wanted to do was go out for dinner. It will just start an argument if I don't agree, so against my selfishness, I quickly changed into the dress and went downstairs to wake him up.

I shook his shoulder. "Caleb, I'm home. And I'm dressed so let's go to dinner so we can get home and go to bed." Oops, hope that didn't imply that we were having sex. If I had to do dinner, I wasn't having sex too. Not after the week I've had.

He popped off the couch and seemed startled for half a second and then his face lit up with a smile.

"Storm, you're home and you're wearing the dress I picked out. Let me go change. "He was practically running up the stairs as soon as he started talking so I moved out of his way. Oddly, he seemed very chipper too.

When he got back down, he grabbed my hand in his and dragged me through the kitchen to the back door.

"Caleb, what's the rush? Where are we going?"

He threw me up in the truck, got in on his side, started it up, and then spoke. "We have reservations at Mona's. We are going to be a little late, but it's okay."

Well, at least it was one of my favorite restaurants. That was the silver lining right about now. I slouched down in my seat and settled in for the twenty-minute drive.

At the restaurant, Caleb was around to open my door before I had even unbuckled. "Madam," he said with a smile, grabbing my hand and helping me out.

I couldn't help but giggle. Here's my burly man, acting like the true gentleman that I knew him to be. Although lately, I hadn't been feeling the love. I couldn't put my finger on what it was exactly.

He put his hand on the small of my back as we walked inside. Once there, he gave the hostess our name and she showed us to our table. He pulled out my chair for me and when I sat down, he pushed it closer to the table and then popped a kiss on the top of my head. Also weird.

When he waved off the menus, I looked over at him. "Okay, what gives?"

His face fell slightly. Perhaps I had better tone it down with my bad attitude. It wasn't his fault worked suck this week. Or that my mother kept calling me even after she visited this past week.

"Sorry. It's been a rough week. Don't mean to take it out on you." Did I really mean that though? I should mean it; he was not my personal punching bag.

He placed his hand over mine and started to rub it. "It's okay. Let's just try to enjoy dinner."

Leave it to him to gloss over my feelings and focus just on dinner. Add that to the list of what's been happening a lot lately. And while I don't want to actually discuss work, it would be nice if he asked every once in a while.

And so began the inner war with the demons inside me. To bat them away, I asked, "How was your day?"

"Fine." While it wasn't uncommon for him to be so short with his answers, I would have thought he would be a little more jazzed tonight, since he planned this dinner and all. But then as I took him all in, there was something off. More so than just the feeling of being off I'd had lately.

"Is everything okay? You seem nervous." Come to think about it, his hand was a little clammy as he rubbed mine in his.

"Fine." Yep, that word again.

Grabbing a sip of water, I noticed as he looked around the restaurant. I followed his gaze but didn't see anything out of the ordinary. This awkward conversation, or lack thereof, was certainly not helping my mood.

"I'll be right back. Have to run to the ladies' room." I went to stand up, but he stopped me, with both his eyes and his voice.

"No. Not yet."

Okay, seriously? What was his problem?

I sat back down temporarily while I waited for an explanation. When none came, I started with, *"Caleb, I really need to pee."*

He was still looking around the restaurant and when his eyes locked on someone coming over the table, he told me, *"Five minutes."*

As the waiter made his way to our table, Caleb's face broke out into a smile, but he seemed even more nervous. The waiter dropped the plate with the silver cover down on the table and before I even knew what was happening, Caleb pushed it toward me.

"You already ordered for us?" My tone was clipped, my stupid emotions clearly all over the map tonight.

"Just appetizers. Dig in."

He lifted the cover off the plate and the minute my eyes conveyed the message to my brain, I couldn't breathe. And not in a good way.

I couldn't stop staring at our *"appetizer"* and didn't even realize Caleb was kneeling on the floor. Before he could even say anything, I stammered out, *"No."* I should have added something else, something to let him know where my head was at, but I just said it again. *"No."* Because I couldn't breathe and it felt as if I might start to hyperventilate. I could already feel my pulse quickening, my body heat rising, and my palms sweating. It was not a good feeling and by the look on Caleb's face, not how he thought this would go over.

"I'm sorry." Knowing I had to get away from him, the haunted look on his face, and the diamond that was blinding me, I pushed out of my chair, practically knocking him over. Once I was free of obstacles in my path, I ran straight for the entrance of the restaurant.

I barely heard the hostess calling out to me as I pushed out into the cold air. Grasping for breath, I found a bench and took a seat. It took me a full five minutes to calm down and process what the fuck just happened.

The ring, Caleb kneeling before me, he was going to propose. And I didn't even let him ask the question, but I sure answered it all right.

Just as I caught my breath, Caleb came barreling out of the restaurant. From my spot on the bench, he couldn't see me right away, but I could see him. I watched as his eyes frantically took in every inch of the parking lot, desperate to find me.

"Over here," *I finally called to him.*

"Natalie, what the fuck?" *he asked as he stormed over.*

"Don't start with me, Caleb."

"Don't start with you? You just ran out of the restaurant when I was going to propose to you. You didn't even let me propose. You just told me no. But I shouldn't get to ask what the fuck is going on?"

I contemplated how much to tell him. I should tell him why I ran; I owed him that. But I don't know if he would understand it all. But instead, I said, "I can't marry you, Caleb. Not now. I can't even be engaged to you." *I could have added 'it's not you, it's me' but that would be a total asshole move on top of the dick move I already pulled.*

"Do you want to explain why?" *I could tell he was pissed, but his anger was overridden by the fact he was hurt. So I had to turn away from him, because despite my actions a little while ago, I wasn't completely devoid of emotion.*

"I can't." *It's all I could muster at this point. And it had multiple meanings, none of which I could share with him now.*

"You can't what, Nat? Look at me." *I shook my head. I could feel the tears hiding at the corners of my eyes.*

He tried again. "Look at me." *I couldn't react this time, not even with a shake of my head, but I couldn't avoid his next attempt.* "Storm." *The one word was all I needed to crumble, and when I looked at him, the tears were unleashed.*

"Please don't make me explain. I just can't. I can't explain. I can't marry you. I would suck as a wife, can't you see that? Why now, Caleb?" *Why ever? I wanted to ask.*

"Because I love you, Nat. And I want you to be my wife. I kind of thought you knew that already. This really shouldn't be such a shock to you." *His expression was sad. Seated on the curb, he faced away from me, not that I could blame him.*

I couldn't argue with the man. It shouldn't be a shock; it's where our relationship was headed, but I wasn't ready, especially tonight. I felt like he had ambushed me. While rational thought told me him proposing wasn't an ambush, my emotional side won that argument.

It wasn't that I didn't want to marry the guy; it was just that I didn't think I could nor would I be any good at it. At all. The last time we discussed it, I thought I made my intentions clear, but I guess I was wrong.

What a clusterfuck I've made of my life! I hated to admit my mother was right, but she was.

"I need to go home. Please just take me home."

He sighed heavily, but got up off the curb and walked away. I followed behind him, like I was walking through mud. I didn't even know what to say to him.

As I wiped the tears that were still falling, I muttered, "I'm sorry" as we walked. I intentionally didn't make it loud enough for him to hear, but when he responded with, "You're always sorry, Natalie," I knew he heard me. And all traces of sadness were gone; he was just pissed now.

Back at home, he stomped into the house and headed straight out into the garage. Since we didn't use it for cars, he used it as his "man cave."

Before I even had a chance to make it past the kitchen, he was back. He was still angry, but the softer expression on his face showed he was struggling with his emotions. "Sit," he ordered.

Caleb didn't lose his shit often; in many ways, he was the perfect balance to my emotions that were all over the place. He grounded me when I needed it most and he had always given me the space and time I needed to get my head on track. So, when he said sit, I sat.

My eyes followed him as he paced around the kitchen. His footsteps were heavy, but today it wasn't only because he's so tall. He's emotional, angry and letting me know it.

When he finally took a seat, he huffed out a large breath. I figured he would yell next; it seemed fitting for the situation. But he shocked the hell out of me when he started giving his proposal speech.

"Nat, you are one of a kind. I've never loved someone the way I love you, I've never needed to love someone like this, but if I'm honest, I've *never wanted to love anyone else. You drive me crazy almost every day of the week, but it's usually a good kind of crazy. Then there are the times when you totally go off the rails and pack it in because you are overwhelmed. That's when you drive me the most crazy, girl, because you always come back. No matter what you feel about yourself, you always come back to me.*

"I thought we had finally crossed the bridge to a place that you weren't going to run anymore. I thought you were with me, which is why I proposed tonight. I'm not going to lie and say it didn't hurt when you refused to not only listen to me ask you something important, but that you didn't even give me a chance. It sucked, Nat, big time. Because I love you and thought you were there too. Clearly, you aren't there, but seriously, are you ever going to be there? Like, if I ask again in a week or so, would that make a difference? If you had warning it was coming?"

He looked across the table from me. And I saw it. This was breaking him. This was his breaking point, me not wanting to marry him. The only problem was I did want to marry him, so much, that it terrified me, but so much more than just having cold feet. Like I started sweating again and my palms grew clammy. Like I couldn't control my breathing.

I'd learned a long time ago that when in fight-or-flight mode, my body always chose flight, no matter what was rational or what I thought. So I managed the only thing I could at the moment: "I don't know."

Any other guy would have yelled. He would have walked out of my life a long time ago. But Caleb? He fucking stayed. Every. Time. So, against everything my body was telling me, I went with my heart. Because he's right. My heart always came back to him, once my head was done freaking out.

"Give me some time. Please."

He sighed in relief. I thought that was going to be the end of it, but he added, "Nothing has to change. I just want you to know that when you wear my ring, it's forever. I'm not going anywhere. Ever. Even if you think I should. I'll stay because that's what you do when you love someone. And, damn it, Nat, I fucking love you. Please just let me."

I could feel the tears running down my cheeks. I got up from my seat and curled my body into his. "I love you, Caleb, more than you will ever know or I'll be able to show you."

And we sat like that for a little while, his strong arms enveloping me as I cried against him. I'd found the one man who would stand by my side, no matter what. He was here for me because he loved me. And as much as I never felt I could return his love, he loved us enough for the both of us.

Until I went and fucked it all up, yet again.

Literally.

Bringing me out of my memories, he hands me the box. "Do I need to ask again?"

I look up at him, standing in front of where I'm still sitting on the couch.

"You never asked in the first place so how can you ask again?" I can't help the chuckle that falls from my lips. But it's true. I never let him ask.

Without a word or any indication of what my words meant to him, he down on the ground. "Nat, no matter what storm you bring my way, I want to weather it together. What do you say? Will you do me the honor of being my wife?"

I nod. "Yep." He cracks up at my answer but slips the ring on my finger. "I love you, Caleb. I'll never know what I've done to earn not only your love, but your respect, support, and everything you give me, but maybe it's finally time to just accept it."

He cuts me off. "You think?" he asks with a smirk. "Storm, it's about damn time that you just accept the fact that you are lovable and while you have the funniest way of showing your love, there's no one in this world better suited for the recipient of mine."

Well, when he puts it that way...

"Okay," I whisper.

Looking down, I notice his hands are laying on my belly. As if to assuage my fears, he replies, "This baby will know love, Storm, only love."

I'll hold him to his word.

9

CALEB

I couldn't sleep that night. She's pregnant? I don't even know how to grasp that fact. I never really thought about having kids so much. Until I met Natalie. Then I changed my mind and was pro kids all the way. With her. *Only* her. I didn't have an "aha" moment, but over time, I realized that if I was going to have kids, Nat would have to be their mother. We talked about having kids from time to time during our relationship and at least were on the same page.

While the timing was certainly not ideal now—it always seemed like parenthood was more of a "future" thing—I'm not sure there was such a thing as the "perfect" time to have a baby.

It brings me back to the second time Nat left.

The girl was under my skin, in the best possible way. I learned so much about her the past year of dating: her likes and dislikes, what makes her tick, how she handles stress, when to push her buttons and when to leave her alone, among other things of a sexual nature. The big one was she convinced herself she didn't know how to be in a relationship. She knew more than she let herself believe. And that, right there, was my biggest challenge.

She'd bared her soul to me, when I least expected it, and despite what she believed, it was a beautiful soul. But she wouldn't take my word for it, no matter what I did. So I tried showing her with my actions, which worked slightly better. Now, we were in a "relationship," in new territory for both of us.

While I was ready to take a leap, she dragged her feet at every move. I had never gotten this far in a relationship before and hell, neither had Natalie. Don't get me wrong; I loved getting so many of her firsts as we navigated these usually stormy waters. But there were plenty of times I wished it could be a heck of a lot easier. If only she'd let it.

Pretty sure I knew I loved Nat a few weeks after knowing her, but I'd kept my feelings to myself for a while. She couldn't handle my admission.

After she ran the first time, I knew I had to tread carefully lest she run again. I wasn't ready for that. I wanted more, and in my subtle ways, I tried to let her know my feelings. Some days, I thought she was there with me, until she'd make a comment letting me know she wasn't anywhere near where I thought she was. Like this comment. "I don't believe in true love; it only exists in books, movies, and fairy tales." How did I argue with that illogic? I had seen true love; I had never experienced it for myself, but I saw it. My parents and both sets of my grandparents all had shown me true love most certainly did exist, but I held my tongue with Natalie. We argued enough about stupid shit; I wasn't going there with this too. Until I knew she was really ready.

I thought sometimes for Natalie, it was a constant war between her head and her heart. Whether she knew it or not, and whether she believed it or not, she already gave her heart to me. It was there in the way she kissed me, the way she came undone with a certain look, the way she reacted to my nickname for her, Storm. Her heart was there, but for Natalie, her life was ruled by her head, and sometimes, her head was a damn idiot and steered her all wrong.

I took her away to Boston to see some old friends. It was just for a long weekend, but it was what we needed. She'd quit her job at the coffee house and started working more toward her career, rather than just a job, at the marketing firm. She was low girl on the totem pole, but most days, she loved being in the thick of it. However, lately, the days were long, working on an ad campaign for a product she couldn't get on board with, and so we needed the time away. She needed the time away to clear her head. And it worked.

My buddies from college, and their wives, all adored her, naturally. She had a charm that drew you in, the charm she hid behind unless you're Caleb. I stopped trying to understand why she let me in when she kept even her closest friends from elementary school at arm's length. And while she was all "lovey-dovey" while we were away, it wasn't an act. For some reason, she let down more of her walls that weekend and let them see more of the real her. Maybe it was because she didn't have to see them daily, so she wasn't going to have to pretend to be someone else all the time. It must get tiring.

When we got home, I dropped her off at her place. As I sat in the car, prepared to say goodbye and goodnight, she looked at me from the passenger's side, looking hurt I wasn't coming in. When she turned on her puppy dog eyes, I parked the car in an actual spot and followed her inside. She had me whipped.

"You want a beer?" she asked from the kitchen. I dropped her bag by the front door and wandered over to have a seat on the couch.

"Yeah, sure. Thanks."

Her place was small, but she loved it, especially because it was her little sanctuary. When she was drunk one night, she explained her childhood, growing up in an old, dirty trailer, and how her room was her way to escape the poverty of her life. In the same way, her tiny apartment represented an escape from life itself.

She often sequestered herself to her place when she was feeling low or was having a rough time with life. She'd let me in a few times, but I'd learned to give her some time. We slept at my house most nights of the week since it was bigger, and while I would have asked her to move in already, she wasn't ready. So I kept the status quo.

When she set my beer down on the coffee table, she climbed onto my lap and straddled her legs on either side of mine. "Thanks for taking me to meet your friends. I had a really great time."

"You're welcome. Hope it was what you needed to avoid work for a short while."

"It was perfect. I hope we can visit with them again." Her expression *fell slightly and while I wanted to ask for an explanation, deep down I knew. Natalie didn't talk much about our future beyond a month or two at a time. I'd never understood it completely, but as long as she was in my arms at the end of the day, I didn't push her.*

I gave her my usual answer. "We'll see what the time brings." She gave me her crooked smile, the one that hit my heart on its way down to my dick. Every damn time. Feeling me underneath her, she looked up at me.

"Bedroom?"

I thought she was going to give me a wink, but I didn't even give her a chance. Nor did I give her a chance to hop off my lap; I whisked her away to her bedroom, her peals of laughter echoing off the hallway walls.

Once we made it to her bedroom—I almost faltered once during the short walk there as she nibbled on my neck while releasing audible moans—I tossed her down on the bed.

"Clothes off, Storm. Be right back." She started to undress as I made my way to the bathroom closet for condoms. I told her time and again to leave them in the nightstand drawer for easier access but she seriously had some vendetta against it. And something for making me wait.

Back in the bedroom, I slammed the door, even though it was just the two of us; she preferred it shut so I obliged when I remembered. She crawled under the covers, but her clothes were strewn along the floor. I tossed two condoms on the bed (always be prepared, right?) and started to undress.

"Hurry," I heard her mumble.

The girl was insatiable when it came to sex; she was always ready to go, no matter the time nor the place. In fact, there were probably times when I stopped her for being so tired. Only a few times. Times I could definitely count on one hand, but still. Insatiable.

I quickened my pace so that I could join her on the bed. Although I couldn't see it to make certain, I noticed her hand had slid down under the covers, most likely getting herself warmed up for me. She had no inhibitions when it came to sex either, nor much shame, something I couldn't help loving about her.

When I had finally shed all of my clothes, I joined her on the bed, pulling down the covers, confirming my initial thoughts. Her fingers of one hand circled her clit, while the other hand pinched and squeezed her nipple. I admired the view of her getting herself off for just a moment, and as she was about to come, I yanked her hand from her clit and laid it to rest on her thigh.

Her eyes had been closed, but they suddenly flew open, a storm in the blue hues. She picked her head up off the pillow it was thrown back on, glaring at me, her breathing already out of control. "Caleb," she started, the hunger and desire to come written all over her face. "Please."

I held her stare for a few moments, just long enough for her to beg again. And then I set to work.

My hands nudged her thighs open, pushing her hand off of her thigh. I slid my body down the bed to rest my face in between her legs. Once I settled into a comfortable spot, my tongue licked from her clit to the bottom of her opening, drinking in all of what was already leaking out; she had gotten herself practically soaked. She moaned and her legs twitched slightly. I brought my tongue back to her clit and made circles around it, just to tease her. Even though she may have been ready to come, I wasn't about to let that happen. Yet.

I continued my assault of her clit, dipping lower every so often. She tried to buck her legs off the bed, but I put my hand on top of her abdomen to hold her down, hold off her release. She continued to groan at me, but a moan slipped out every other breath. She wasn't going to last much longer before she was truly begging me to come. I buried my face in her sex, lightly sucking on her clit and lips. When I had her where I fully wanted her, I pulled my mouth back, and instructed, "Nipples, Nat."

Immediately, her hands found the taut nipples and she rubbed, pulled, and twisted them until, my tongue lapping up her juices, her toes curled and she finally came. She lifted her hips off the bed, and I steadied myself with my hands on her waist as I finished eating her out.

"Caleb," she moaned, all out of breath as she came down from her high as I pulled my face away. I knew she was looking at me, but I couldn't look at her. I focused on sheathing myself so that when she was

completely down from that orgasm, I could immediately start on the next one.

Once the condom was rolled on, I glanced in her direction. Her head back on the pillow, her hair completely wrestled out of the ponytail she had it tied back in. Her eyes were closed and one hand rested on her heart, the hand moving up and down as she breathed slower and slower.

I climbed up on top of her so that my palms were planted on either side of her face, my legs straddling hers. I gently lowered myself down to plant a kiss on her lips, yet instead of attacking my lips with hers, she demanded, "Take me." It was all the direction I needed.

Keeping my arms planted, I aligned my lower body with hers so that all I needed to do was thrust inside her. One push in, and she was arching her back, welcoming me in.

"Oh, fuck yes," she stammered out. "Don't stop, BG."

I cracked a smile at the use of my nickname but was able to continue to thrust inside, pulling myself in and out every so often. I felt myself getting closer to the edge of my impending orgasm as her vagina gripped my dick, tighter and tighter.

I studied her face as we both got closer to our release. She kept her eyes closed, but her face scrunched up, and she had drawn her lower lip into her mouth, biting down slightly.

As I continued to push inside and forced her hips up, she matched me, thrust for thrust. I lowered my face down to her lips and gently tugged her lower lip from her mouth into mine. I could only hold onto it for a second before I heard her screaming my name. At the same time, my already swollen dick was gripped tighter, my balls pulled up, and I found my release, riding our ecstasy out together.

Panting, I stayed inside her but rested my head on her chest. "Fuck, Nat. You are incredible."

She responded only with a grunt. Somehow her hands found my hair, and she tangled her fingers in it. "You bring it out of me."

Her breathing was labored, still recovering from the orgasm. I gave us a few minutes to just revel in each other, but then I pulled myself out of her and wrangled off the condom. Tying it off, I tossed it in the garbage can next to her bed. Once it was disposed of, I climbed back up next to her. Her eyes were still closed, her hunger for sex sated for the time being. Instinctively, she curled her body into mine as soon as I lay down next to her. Wrapping my arms around her, I pulled her in closer to me.

"Hmm," she mumbled, along with some incoherent shit that I couldn't make out. And one word that I could: "Stay."

I'd never slept at her place before, but I took this as a big step for her. Not only wanting me to stay but also asking me. My love for her grew a tiny bit.

I wasn't sure how long we lay there, naked, just relishing in the closeness of each other. Nat wasn't much of a cuddler so when she wanted to cuddle, I soaked it up in spades. Not that I was much of one before her either, but I soon learned there was nothing better than cradling her tightly next to my body.

Some time later, she finally got out of bed to use the bathroom. On her way back, she brought me my beer from earlier and some candy bars for us to snack on. She slipped into comfy PJs and threw me my boxers and pants.

"What's on the agenda for tomorrow?" she asked mid-bite of a Snickers bar.

"I have to be at work early so I'm skipping the gym and will go after work. I could grab us some pizza for dinner. Unless you had other plans."

She shook her head no, swallowing the bite. "I'll be home later because tomorrow is the day the campaign launches." She went quiet after that, and I was sure it was because she was stressed.

"It will be great, Nat," I told her, laying my head on her legs. I had finished off my candy in two bites, and I wanted to be closer to her.

"Glad someone thinks so."

It was a huge project, but one I was certain wouldn't have been passed to her if the managing partners didn't think she could handle it. I hated how down on herself she got, especially when it came to work, but it was another balancing act of what to say. Mostly, I kept my mouth shut, my opinions staying in my head.

When she was done with her snacks, she threaded her fingers back in my hair and twisted my locks in her fingers, pulling gently every so *often. Her massaging nearly put me to sleep, my eyes drifting closed. And then, I swore, it just slipped out.*

"I love you, Nat."

When I realized what words had filtered out of my mouth, I coughed and tried to play it off like I didn't say anything. When her fingers stilled and her entire body tensed, I knew it was a huge mistake.

"What did you just say?" Her voice was barely a whisper. She was also pulling away, pushing my head off her lap so she could escape the bed, escape from me.

I contemplated telling her I didn't mean it, but that might just make it worse. Who says I love you and then takes it back?

I sat up and observed her. She started pacing and from the way her mouth was moving, mumbling to herself. Great, just great. *Now what did I do?*

I ran my fingers through my hair, trying to decide how best to play this off. Ah, fuck! Why did this love thing need to be so complicated? And why wasn't my brain coming up with a better solution than just sitting here, in her bed, watching her freak the fuck out? These were the times I wished she wasn't so under my skin.

I got pulled out of my thoughts when I heard her say, "I need to leave," forcing me to act.

"Nat, you live here. Where are you going to go?"

She reacted like I didn't even speak—muttering something about being unlovable.

I raised my voice a little. "Natalie."

She continued pacing, but now, she looked like she was searching for something.

I tried once more, already throwing on my shirt knowing what was coming. "Storm." That got her attention; it always did.

She stopped moving for a brief time and looked over at me. Her face was tormented, that damn battle waging again.

"I need you to go." It was a demand; there was no quaver in her voice. And there was no arguing with her.

I walked up close to her and tilted her chin to look up at me. Her eyes were stormy, no tears in sight, but she was at war within herself. All I wanted to do was hug her, kiss her, make her realize that there was nothing "unlovable" about her. But if I didn't want to push her away completely, I had to just leave.

But not without this: "For what it's worth, Nat, it's all true."

I kissed her on the forehead and as I pulled away, she fisted my shirt. My look of shock didn't even register in her mind. She continued to cling to me, tightly, almost as if she didn't want to let go. Her heart didn't want to, but when she huffed out a sigh, her head won out.

"Go. Now." Again, it was a demand, a pleading for me to just let her be. And against my better judgment, I left. But not without letting her know to call or text if she needed me.

I strode down the hallway to the kitchen and swiped my keys off the table. I went out to my truck but couldn't make myself start it up. Furious with myself and my stupid admission, I pounded my hand on the steering wheel. I knew she wasn't there yet. Her asking me to stay and the sex coma made my mind stupid. Fucking stupid.

"Argh," I yelled into the confines of the truck. "Fucking asshole."

I debated whether or not to text her, but in the end, I started my truck up and headed for home. It was not only going to be a long night, but who knew how long until she figured some stuff out. All because I was an eager son of a bitch who just wanted to profess his love to his woman.

Fuck me.

It was a long night, followed by a long three weeks with radio silence from Natalie. Some days, I barely functioned. Thank goodness it was boating season. Pretty sure I logged hundreds of miles taking it out on the marina. Pretty sure Grayson knew something was up around day three. He never once asked, and since he was in contact with Natalie, he probably assumed I was at fault. I was fine with that; the girl needed her space and time.

It was Friday night, I thought. But it could have been a different day; I lost track of all time. I couldn't even remember the last time I shaved, but I at least knew I showered earlier today. My work was sloppy this week, but thankfully no one had said anything. Yet. I knew I had to get it together. But damn, I missed her. Like a whole hell of a fucking lot. I wouldn't let myself believe that this was the end. It couldn't be. I was grasping at air holding onto that thought. And I wouldn't let go.

My phone pinged with a text. Didn't even know where the phone was at this point. I figured I would search for it later, when the mood struck me. But it went off again. And then a third time almost immediately.

I lumbered off the couch in pursuit of it, finally finding it under the table. Hmm. Wonder how it got there. Didn't really have to continue pondering it because I suddenly noticed Natalie's name on my phone. And all of a sudden my day looked brighter. It didn't matter that it was nine p.m. There was light at the end of this godforsaken tunnel I had found myself in.

Need you

Please

Now

I didn't even bother with a jacket; I stepped into my shoes, grabbed my keys, and raced out the door. Once in the truck, I checked her location.

Don't worry; she knew I could keep tabs on her; I'm not a total creeper. It was for her safety, so I could find her when she texted me that she needed me. She was the one who set it up so that I didn't ever have to ask where she was; I would always know.

She was at a park near her apartment, a good fifteen minutes from me.

On my way

I made it to the park in just under twelve minutes. There may have been a few yellow lights I ran and at least one that was red with no one else in sight.

Upon pulling into the park, I spotted her car right away. It was empty, but I pulled up beside it since the parking lot was otherwise vacant. I hopped down from the truck and started walking in the general vicinity of the park. It was a popular park by day, but at this time of night, there was no one here. Well, except for Natalie once I found her.

After walking a couple of minutes, I finally saw her sprawled out on the ground, looking up to the sky. I quickened my pace, trying to get to her that much faster. Once I reached her, I stood at the top of her head, gazing down at her. I didn't say anything, nor did she, but when she opened her eyes, they were hollow and wet.

"Storm?" I questioned. Without taking her eyes off me, she tapped the ground with her hand, indicating I should join her on the blanket. Once I was lying next to her, she inched herself closer to me. And then she spoke.

"I love you, Caleb." That was it.

To say her words shocked me would be a lie. I was flabbergasted.

She turned to face me, and I knew she saw the surprise registered on my face. Even though she remained pretty stoic in her expression, she wanted to crack a smile or at the very least, a smirk.

"You want to know how I know?"

All I could do was nod. I couldn't think.

She fucking said it. Out loud. To me. And she wasn't freaking out. It was a lot to process; I may even be freaking out. Pretty sure I stopped breathing for a split second at her admission.

"Every day when I woke up, I wondered how you slept, if you were sprawled out, taking up the entire bed, or had stuck to your side. Then when I ate my meals, I pondered what you were eating, if you were enjoying it. Before I went to bed, you were there again. I was curious how your day went, how the boat was, were you thinking about me? Every single day. But I couldn't bring myself to ask you. Because I was terrified of admitting I was in love with you."

She paused for a moment, scooted closer to me, and laid one hand on my stomach. Her voice dropped to a whisper. "I had convinced myself that I could be with you and not fall in love with you. Because love doesn't exist. But I was wrong; you prove that to me all the time. All the damn time. It does exist, and we have it. I'm not sure how or why, but we do."

"*Damn straight,*" *I told her after she was quiet for a time.*

Her hand started caressing my stomach, and it felt good. Too good to have her stop anytime soon.

She cleared her throat and continued speaking. "I owe you an apology and an explanation." When I shook my head, she was adamant. "Yes, I do." She stopped rubbing me so she could sit up and look me in the eyes.

"*I'm sorry. I'm sorry for freaking out and demanding you leave. Please know that was all on me; you did nothing wrong. I was wrong for reacting that way. And deep down, I knew it was coming; I had been preparing myself for it, but it still freaked me out when you said it so nonchalantly. Like you had no cares in the world, like loving me was something you were supposed to do. I think that's what freaked me out the most; the casual way it just slipped out of your mouth. That's what I love about you, Caleb. It's so natural for you. I hope that one day I'll meet you at that place, and we will both be there together.*"

At that, I nodded. I didn't want to interrupt her momentum so I continued to keep quiet.

She took a deep breath and told me her explanation. It gutted me, and it definitely broke me. Because with one story, I understood it. I understood it all. And when she was done, all I could do was hug the shit out of her.

* * *

NATALIE

*S*o I guessed I was doing this. Letting Caleb know my secret, the secret no one else in the world knew. The one that had kept me up all night so many nights years ago and still haunts me. THAT secret.

I knew I couldn't look at him when I told my story. I couldn't watch his facial expressions. He was tough on the exterior, but behind his façade, a softie hid. He didn't let that guy out much to most people, but I

*knew he was in there. I also knew what this story was going to do
to him.*

*I cleared my throat before I began. Several times. I'd never told this
story to anyone. Not even my closest friends. Not even my mom knew.
She knew something happened when we had breakfast the next morning, but I wouldn't talk.*

*Even before tonight, part of me knew that Caleb would be the one
person to ever hear this story because he deserved to know, regardless of
my feelings toward relationships*

After one deep breath, I began.

*"It shouldn't come as any surprise to you I lost my virginity earlier
than most girls. Between the parade of men in and out of our house and
the fact that I was alone most of the time while my mother worked to
support us, I was sexually curious at a young age. I used to sneak into
my mother's room and steal her Danielle Steele and Nora Roberts
romance books. I devoured them, looking for clues about sex.*

*I didn't have many girlfriends in high school, well besides Bella, and
she came out of the closet early. We spent hours watching porn and
researching stuff on the Internet. Even though I had almost three years
on her, she was even more of an early bloomer than I was.*

*She hid it all from her parents and Grayson too, swearing me to
secrecy. I'm highly certain that she wasn't as experienced in the actual
sex department until she was older, but boy could she talk about it. The
girl made it sound like she had the experience, but it was mostly all for
show. To gain attention from the older girls, even if they weren't gay.*

*"Anyway, I won't bore you with the details about how I lost my
virginity at fifteen or how I slept with a bunch of guys over the next
year. I knew I was a slut, but since the girls had been calling me that for
years, I figured I would live up to their expectations." He actually
cringed at this part of the story. "Don't worry. I'm a reformed slut now."
I laughed, mostly to relieve some of the tension I could feel in the air
between us, but also because I knew what was coming.*

*"I slutted it up for a year then practically shut down the next year.
Junior year was a rough year in high school, and I mostly retreated into
myself. I decided the mean girls didn't need any more ammunition to use*

against me when they tossed around the word *slut*. But more than that, I gained a sense of my self-worth that year. Grayson may have had a hand in that even though he doesn't know it.

"Senior year, I met Daniel. He was from the 'wrong side of the track' and had that "bad boy" attitude and look to match. At first, we were just friends: going to the movies, hanging out at the diner, thinking we were cool by smoking cigarettes. We weren't cool by any means, but at seventeen, what did I know? Somewhere along the way, we made the transition from friends to dating. No, not dating, but it wasn't just fuck buddies either. Not that we would have called it that back then, but you get the idea."

I paused there. Caleb stayed quiet, but I could tell his breathing was heavier than before. He was anxious to know where my story was going. Surprisingly, I wasn't nervous to continue. It was almost cathartic to get it off my chest, for at least once in my life. And even though I knew the worst parts were still to come, I was doing okay. So I continued.

"At first, he seemed sweet about the sex. It wasn't at all rough, and while up to that point, I never knew it as rough as we've known it, I'd experienced my fair share of wild and dirty.

"Things started slow but quickly escalated. I don't remember exactly how or when, but all of a sudden, he was sneaking into my room to have sex. With my mom home. That didn't sit right with me for many reasons, but one night I gave in. Sort of."

And here was where the story got worse.

I stole a quick peek at Caleb. His hands clasped behind his head, his breathing still heavy, and he stared up into space. His biceps popped out of the sleeves of his T-shirt and his hat had fallen off his head. He was deliciously handsome, even with the days-old scruff that was more on the verge of beard.

I shook my head, trying to shake off the thoughts of what I could do to this man right now. I had a story to finish.

"It was a warm night, so my window was open. The screen was down, but that never stopped Daniel before. I think it was a little after ten, and even though it was a school night, I couldn't turn my brain off to get to sleep. Even back then I had that problem." I chuckled. Caleb was always on my case about my head doing too much thinking all the time.

"I heard the screen being slid up and when I looked over, I wasn't too surprised to see Daniel climbing through. I was a little surprised at his look though. His hair was rumpled; we'd call it the 'just fucked' look now, but back then, it didn't even occur to me that he'd been with someone else. I just chalked it up to the time of day and the fact that he looked tired. His button-down was unbuttoned and his T-shirt untucked. He was usually more put together.

"As he walked closer to me, I could tell he had been drinking. He wasn't drunk but had definitely had a few. It wasn't too shocking; we would drink together sometimes even though we were underage. He always "had a friend" who could get him beer. Still, he looked, I don't know how to put it into words. Disturbed, almost. He climbed into my bed; again, not unusual, but instead of asking me to move over, he kind of pushed his way into the middle of my twin bed, leaving me little space between him and the wall.

"'Hi,' he said, placing a kiss on my lips. That was odd. He hardly ever kissed me; it was always about the sex with him.

"'Hey. Rough night?' I asked in return. The alcohol on his lips—vodka I think it was—made my stomach turn. When I added everything up, there was something wrong, but I couldn't figure out what it was. I turned away from him to face the wall. Even though I couldn't turn my brain off, I wanted to sleep. But he wasn't having it.

"He crawled on top of me and laid down. I remembered thinking that his body was heavy, that he was crushing my chest. If I only knew!"

My nerves kicked into high gear, and the laugh that escaped my throat was nervous. Caleb sensed it; he grabbed my hand which was closest to him and squeezed my tiny fingers in his. He didn't let them go.

"So, he was lying on top of me, and I knew what he wanted. But I didn't want it. So I told him that my mom was home and that she could hear us.

"'You can be quiet, sweetie.'"

At that, Caleb interrupted me. "Got that one now."

He once called me sweetie, and I flipped the fuck out on him. Not on purpose, just because I couldn't have him calling me that, dredging up the memories of Daniel and that night every time he said it. He never once asked me why I flipped out; he never uttered the word again.

"I tried again, a little stronger this time. 'How about tomorrow night? It's late and I'm kinda tired.'

"'It's never stopped you before.' He shimmied himself a little farther down on top of me, and started to undo his jeans. On the one hand, he was right. I'd given in to him when I was tired before, but tonight seemed different for some reason.

"'Another night. Please.'

"I was practically begging at this point and did my best to push him off of me. But he wasn't listening. I tried to push him off of me, but he was bigger and stronger than I was, and he wasn't having it. 'Daniel, I said no.' It was just below a scream. I was somehow still conscious of the fact that my mother could potentially hear us, but at the same time, I was hoping that she did.

"He didn't stop. He had his pants around his ankles now and was trying to remove my shorts. I held onto the waistband with all my might, stupidly hoping they didn't rip. Not that he couldn't get them off; that they didn't rip. God, I was such a mess. Well, not was; still am."

I stopped, mostly to catch my breath, but it gave Caleb the in he needed. "Don't beat yourself up, Storm. You've always done the best with what you had to work with."

That hit the nail on the head.

And then, just to prove the guy's devotion, he pulled me closer to him, tucking me into his side, whispering, "You don't have to finish if it's too much."

But I did. I had to get it all out. I had to let him know why hearing him say "I love you" was my kryptonite.

I shook my head, inhaled again, and continued. My voice was a little shaky now, and it was practically a whisper as I finished the narrative. Granted, I glossed over it enough so I didn't have to relive it all, making sure to give Caleb just what I needed him to know.

"He was able to get my shorts down to my knees at least. He ripped *through my underwear, and I remember thinking in no way is that sexy like all the books portray it. He didn't even warn me when he was entering; he just barreled himself inside. My gasp echoed around the room; despite the fact I had experience, it still hurt. Most likely because he gave me no warning, and I was not even the slightest bit wet.*

"I took no pleasure in any of it but even my protests and cries went unheard. So I stopped voicing my disdain and retreated inward.

"It fucking hurt, as he pushed inside deeper and deeper, not even pulling out; he just kept pushing deeper. Tears spilled out of my tightly shut eyes, tears I'm sure never even registered for him. I just kept wishing for it to be over, for him to hurry up and finish already. And then I felt the familiar twist of my stomach and felt myself getting wet. And it made me sick, but I was so paralyzed with fear, I just continued to lay there, praying to anyone who would listen for this to just be over.

"I don't know how long it lasted; it felt like hours, but I'm sure it was just a few minutes. Eventually he was screaming out, 'Fuck yeah,' and I knew he was climaxing. It hit me then he wasn't wearing a condom, but at that moment, it wasn't my biggest worry. Because what he said next would come to haunt me for years.

"'I love you.'

"Just three little words, as he pulled himself out after assaulting me. That's when my brain registered what he said. And with my limited experiences with the matter, I decided right then if that's what love was, no thanks. I'm good without love. And I've managed to avoid it ever since. Until you came into my life."

He interrupted me again but this time, it was just to pull me into him. He somehow sat us both up, and his arms wrapped around me. And he didn't hold me; he squeezed me, like he was never letting go. Like he was trying to take the pain of my story away from me. Like he totally just understood everything, and I mean EVERYTHING, about our relationship and where I stood. And I let him.

I couldn't move; I didn't want to move. I needed him to hold me, to let me know it was okay. Because even though it happened over ten years ago, the repercussions of that experience never went away. But I'm glad I told him, not for him to feel like he had to take my pain away,

but for him to know why I freaked out. Why when he said, "I love you,"
especially so casually, the memories of that night came flooding back. It
didn't matter that it was Caleb and that I loved him too; all I heard was
Daniel's voice. And I panicked.

He didn't let go of me for a good long while. He eventually asked if I
wanted to finish the story so I told him that Daniel left soon after the act
was done.

"I was literally a mess and didn't get any sleep that night. When it
was day, I saw the blood on my sheets. I'm pretty sure it was more blood
than when I lost my virginity. I just tossed my sheets in the outside
garbage bin, hoping my mother wouldn't find them.

"She noticed something was up with me, but she never really asked
what was wrong, just if I was okay. I was able to convince her I was; it
wasn't hard to do. I'd been lying to everyone my entire life, and even
though she was my mother, she was no different.

"When Daniel walked out of my room that night, I never saw him
again. I never questioned it because I needed him out of my life. My
mind had enough of a constant reminder of what he did; it would have
been too much to face him.

"Grayson and Bella both saw through my act, which is odd because
they never had been able to before, but even Bella was smart enough not
to pry. She still doesn't know what happened, and she never will."

Caleb's hold on me loosened slightly, just enough to cup my chin in
his fingers. "I'm so sorry, Nat. You should have never had to go through
any of that, let alone deal with the aftermath of it all on your own. I get
why you didn't let people in, but you gotta know that it only made it
worse for you, right?"

I nodded. I couldn't really speak. Not only was my mouth dry from
sharing my story, but there's a huge lump in my throat.

"You know I won't let anyone hurt you? Ever again. Never."

I nodded again. Sometimes I couldn't believe my luck that I had
found this man, after everything I had been through, this man who
recognized me for who I truly was, and knew exactly what I needed, no
matter what hell I put him through. I truly was his Storm, in every
sense of the word.

I went to speak, but he put his fingers over my lips. "Will you let me take you home now, please?" He didn't allow me to even answer, simply scooped me up in his arms, dragged the blanket behind us, and walked me to where our cars were. Setting me down next to my car, he spoke. "Are you okay to drive? I don't think it's such a good thing to leave your car here overnight. But you have to be okay."

"I'm okay," I muttered. "Thank you. And not just for that. For all of tonight. For the past three weeks when I bailed. For the past year of knowing you. Let me say it again. I love you, Caleb Washington. More than you will ever know."

He pulled me into him again, anticipating what I needed. When I saw him wipe the corner of his right eye, I realized it wasn't for me; it was what he needed at the moment. To feel me close to him. To know that I was protected and that he was the one protecting me. It was all there in his hug, in the way his arms crisscrossed over my back and almost met at my front again.

It was at that moment that I made a promise to myself not to run again. That this man was it; he was the prize for everything that I had endured up until this point in my life.

I kept that unspoken promise to myself for over four years. I didn't run when things got difficult; I held my ground, and we worked out shit between us and shit within ourselves.

When he asked me to move in with him, it wasn't a no-brainer, but I also knew it was inevitable, and so after a few days of hemming and hawing, I agreed.

And life was good, never perfect, but I was happy and content. Until he propositioned forever with him. That one threw me for a big loop, and I blew my promise to myself out of the water.

Because let's face it. Forever is a long ass time; it's for eternity, and no matter how much you can prepare and set yourself up for something like that, it still could come as a shock when it happened. Especially for someone like me.

10

CALEB

$\mathcal{T}$he next morning, I'm up early to make Natalie's coffee run for winning. She informed me last night, after dropping the pregnancy bomb, that she could only have coffee, nothing fancy, "but make it a big one." She was still sleeping when I snuck out of the bed and got ready.

When I get home, she's still asleep. Nestled snuggly on my side of the bed, I couldn't just leave her there by herself. I crawl onto her side and snuggle in next to her. My arms barely wrap around her and suddenly, she pops out of the bed.

"Oh, you did good, BG. I can already taste it." She turns to look over at me, gives me a cheesy smile, and swipes the coffee from my nightstand. Before taking a sip, she carefully situates herself to a sitting position in the bed. She pats her thighs, motioning me to lay my head down.

"Hmmm, this is the taste of sweet victory." I turn my head to look up at her as I can see the liquid traveling down her throat.

"Enjoy that cup, Storm. Only six more days of this."

"That's plenty of days to still enjoy." She licks her lips after taking her sip and puts the cup back down. "What's on the agenda for today?"

"Dinner at Grayson's, I think. I thought maybe we could take a drive out to my sister's this afternoon. My parents will be there to see the kids too. If you want."

My family loves Natalie. The Nat they know. I've never shared much of her history with them and don't intend to start now.

My sister lives about thirty minutes away, by herself with three kids. Her asshole husband picked up about six months after the baby was born, said he couldn't handle life with three kids, a wife, and a mortgage. It turned out he had been cheating on her off and on for at least two years and decided he had had enough. I never really liked the guy, but once he walked out, I lost all respect for him. Unfortunately for my sister, she's stuck in between a rock and a hard place because he's the father of her kids, but she can't stand him either. I try to visit as much as I can, not only for the kids' sakes, but to help out around the house. I'm pretty good at fixing stuff, so she usually leaves me a list of stuff to do when I'm there.

"Sure. I'd love to see the kids," she exclaims. "I don't think we should tell people yet about our baby. Not until I go to the doctor's next week. Just to make sure everything's good."

"Okay," I agree. "But the engagement?" My eyes drift to her left ring finger. As if she follows my gaze, she wiggles it.

"For sure. This looks really good on my finger." She admires the ring, with a huge grin on her face, a complete one-eighty from when I first presented it to her. She turns to look at me, as the grin slides off. "We all good?" she asks in a whisper.

I want to say yes. We have hashed out our issues—okay Nat's issues mostly—she's taken her responsibility in all of it, including the cheating, and we are in a good place. But I'm hesitant to voice my opinions. Not because I think we aren't all good; I can't put my finger on the way I feel.

Trailing my fingers up and down her thighs, I answer, "I think so." I hesitantly wait for her reaction. It could go either way, but I'm hoping it goes the way I want it to go, the way I *need* it to go.

Her expression remains the same, not quite happy but no signs of anger or real unhappiness either. She shrugs and responds, "Okay. I'm good with that. Let me know when you're sure."

I let out a sigh of relief. It's mostly inaudible, but I'm pretty sure she hears me. And she adds, "I love you, Caleb. Thank you. I'm highly certain any other guy would have run for the hills by now with all of the destruction I've caused. Thank you for not being that guy."

She plops a kiss on the top of my head, gently pushes my head from her lap and gets out of bed. She makes her way out of the room and after hearing the toilet flush, she returns.

"You want waffles?"

With the lump in my throat, all I can do is nod. She turns on her heels and heads downstairs for breakfast. I lay back on the bed, staring up at the ceiling. The girl has no idea what her words do to my heart, no matter what I'm able to get across to her. Sometimes they have negative effects, and then there are days like today that have such a profound, positive effect, I think my heart might burst.

It was her simple declaration of "not being *that* guy" that did me in. She would never believe me, but she's made me not be "*that* guy." Pretty sure my high school and college girlfriends would say I was "*that* guy." Natalie changed me, for the better. There's something about her that makes me stick around for the long haul. My life might be less complicated without her, but it would suck nonetheless. Am I too naïve to believe that she's truly done running this time? Only time will tell

By the time I make it downstairs, she's got the batter all ready made and the waffle iron heated and ready. I grab the chocolate chips from the cabinet and dump a bunch in the bowl. She goes to protest, but I wrap my arms around her from behind, my hands landing on her belly, and I whisper in her ear, "They are for the baby." She places her right hand on top of mine and squeezes it gently.

"Okay," she whispers.

Natalie doesn't have much of a sweet tooth, beyond treats made by Grayson and Ainsley and select other items, including Trephines cheesecake. The only reason we have chocolate chips in the house at all is because I like to eat them by the handful and occasionally throw them in the batter for waffles, pancakes and muffins. She gives the batter one last stir before pouring it into the iron.

"Dinner might be canceled. Apparently Ainsley's really sick from last night. Grayson texted me to let me know she was throwing up all night long. Pretty sure he's not too happy with me. Oops."

And then it hits me why Ainsley drank so much.

"Does she know you are pregnant?" I ask. The tone is harsher than I mean it to be, but Nat takes it in stride.

"No, I didn't tell her. I just kind of kept filling her cup so she wouldn't notice that I wasn't drinking. I would have done the same for the girls, but they were more interested in bowling than drinking." She goes quiet for a minute, as the waffle maker beeps. "I told Kylie," she mumbles, setting a plate in front of me. I barely hear her, yet she continues. "I needed to confide in someone when I first found out, and I couldn't put Ainsley in the middle of Grayson and me yet again." She watches my expression carefully. I'm sure my eyes are wild, because when she adds, "I'm sorry, but I'm not, because I couldn't tell you, but it needed to be said aloud. I know that's not my usual MO, but I was still so screwed up and didn't know what to think or how to process it." By now, she's walked back over to the counter to continue making the waffles, ignoring the heaviness in the air.

I cut into mine and take a huge bite, making sure to get a chocolate chip. Once I've devoured at least half of the waffle, she joins me at the table with one of her own.

"Okay." It's all I can say, and it feels like it's been our go-to response in the past few weeks for almost everything. But I really can't be mad, especially because she figured out a way to process her shit, even finding out she's pregnant, and the outcome is the only one I wanted.

"Okay," she echoes, as she digs into her waffles.

*　*　*

*I*t's quiet on the drive to my sister's house. Her bare feet rest on the dashboard, having abandoned her shoes the minute she got in the truck. She's wearing her leggings and a long top and she twisted her hair into a braid. Most days, she does minimal makeup, but today she's not wearing any.

I can't tell what they are, but thoughts are rattling around her brain. Every once in a while, she sighs. It's subtle, but something's going on.

"Talk to me. What are you thinking?" I rest my hand on her thigh, and while she doesn't shove it away, I can tell it makes her a little uncomfortable.

She stays quiet, and I don't think she's going to talk, but eventually she opens up, and her thoughts explode into the quiet of the cab.

"Your family would hate me if they knew of my actions the last few weeks. H-A-T-E me. Especially Kate. I mean, really. I don't know how I'm even going to face her today. Like, she's going to know exactly what I did and then probably ask me to leave. Are you sure you want me to come?" She inhales when she finishes her stream of consciousness.

"Nat, they won't know. I won't tell them. You know I would never tell them."

She considers my thoughts for a moment, then quietly asks, "Why have you never told anyone my secrets?"

"Because they aren't mine to tell." It's the prepared answer I've had at the ready for this moment. She's never asked me before why I don't tell people; she's always accepted that I don't share all of our lives with others. It's just one of the reasons why we work. "It's really not anyone's business but ours, Storm."

"Okay." There's that word again.

She's quiet the rest of the way to my sister's. Once we get there, my parents are already there, which isn't too surprising. They live closer to Kate than I do. And I'm sure they were here early this morning.

Pulling up behind Kate's minivan, I park the truck as best as I can so it doesn't take over the entire driveway, not an easy feat with this truck. Before I open my door, I look over at Natalie one more time.

"Everything's going to be fine. Plus, you can distract them with your shiny new bling."

At my words, she glances down at her ring. It totally sparkles, especially with the sun beating down on the windshield. And then she gasps.

"Caleb!" she practically shouts. "They are going to want to know how you asked me. I can't tell them the story. I just can't. I know it's how it happened, but how the hell do I tell that story? That I didn't even let you ask, and I turned you down? I'm a fucking bitch and now everyone will know."

She drops her head into her hands, her body starting to shake with her silent sobs. I knew she'd realize this eventually, and truthfully, if we told it the way it happened, it would cast her in a bad light. And I don't want that for her, even if it is the truth. Other people just won't get it. And while lying is pretty much up on my hard limits list like cheating, I know I have to protect her from the truth.

"I'll handle it," I tell her, wrapping one arm around her as I lean over. I can't drag her close to me because of the console. "Look at me." When she doesn't immediately find my gaze, I direct her again. "Storm, eyes up here." That does it.

Her eyes are filled with more regret now than I've seen lately. Because as much as she thinks she's gotten her shit together, she truly hasn't faced all of her demons yet. I blame the pregnancy. But I also know the pregnancy has been a blessing in disguise of some sort, and she'll be okay. She'll get there, and we'll be okay. Better than okay, even.

"I'll. Handle. It. Just follow my lead." I wipe the tears that have slipped out of her eyes with my thumbs. She nods. Just as she's about to speak, I tell her, "And don't say okay. Just smile."

She smiles weakly in my direction, and it's enough for me to know that she understands and will follow my lead. I drop a quick kiss to her lips, one on each cheek, and top it off with one to her forehead. Her eyes drift closed with that one, she inhales deeply, expresses it, and when her eyes open again, there's less regret in them. The storm has passed.

"Come on. Let's go see your family."

She slides out of the truck before I can get over to open the door but then waits for me. Her small hand fits into mine, for comfort and everything else she may need at the moment. I give it a gentle squeeze as we stroll up to the front door.

From inside, I can hear my niece and nephews. They range in age from four to eight. The door opening is a beacon calling out to them like a lighthouse in a storm. I hear shouts of "Uncle Caleb" before I see any of them. And then all of a sudden, all three of them are there, fighting for my attention.

I pick the littlest up and toss him on my shoulders, grab my niece and toss her on my back, and then ruffle my oldest nephew's hair. Since there's no room for him anywhere on my body, he turns his attention to Natalie.

"Aunt Nat, come see my newest Lego creation." He grabs her by the hand, dragging her down the hall. She laughs as she follows behind him, trying to keep up.

Owen brings his face down in front of mine. "Boo!" he shouts when he has my attention.

"Boo!" I bellow back to him, while I feel his sister trying to climb higher up my back. With the kids still attached, I start my walk to the back end of the house and find my parents and my sister sitting down at the table in the dining room, each with a mug of coffee in front of them. I attempt to say hello but am thwarted in my abilities by the monkeys crawling all over me, squealing with delight as I tickle and gently pinch their legs.

When I get to my dad, I lean forward and he grabs Owen off my shoulders. I quickly slide Quinn around to my front, pop two kisses on her cheeks, and lower her to the ground. I wrap my arms around my mother's neck and when she turns to look back at me, I kiss her cheek. "Caleb," she croons lovingly. "So glad you could make it. Where's Nat?"

"She barely had one foot in the door, and Aiden dragged her off to see his Legos. He's not too excited or anything."

I make my way over to my sister. I don't even have a chance to give her a kiss or hug, before she shoves a piece of paper in my face, a list of things for me to do.

"I can't even get a proper hello nor a cup of coffee before you are forcing slave labor on me."

She laughs, pops out of her chair and wraps her arms around my waist, laying her head on my chest. "So good to see you, baby bro. Glad you could come to visit." She squeezes my body in her arms before she lets go. "You want a cup of coffee? The 'rents didn't skimp on the cheap stuff this time."

Before I can answer her, Natalie and Aiden come into the kitchen. He's still got her by the hand. His hand keeps fidgeting, but he doesn't let go. I realize he's holding onto her left hand. She looks to me for help, especially when he says, "Aunt Natalie, what keeps poking my hand?"

All adult eyes turn to look at the pair, and Natalie actually freezes in her position.

Knowing I have to rescue her, I hurry over to them and tug his hand out of hers. And then I put hers on display.

Before I can say anything, Kate chimes in, "About damn time, brother." She pushes me out of the way and throws her arms around Natalie. Nat's eyes go wide, jumping from me to Kate who's not letting her go anytime soon. "Congrats. I've always wanted a sister."

"Um, thanks," Natalie manages to sputter out. And then as if a switch is turned on or off—because I haven't quite figured out which best applies to Natalie—a huge grin overtakes her face, the Natalie my family knows and loves shining through.

My parents are up out of their seats too, my dad shakes my hand with a pat on my back while my mother gushes, pushing Kate out of the way so she can hug Natalie too. When they finally are done with her, they inspect the ring. Nat just takes it all in stride, that grin still plastered on her face.

When my mom asks, "So how did he do it?" the grin fades, and I know the panicked look is coming. So I answer for us; I tell the story of how it should have gone: the ring came out as the appetizer, I got down on one knee, she said yes, I slipped it on her finger, and she cried. It's not too hard to swallow the lie because truthfully, it's how I imagined it would go.

"It's a beautiful ring." My mom fawns over it.

"Yeah, he did good." Natalie glances over to me and mouths, "*Thanks.*" I smile back at her in return.

"Okay, apparently I have a list of things that need my attention. Who's going to help Uncle Caleb?"

Shouts of "me!" reach my ears as all three of the kids jump up and down and surround me. Blowing a kiss to Natalie, I grab the list off the table and like the pied piper, lead my helpers out to the garage to tackle my list.

The kids and I knock out Kate's list in about an hour or so. It probably would have taken me about thirty minutes on my own, but I don't complain about the help. I love that they want to help me; I wouldn't have it any other way. I want them to know there are good guys in the world, unlike their father, but also, I want to teach the boys that sometimes you have to take care of your sister when she needs help. And heck, lord knows I could use the practice for my kid.

"Uncle Caleb, when are you and Aunt Natalie going to get married?" my niece asks as we finish up the last item on the list: hang pictures.

"We haven't really talked about it. Why?"

"Just wondering." Her voice drops to almost a whisper, like she's telling me a secret. "Did you know Mommy's sad?"

I herd the boys inside so I can talk to Quinn alone. I sit down on the Adirondack chair on the back porch and pull her onto my lap. Instinctively, her head falls onto my chest.

"Did she tell you she was sad?" She shakes her head. "How do you know?"

She pulls her head off my chest and turns to face me. "She cries at night. I hear her down the hall, when she thinks I'm sleeping." A sad expression slips onto her innocent face.

Pushing her dark curls out of her eyes, I study my niece. My ex-brother-in-law's leaving has taken the hardest toll on her. She's always been a Daddy's girl and with him not around anymore, she's had a hard go of things, at least according to Kate. I've tried to fill his shoes, but there's only so much an uncle can do to replace a father.

I pull her back closer to me for a hug. "I bet Mommy is sad sometimes, but you and your brothers do a great job at cheering her up." Because I don't really know what else to say, I start to tickle her. The sound of her giggles makes me smile, giving me another idea. "I bet tickling Mommy will make her less sad. You should try that one night."

Her giggles subside, and she looks back up at me. I see so much of Kate in her face, including the sadness that hasn't left my sister's eyes for years.

"But then she will know I'm not sleeping." Her face conveys she's more worried about her mom knowing she's awake than the fact that her mom will know she's sad.

"Oh, right. I'll think about how I can help her be less sad. How about that?"

"You should come over more. She's never sad when you are here."

From the mouth of babes.

I wish I could come more, and I vow to try to get here more often.

In an instant, Quinn flashes me a smile and hops down off my lap, like we just didn't have that heavy conversation. Shaking it off, I head back inside to see what everyone is up to. Before making my way to Nat, I grab my sister from her chair and hug her. When she asks, "What's this for?" I simply smile and kiss the top of her head.

"I love you, Kate. That's all." Looking over at Natalie, her questioning eyes travel back and forth between Kate and me. After letting Kate out of my embrace, I do the same to my future wife. "I love you too, Natalie." She doesn't fight my hug; instead, she melts into my embrace and suddenly I know—everything's truly good between us.

Leaning down so only she can hear me, I whisper in her ear, "We're good. Be prepared for hard and fast tonight."

The shocked expression on her face lets me know she's good too.

11

NATALIE

*a*fter the visit with Caleb's family, all is right in my world again. I'm pretty sure our sexathon that night more than made up for the weeks of sex we had abstained.

I feel like I'm in a good spot with most parts of my life: my relationship with Caleb is back on track, in the direction it should be heading; I've officially accepted the baby; I'm managing work (but avoiding Scott at all costs); and well, I'm proud of myself for getting to this point. Which I get may seem frivolous to most, but the fact I managed to "get my shit together" as Caleb is fond of saying, is a small miracle in some ways. But I've made it a point not to dwell on the past and am facing the future with a more positive outlook. Because Caleb is "not that guy" and I need this guy in my life, by my side, and this is it. I'm officially, officially done running, and it's the *last* time I'm going to make that promise to myself. I owe it to our baby, but more importantly, I owe it to Caleb and myself.

The girls and Ainsley were ecstatic with the news of our engagement. Hell, so was Grayson. I didn't get into details about any of it with them; that may be one thing I'm still processing: my reaction to Caleb's non-proposal. I used what Caleb had said to his family, and I'm sticking to that story. Thank goodness for the levelheadedness of my fiancé at times. And the fact that his love for me is so strong he would do just about anything to protect me.

Caleb and I decided we would wait until after the first doctor's appointment to tell everyone about the baby. The appointment was great; we heard the heartbeat, got my approximate due date in May and even got a picture to share. It made it all real, more real than almost anything in my life has ever been. Except for Caleb.

I can't help but stare at the ultrasound picture of the baby on the way home from the appointment. "This is really happening, isn't it?" I whisper, tracing my finger over the tiny being.

"Natalie," Caleb starts. There's an edge to his tone, a warning almost.

I peek over at him as he drives us home. He's just got that hint of stubble growing on his chin; it's at the length that I love most, especially when it rubs up against my thighs or chin. His eyes are fixated on the road, blinking only every so often. His brows are furrowed, almost as if he's thinking hard about something, which if I had to guess, relates to my comment.

I reach my hand out and rest it on his thigh. With a sigh, I give him not only what he needs to hear, but the truth of the matter.

"I'm excited, Caleb. I'm excited to know that in several months, this little nugget will be a part of our world, more so than he/she currently is. I don't know if I'll make the best mom ever, but I know that what I lack, you'll make up for. And that fact alone makes me want to do my best. It's safe to say I grew up with a shitty mom, and if all else fails, I will be better than her, so there's that."

"Oh, Storm. Why are you always so hard on yourself?"

I let the question linger for a few minutes. I know it's not completely rhetorical, but I also don't have a good answer for him. "Because it's the way I am" seems like a cop out. So I stay silent, my gaze focused back on the nugget's picture.

He sighs heavily. "For what it's worth, you're going to make a great mother."

It's how it's conveyed more than the meaning behind the

words, like no truer words have ever been spoken. And for now, it's everything I need to hear.

"Okay."

He chuckles and smirks at my response, which in turn, makes me giggle too.

"It really is our go-to answer, isn't it?"

"Yep," he confirms. His hand leaves the wheel and finds mine, still resting on his thigh. "Love you, Nat. You'd be wise to always remember that."

It's something he reminds me often because apparently—at least according to him—it seems to slip my mind sometimes. And so I echo, "Okay."

When we get home, we call his parents to tell them the baby news. His mom is thrilled; I'm sure her down-the-street neighbors could hear her squeals. Kate has a similar reaction and when she tells me to take it off speakerphone so she can speak only to me, I'm a little nervous.

Kate and I have always gotten along. Despite not knowing all the shit that's gone down with my past and with my relationship with Caleb, she knows her brother well. She's always known there's more to my story than I've let on, but she's never once broached the subject and pressed me for more than I've ever given her.

"Congrats. How are you feeling?" she asks to start the conversation.

"Not too bad. So far, the first trimester has been pretty easy thankfully. Sometimes I even forget I'm pregnant at times." I laugh, a hint of nervousness accompanies it.

"That's good but not what I meant."

When she doesn't clarify nor continue, I say, "Oh." And I think about my answer before speaking. Even though I can't see him, I feel Caleb watching me, listening for my answer. "Um, I'm okay." I hear Caleb's chortle because I said "okay." "It's not like I planned for this, well neither of us did, but once I got over the initial shock and after seeing the nugget on the screen, it's becoming more real."

"He's listening, isn't he?"

I nod but realize she can't see me. "Yep."

"Walk away." Her tone is kind, but direct and to the point.

I follow her direction and make my way to the bathroom, conscious of the fact Caleb is probably questioning my actions even though he hasn't said anything or made a peep.

After closing the door, I tell her, "Alone."

"Okay, so spill it for real. How are you doing with it all?"

I sigh. I don't know how much to even tell her; I've always been guarded with my personal shit, even though I know she's a great person.

"I freaked out a little when I first found out. No, a lot. I was already going through some shit I was working on and this totally threw me for a loop. It took me a while to process it and believe it was really happening, and to even tell Caleb. Not that I would have ever kept it from him forever, but it didn't come at a great time. Now that I've had weeks to process it, I realize there's a reason it's happening now." I stop there; I've already said too much, but on the other hand, it feels good to get it off my chest.

"He's going to make a great dad. And husband," she adds quickly. "Not like my ex."

"Caleb has staying power, even when I don't deserve it."

Oops, that kind of just slipped out.

Kate doesn't say anything for a few minutes. I just listen to her breathing on the other end. "Can I ask you something which may be none of my business? Feel free to tell me to shut it if I'm out of place or it's too personal."

"Okay."

I start to pace around the bathroom. It's not big by any means so I'm essentially walking in circles. What the hell is she going to ask me?

"Do you have staying power?" She's hesitant with her question, almost as if she knows the answer already.

I consider my options: I can lie and tell her I absolutely do. I can tell her a version of the truth. Or I can be completely honest with her for the first time in my life.

Hiking up my big girl panties, I go for option three.

"If you had asked me a few months ago, my answer would be different. But yes, today I have staying power."

And she picks up on the one word I should have left out.

"And what about tomorrow?"

"Yes," I declare confidently. "I'm done running."

When I realize the words that have just left my mouth, I clam up and smack myself in the forehead. *Shit!* Didn't mean to give her that much truth.

"Look, Natalie. Even though he's never said anything, I know my brother. Your relationship has had rough waters. With that said, he's also the happiest I've ever seen him. That man loves you. He's not going to give up when things get too rocky. I know you must know this already, but I just want to make sure you truly understand. He would do anything for you. Just let him."

Wow. I never realized how much alike the two of them truly are. I contemplate what to say in response, but she keeps talking.

"One day, I hope you will let me in deeper into your life." She takes a breath but continues, changing the subject. "Okay, now that that is out of the way, anything you want to know about pregnancy? I'm an expert by now."

I can't help but laugh. "Um, I don't even know where to begin."

She laughs too. "Been there. How about we meet for lunch one day, just the two of us, and go from there?"

"Sounds great, Kate. Thanks." And then before I chicken out and talk myself out of it, I add, "One day, but not at lunch."

"Deal. Love you, Nat. Congrats again."

She doesn't let me even say goodbye before I hear silence on her end.

Well, that was interesting, to say the least. I'm not sure how to process the whole of our conversation, so I don't even bother trying. Instead, I walk back out to the living room and find Caleb lounging on the couch. He's got the remote in his hand, but he's not really focused on the TV. As I approach him, his eyes follow my movements, almost as if he's stalking me. Plopping myself down on the floor between the couch and the coffee table, I make myself as comfortable as possible.

"What did Kate want?"

I already made my decision not to tell him what we talked about.

"She wanted to make sure that if I had any questions related to pregnancy and the nugget, I can call her anytime. We are going to go to lunch soon."

"That's good." Then he gets a questioning look in his eyes. "Nugget?" he asks.

"Just go with it." I couldn't tell him where the nickname came from, but as soon as I began thinking about our baby as "Nugget," he/she definitely became more real.

He starts to say, "okay" but quickly catches himself, instead saying, "Works for me." He turns the TV off, places the remote on the table and motions me up on the couch, lifting his legs so I can slide underneath them. When he's comfortable with my position, he gives me a stare down. "Are you calling your mother?"

"Ugh," I start.

I know it's not a real answer, but I have no desire to call my mother to tell her our news. She wasn't even thrilled to learn about our engagement. She just wanted to make sure we gave her plenty of notice so she could take the time off to come for the wedding.

Thinking about my mother has me instinctively rubbing my belly. Call it mother's intuition, but Caleb's right. This baby needs to know only love. And that starts now.

I can do this. It's not just because I have Caleb by my side; that's an added bonus. It's because I know what kind of mom I don't want to be. I will be better for my nugget.

"I'll call her later over the weekend. No use bothering her at work this week."

Caleb grunts in response. He doesn't get my relationship, or lack thereof, with my mother. I've learned to accept it as he has learned to just let it be.

"Now that we've told your family, can we tell our friends tonight? Please? I can't keep this from Ainsley anymore." I've almost slipped a few times, catching myself at the last minute.

"Sure thing, Storm."

I crack a smile. The nickname gets me, every damn time. "I love you, BG."

He maneuvers himself to lie down and pull me next to him. It's not an easy feat; the couch is barely big enough to hold him. When he notices this position isn't going to work well, he pushes off the couch, and then I'm being lifted in his arms as he makes the way to our bedroom.

"What time do we need to be at Grayson's?"

"We've got enough time for whatever you're planning," I state. "Plenty of time."

* * *

*A*fter a round of hot sex, a short nap and a shower, we finally head over to Grayson's. I texted Kylie to let her know we were sharing the news and to act surprised.

Once Caleb parks the truck, I hop out and don't even wait for him before heading inside. Since I know the girls are already here, I don't bother knocking.

When Gray and Ainsley are alone, it's a gamble to just walk in, even if they are expecting company. Hey, I get it. I was there with Caleb once, and we are hopefully working our way back there. And as far as relationships go, theirs is still in the honeymoon phase. They just mesh in so many ways, including the bedroom, or whatever room they find themselves in. I'm not going to knock the way they conduct themselves in their own house; I'll just knock on the door.

I find all four of them in the kitchen, Ainsley taking something smelling divine out of the oven, the girls at the table, and Grayson pouring drinks. They are the perfect hosts, and it doesn't suck that they serve the best food and desserts.

"Hey," I call out to Ainsley. After setting the tray on top of the stove and shutting the oven, she turns to me.

"Hey. Glad you guys could make it."

Caleb comes in behind me and immediately takes a seat at the table, making himself comfortable as one does at a good friend's house.

"You want a beer?" Grayson asks him. Nodding his answer, he grabs a handful of chips and shovels them into his mouth. Grayson turns his attention to me. "Nat, what can I get you?"

Before I can answer, Bella's up out of her chair, bounding to the fridge. "Ainsley and I made a winter sangria." At Ainsley's throat clearing, Bella corrects herself. "Fine. Ainsley made sangria. It's really good. I'm already on my second glass. You should try it."

Knowing it's now or never, I state, "Just water for me."

My comment elicits stares from almost everyone.

"Are you hung over?" Bella asks, which actually isn't a bad guess.

I shake my head, thinking that one of them will come up with the real reason. When they are still silent after a few minutes, I can't take their stares any longer.

"I'm pregnant."

I'm not sure what I expected their reaction to be. I guess I haven't really given it much thought. So I shouldn't be surprised when both Bella and Ainsley rush over to me, nearly knocking me down, grabbing me into some sort of odd three-person hug.

"Oh my gosh!" Ainsley squeals. "How exciting."

And then there's Bella. "A baby. Wow. I can't even believe it. You. And a baby. Wow. Just wow."

They somehow manage to wrap their arms around each other and me as well, so when Kylie comes rushing over, she can't even figure out how to get in on the hug. She shrugs and throws her arms out into the mess of tangled limbs, somehow managing to drape them around me.

"Congrats. Such exciting news." When she's positive no one is looking, she winks in my direction, a sly smile sliding onto her lips.

"Thanks, friends. Caleb and I are excited."

Once we untangle ourselves from one another, Bella asks, "So wait, which came first? The baby or the engagement?" Leave it to Bella.

Technically it was the engagement, but that's not going to make any sense to them, especially once they find out how far along I am. I'm about to lie when Caleb joins the conversation.

"If you want to be technical about it, I bought the ring before we found out about the baby, and she said yes before she told me about the baby."

In his roundabout way, he managed to tell the facts. Of course, there were things he omitted, but he didn't lie.

"What he said," I respond. "And before you ask, I'm nine weeks along. Here's a picture of the little nugget."

I whip out the ultrasound picture from my back pocket. Of course, the girls all ooh and ah over it.

While they do that, Grayson comes up behind me, pulling me into him. When he turns me around to face him, he doesn't give me any other option than to accept his hug. I can't help my body's reaction to naturally meld into him. Given our history, in many ways, he feels so much like home, more so than Caleb sometimes.

"Congrats, Natalie. I'm happy for you." His voice is sincere, and I know he means the words he says. "Your kid is lucky to have you for a mom."

When he says stuff like this, it kills me that he doesn't know the entire truth of who I am. I wonder if he would still agree if he knew all of my deep, dark secrets.

Without much thought, I respond, "Thanks, Grayson. That means a lot." His arms tighten ever so slightly. When he finally lets me go, it's only because Ainsley has handed him the ultrasound picture.

"So, how big are you going to be for the wedding?" It should totally come from Ainsley, but it's Grayson who asks the question.

I can't get a good read on Ainsley's take on Grayson's opinions on the wedding. Some days she seems thrilled he's taken most of the lead, yet other days I think she wishes he would back down. I've stayed mostly out of it except to accept my role as bridesmaid.

"Pretty big I would gather. Like almost eight months."

Not going to lie—it's a little freaky to think about how big I'll be at the time of the wedding. Or even at the end of the pregnancy. To deter this line of thinking, I bring the focus back to the wedding, not my part in it. I look at Ainsley. "So, what details have been decided on?"

She hesitates for a minute. "Um, we have the date picked out. Grayson booked the photographer. That's about all we've got."

Grayson comes up behind Ainsley, takes a seat in a chair, and pulls her onto his lap. He puts his hands over her ears, and while she silently protests, she's got a huge smile on her face.

"Please don't ask any more details. I can't have her freaking out on me. Again." He uncovers her ears, she turns to look at him, whispering something in his ear.

This time, it's Bella that speaks up.

"Not. Now," she hisses through gritted teeth. "We won't be here forever."

Both Grayson and Ainsley look over at her, not in the least bit embarrassed, but they do tone it down.

"What did you decide on the cake?" Kylie joins the conversation.

It seems like a simple question, but with the way Ainsley's scowl appears on her face and Grayson's insistent shaking of his head, clearly there's more to the story.

"We are not allowed to discuss that," Ainsley mutters.

"Why not?" Bella asks the question I want answered as well.

"Ainsley, we are not making our own wedding cupcakes."

Grayson's tone is adamant. "I will order whatever cake, cupcakes, cake pops, etc you want, but I'm not baking the cupcakes myself. And neither is the bride," he quickly adds when Ainsley goes to protest.

"But," she starts.

He shakes his head. "No."

While I don't want to get in the middle of their fight, I can't help but add my two cents. "Why can't she make them if she wants them?"

Grayson's eyes shoot to mine; it's almost enough to make me feel the stab of his daggers. "Don't encourage her, Natalie. She's the bride. Brides don't make their own wedding desserts."

"Says who? I'm sure they do if they are as delicious as Ainsley's."

In solidarity, Ainsley gives me a weak smile.

"I've tried telling him this, but his stubborn ass won't listen to me. I've been agreeable to his demands."

Grayson guffaws. "Agreeable?" he questions with a raised brow. "Darling, you couldn't even talk about the wedding without breaking into a sweat up until a short time ago. That does not make you 'agreeable.'"

His quotes on the word agreeable are spot on. "Agreeable" would imply she's made decisions, and from what I can tell, she has not.

Leave it to Caleb to table this for now with his question of, "Um, can we eat soon? I think my baby is probably hungry."

That garners a laugh from everyone, even Grayson and Ainsley. I can tell by their expressions that the conversation is nowhere near over. I certainly hope Ainsley wins this battle.

* * *

I put off the phone call as long as I can, but it's inevitable to eventually make the call. She's my mother, for goodness sake. The baby's grandmother. For most people, she would have been their first call. But let's face it. I'm not most people and neither is she.

Knowing my mother, there's no real "good" time to break this kind of news. So I figure I will do it when it's convenient for me. Which equates to around eight at night.

Caleb's working late so after I made myself dinner and cleaned it up, took a shower, dried my hair, and got mostly ready for bed, I plop down on the couch and settle in. After dialing, the phone rings four times. On the fifth ring, it goes to voicemail.

With a curt, "Hello?" my mother's voice rings in my ears.

"Hi, Mom."

"Natalie. What's wrong now, dear?"

She always assumes there's something wrong when I call her. Always. I guess she has a point because I don't call her often; when we do talk, it's her calling me. But it still irks me. This time, there's nothing wrong, not that she will see it that way.

"Nothing. I just have some news I wanted to share with you."

Fiddling with the blanket on the back of the couch, I take a deep breath and let it out before sharing my news. In the time it takes me to do that, she's already asking, "Okay, what is it?"

Here goes nothing.

"I'm pregnant."

Despite having given serious thought to what her reaction would be, I came to no concrete option of how she's going to take the news. She's always toted safe sex to me, from the time I was twelve years old. And while she may have never called me a mistake, it was no secret I was unplanned. Unwanted, even. She's the first to tell you she did her best with me and what she had to work with. Fair enough, to a point. Just makes me want to do better for my nugget.

My hand floats to my abdomen. It's too soon to feel the baby but seeing him or her and hearing the heartbeat has definitely made it more real.

I wait patiently for my mom's reaction. She's quiet for a while, but I won't say anything else until she's responded. I hear a sigh, which I'm sure is accompanied by a shrug.

"Guess I'm not all that surprised" is her response. When I think she's done and go to respond, she actually continues. "Is this why you are getting married too? The baby? At least that man is good for something."

I should explain that despite my mother meeting Caleb two times in her life, she's never liked him. She doesn't know our history, the fact I've left, the rocky waters we've faced in the past, none of it. But she also doesn't know he's the sweetest, most loving man I've ever met either. Because it's all or nothing with my mom. If I told her just the parts about how he loves me, protects and supports me, lets me be me, she'd believe there was a catch, that there has to be more to it than that. She does know some of my "slut" history so I've always assumed she thinks he's another one of my bad decisions. At least she did in the beginning. I chalk it up to the fact she's mistrustful of all men, based on *her* history, but again, it's not like I've stood up for Caleb to her.

"No, he asked me to marry him before we found out I was pregnant." I want to add more, but without going into everything, I'm not sure how I can at this point.

"Look, Natalie. You're a big girl, so what you decide to do with your life is your business. If that's marrying Caleb and having his baby, then good for you. I'll be at the wedding, as soon as you let me know when it is, and I'll want to meet my grandchild."

"Of course. Thanks."

I'm not sure why I add the "thanks". Thanks for what, exactly? Letting me make my own decisions? Coming to my wedding? Wanting to meet her grandchild? Thank goodness I'm used to this from her, but it's truly no wonder why I've never relied on her.

"Is there anything else?" Her tone is annoyed. Her only daughter is having a baby, and she's irritated.

"Nope, that about sums up my life right now." My tone is sarcastic, but she misses it all. Or chooses to ignore it, I'm not sure which.

"Let me know when the wedding is." Clearly the date is important to her as she's made sure to mention it several times.

I notice the tear as it's about halfway down my cheek. Swallowing the lump in my throat, I squeak out, "Will do."

Her last word, before the line goes dead, is "Congrats."

As I wipe the tear off my cheek and chuck my phone across the room, I notice Caleb leaning against the doorframe.

"Your mother?" he guesses with a head tilt toward the phone.

"Yep. What gave it away?" I try to laugh it off, but when it comes down to it, I'm letting it get to me, more so than I ever have before. I blame the hormones.

He doesn't move from his spot in the doorway, standing with his arms crossed over his chest, a tired expression on his face. He was in the office today, so his attire reflects that. He's already kicked off his shoes, but he's still wearing his khakis and a button-down shirt. The pants are all wrinkled, the sleeves are cuffed to his elbows, and the top two buttons are undone. This look gets me every time. Just the sight of him alone is enough to send more tears down my cheeks, which of course sends him in protective mode as he stalks over to the couch.

"I'm fine. It's just a lot," I tell him so the worried expression that has crept on his face starts to soften, even if it's just slightly.

"You want to talk about it?" He takes a seat on the couch next to me and lays a hand on my thigh. I rest my head against his shoulder.

"Nope, not really." Because truth be told, I don't want to rehash the conversation with my mother. And he'll let me have my way. While I know he doesn't share everything with his mom, the two of them are close, as close as a mom and son who doesn't say much can be.

As he rubs my thigh, he asks, "You want cheesecake? We can go out and get it or I can run out and bring it back?"

Cheesecake sounds amazing right at this point.

"Yes please," I whisper.

I turn my head up to his. The worried look is gone, but so is the tiredness. All that's left is adoration.

As best as I can, I shimmy my arm around his back and wrap my arms around his torso. He dotes a kiss on the top of my head. It's the little moments like this that make me wonder why I ever questioned anything when it comes to this man. And I know it's the hormones and the tiny human inside me making me more emotional than I normally am. Again, I'm counting my blessings things happen for a reason. This baby happened for a reason. I'm just glad Caleb loves me enough to have allowed us to get to this point. No, allowed *me* to get to this point. With him. For us. Because I never imagined myself getting to this point with any man. But here I am. And for once in my life, I know this is where I belong and where I need to stay. Forever.

I hear Caleb talking but his words aren't making any sense until I realize it's because I'm stuck in my head again.

"Huh?" I ask for clarification.

He shakes his head with a laugh. "Do I even want to know?"

I ponder his question for a moment. "It boils down to I love you and this baby. Let's leave it at that." I smile up at him to make sure he knows I'm serious.

"That works. Now, cheesecake. You want to go out or you want me to pick it up?"

I'm distracted again, this time by his hand that has found its way inside the hem of my shorts and inching closer to my undies.

"Um, I want to say pick up," I start, suddenly panting, "but part of me doesn't want you to leave."

He stills his hand as my head falls onto his chest from his shoulder, my eyes slipping closed.

As if what he's doing isn't already turning me on, he leans his head down and rasps in my ear, "Go upstairs and get dressed. I'll make it worth your while later." He doesn't give me a chance to even react before he pulls his hand away, pushes me up off the couch, sending me on my way.

If his promises for later weren't always worth it, I might say screw it. But Caleb always holds true to his promises. My guy is loyal to a fault.

I trudge upstairs and throw on some clothes. Caleb follows behind and quickly sheds his work clothes for more comfy clothes. I smile at him before reflecting to a time when ending the day with cheesecake wasn't always a possibility.

* * *

I'd always been resourceful and for the most part, self-sufficient. Growing up poor in a more affluent town will do that to a kid. I was never looking for a sugar daddy nor someone who had so much money, we didn't have to work.

Caleb grew up comfortable. His parents both worked, and they made ends meet with a little extra each month. His entire life, he never really wanted for anything, whether that be new shoes or the fancy new X box.

When we met, Caleb worked a few jobs, not necessarily to make ends meet, but because he didn't know what he wanted to be when he grew up. He's fairly handy and can fix almost anything. That's how he first got into construction work. It started as a side job, but by the time we had been going out for a few months, he clearly had potential and the desire to do more.

So when his friend offered him an opportunity to branch out on their own, he took it. That's when I knew Caleb was the one. Despite the initial outcome.

Caleb was late. Again. If I was keeping track, it was like the seventh time in two weeks. But I wasn't keeping track. Or so I let him believe. It drove me just about crazy that he couldn't send a text to let me know he was going to be late. Was it really that hard? But considering I had never really been this far into a relationship nor had to rely on anyone else, there was a learning curve. Even after two years in. So I tried to curb my annoyance and cut the guy some slack. God knows he did with me and my issues.

I didn't mind eating alone; it was my normal, yet I had gotten accus-

tomed to him being around for dinner. I took comfort in not eating alone anymore. A comfort I never thought I would enjoy, but if I was honest with myself, something I started to take for granted because I liked it so much. I liked him so much. I had to take a few deep breaths every day so as not to terrify myself. Because I promised myself I was done running.

I more than liked him; I loved him. And I let him know it. Except now that he was hours late, I was upset and wondered if I could hold my temper when he trudged through the door. Whenever that happened to be.

Hours ago, I ate dinner by myself, cleaned it up, and got myself ready for bed. I had a few things to finish up for the ad campaign for next week's presentation so I settled in on the couch with my laptop and a cup of coffee. I had already added coffee to the list for the grocery store this week because my current cup was the last K-cup. Sure, we had the instant shit but who had time to make that on a busy morning? And besides, it sucked. I could run to my favorite coffee shop, but I was on a tight budget lately—how I grew up—so it didn't bother me. But lately, it seemed so much worse. We had to cut back in some areas, but a good cup of hazelnut coffee wasn't going to be one of them.

I lost track of time and when I finally heard the back door open and slam, it was after ten. I got so into my work, I forgot to be angry with Caleb. Until he came stumbling into the living room. Well on his way to drunk.

I took a deep breath and released it before I spoke. Looking up at him, I said, "You're late."

He tripped and almost lost his balance at my words. Somehow he managed to avoid falling; good thing the chair broke his fall. His face lit up with a surprised expression.

"Storm! You scared me. Wasn't expecting you." He chuckled.

"Where have you been? You said you'd be home right after work." The words spilled out of my mouth with no edge to them. Go me.

"I met Grayson at the bar for a few rounds. I meant to text you."

I'm not sure which was worse: that he went out for drinks or that he "meant" to text me.

"How many is a few rounds?"

I watched him, trying to figure out how much he had to drink. I wasn't so concerned with how much he drank (other than how he got home); the guy could hold his alcohol, and if that's how he chose to unwind, far from me to stop him. Drinking was one of my favorite hobbies too. In today's case, it was the cost factor.

"Maybe like five beers." Once he answered, he sank deeper into the chair. Closing his eyes, he added, "No, more like eight."

"Caleb!" I pushed my laptop off my lap, got up and stormed over to him. Despite the warnings in my head, I lashed out. "What part of 'cutting back' do you not get? That's over fifty bucks!"

His eyes remained closed, and for a split second, I thought maybe he was asleep. As I was about to stir him, he bolted upright. "It's fine."

"It's not fine! You don't get it. I'm not sure you ever will. Until you get to the point when you have to choose between lunch or dinner for the day because you can only afford two meals and you already ate breakfast. Or your lights get shut off because your mom 'forgot' to pay the electric bill which also killed the power to the fridge and what little food was in there spoiled."

I started pacing sometime during my speech. When I stopped to take a breath, Caleb was behind me. Even in his inebriated state, I got through to him.

"I'm sorry."

It was how he said it and then wrapped me in his arms. And I got it. He was trying to protect me, wipe away the memories of my past.

But not this time.

I wiggled out of his arms, using the fact that he was somewhat intoxicated to my advantage to push him away.

"No. Sorry doesn't cut it in this case. You knew we couldn't afford drinks tonight, and you couldn't even let me know you were going to be late. That's two strikes."

He cut me off and based on the look on his face, he was pissed.

"Two strikes for what? Like what happens if I get three? You going to run again?"

I didn't even have a chance to react before he realized what he said. *And he tried to backpedal and take it back with his, "Shit, Nat." But I walked away from him, too mad to even give him anything.*

I stormed out of the living room and upstairs to our bedroom, slamming the door behind me. It had only been "our" bedroom for a few months but already I felt at home here. More so than anywhere else I'd ever lived. I both loved and hated that fact. Tonight I hated that I shared it with him, that I had given up my so-called independence to cohabitate with this man. The one who infuriated me more than words could say, especially lately when he pulled shit like tonight. But also the one to who I had given my heart, the one who held that heart like it was the most important thing in the world. And like he would never let it break.

The war in my head raged on. So to try and stop it, I got ready for bed and hoped like hell I'd be asleep before Caleb dragged his ass to bed.

* * *

I didn't even hear Caleb come in last night and when I woke up this morning, he was already up and out of the house. It amazed me every time he could come home close to plastered and not be affected the next day. The only evidence I could find he was already up and out was the box of coffee K-cups sitting on the table. With a note.

It won't always be this bad. Don't count me out just yet. I've got a plan in the works. Just need some time. I know you deserve better. Love you. I'll text you later. BG

Damn him for knowing how to knock down my walls in one fell swoop. Between the box of coffee, the "deserving better" and the BG, I couldn't hate the guy. I couldn't even really be too mad anymore.

I made a large cup of coffee and sent him a text.

> Apology accepted. We still need to talk.

His response was immediate.

> I'll be home by 5. Let's go to the diner.

> You can't be serious!

He didn't get it. Irritated, I went to text more until his response came through.

> We have to eat. And the diner is cheap.

> Dinner at home is cheaper. See you at 5.

Aggravated, I tossed my phone in my bag and finished getting ready for work. Thank goodness for the coffee or else my mood would be worse.

Caleb walked through the door at 4:58 that night. I only knew because the timer was going off at the same time and once I turned it off, the time flashed in my face.

He came in through the back door as I was taking the chicken out of the oven.

"Hey," he called out, toeing out of his work boots. "Smells delicious. Do I have time to shower?"

He came up behind me at the sink and pulled me into him. And damn if I didn't melt into him on instinct. I wallowed in his scent for a few minutes as I allowed myself to let go of everything but this moment.

One of Caleb's best qualities was knowing what I needed, when I needed it and not pushing it. Too far, at least.

He allowed me to stand there before telling me, "I'm going to shower. Be down in ten minutes." When I didn't protest, he had his answer to his previous question.

With a peck to my cheek, he pulled away. I missed his presence immediately.

I finished getting dinner ready and by the time he came downstairs, the table was set and everything was ready.

He sat down, almost hesitantly. He looked as if he had things on his mind but didn't say a word; just dug into dinner. It wasn't uncharacteristic to eat in silence, but for some reason tonight, there was definitely an aura of something looming over us.

When he finished his first beer, he started to push out of his seat for another one.

"That was the last one."

His face fell. "Garage?"

I shook my head. "It's on the list for next week. Not in the budget this week."

It was painful to admit that. Not because of how much he loved his beer; more so because I swore I would never live paycheck to paycheck. And yet here we were.

He stayed sitting, went back to eating, and slammed down his fork. It startled me for a second, but looking over at him, I noticed he wasn't angry. It was almost a look of sadness on his face. Like he was disappointed. And if I had to guess, it was in himself.

"I get paid Friday," he exclaimed, picking his fork back up.

"And that will pay the mortgage and some of the bills. We've been over this, Caleb." I know my tone was clipped but I couldn't help it. He didn't get it. And it was my job to make him understand.

"I know," he said, exasperated. "And I heard you. It's just, there's got to be money somewhere."

Before I completely exploded at the guy, I changed tactics. "You said you had a plan or something."

He put his fork down and his expression changed. The doubt was gone and in its place was more positivity. "So you know Charles?"

I nod. "Vaguely."

"He found an investor who would back his idea for a construction business. And he wants me on board."

I let his words sink in before I said anything, not wanting to jump to conclusions. "So what does that mean exactly?"

Because this could be great, really great, or it could be bad. Really, really bad. And while I wanted to think about the good, life always gave me the negative.

"I'd start with doing the construction work, but ideally we would like to hire other workers and be in charge of the business side. Put my degree to use." He laughed. His "degree" from the "fancy college" he attended was gathering dust in our attic.

Okay, clearly he had put some thought into this, which was a good sign. But then came the catch.

"I just need some of the startup capital."

And that's about when I lost it.

I cut him off, totally flying off the handle. "That's a joke right?"

"No?" he more questioned than said, his eyes probing if I was serious. Then as if he realized it, he cleared his throat and spoke again. "No, it's not a joke. I told him that...."

I cut him off again. "We can barely afford our bills and you want to put us more into debt? That's what you are suggesting?" I fumed. I pushed my plate away even though I barely ate any of the food, suddenly not hungry and sick to my stomach. It was a feeling I knew all too well, but one I never got used to.

Caleb was starting to get angrier too. His face was red and he stopped eating.

"Thanks for the support, Natalie. I always support your career decisions, but I guess it's too much to ask you to support mine. This is really something I want."

"I don't doubt that. And I don't doubt that you wouldn't be great at it. But we can't afford to take a gamble like this right now. It has nothing to do with anything but finances." I thought he was smarter than this.

"So then how do we finally get ahead? How do I get us out of this hole we are in? Enlighten me." He eagerly awaited my response, expecting me to have an answer.

I softened slightly with his words. "While I'm glad you want to accept the responsibility, it's not on you to fix this. We have to work together to get it done." I hesitated with my next statement. Because as much as I knew what I wanted to say, I didn't know how to say it. At least without him taking it the wrong way. "I promised myself I would never get to this point in my life. Ever. Again. Yet, here I am. And I don't know how to fix it."

I all but whispered the last part. It was the truth, but it stung. It stung badly.

I couldn't look over at Caleb. Sure, he had seen me at my lowest, soul bared to him, but this was something different. This was the last piece of myself I had never shared with him. Yes, he knew bits and pieces of how I grew up but this went deeper.

"Do you have a number?" he asked, out of left field.

Confused, I questioned, "A number?"

He pushed his chair back from the table and got up and grabbed some paper and a pen. "A number. To get us back to the black and out of the red?"

Okay, maybe he was starting to get it.

"Not off the top of my head."

"So let's figure it out." His grin let me know he was going to make it work. How? I had no frigging clue, but I knew something had to change and if he was willing to make those changes with me, I had to at least hear him out.

And we did. We sat at that table for over two hours, going over every piece of our financial lives. We made some cuts even I didn't see, and Caleb said he'd take on more side jobs. Even a few small ones each month would make a huge difference.

A month later, he asked his parents for a loan, and his company was up and running within that month. It took about six months to get into a groove and establish clients, but once it took off, we were always in the black. Who knew the guy had such a head for business?

That first night at the dinner table, he promised me I would never be in a position like that again.

I'm not sure I will ever believe it could never happen, but all of a sudden "being comfortable" was in my vocabulary. And that's how I knew this guy was the one.

12

NATALIE

I haven't been involved in a lot of weddings, but Ainsley is one of the most laid-back brides I've ever seen. I think it has something to do with the fact that Grayson has over-shadowed her at almost every turn. She just goes along with pretty much whatever he's suggested. Thankfully, his suggestions and requests are actually pretty great. And well since he's footing the entire bill, I think she feels he needs to have more of a say than she does. I have to believe that deep down, she knows he would do anything for her, but seeing as I know a little bit about those feelings myself, I just showed up when they told me to show up.

The night of the rehearsal dinner arrives. Being eight months pregnant, I hate how everything looks on me. I've basically been wearing the same five outfits to work every week, and when I'm home, I lounge around in one of Caleb's old sweatshirts and a pair of maternity yoga pants. When I finally found a pair I liked, I bought several pairs. I've decided I may never go back to wearing real pants again.

I look over at the clock; I have to start getting ready. It's a struggle to just get out of bed some days, and I know it's only going to get harder these next months.

The doctors have told me that the nugget is going to be big; I blame Caleb for that. I mean, the guy is six-three and built like a linebacker. A sexy, fit linebacker, but still. He's big. However, I can't focus on that right now.

At the moment, I have to focus on getting out of bed and getting dressed. Ainsley and the girls picked out my dress for tonight. I'm taking their word it looks "great" because I don't see it. As I'm willing myself out of the bed, Caleb comes into the room.

"Need some help?" he offers, rushing up to the bed and helping me up and out.

Once I'm up, I waddle over to the dress hanging on the outside of the closet. Before I can grab it down, Caleb's reaching over my head for it. He carefully slips it off the hanger and motions for me to go sit on the bed. I willingly take his lead.

Over the past months, I've learned to finally give myself fully to him. I need the support, in every way that it counts: emotionally, physically, mentally. He's taken care of this baby and me like a champ, not that I would have expected anything different of the guy. It's amazing how much more vulnerable you become when you are carrying a tiny human inside you. Let's just say any and all doubts about Caleb's love and devotion for me have been put to rest. I've accepted this fact. It's what has gotten me through this pregnancy. This man. My future.

And then I realize I'm crying again. *Stupid hormones.*

"Storm, what's wrong?" Caleb sees the tears after he's helped me out of my T-shirt.

I wipe them away with the back of my hand. "It's nothing. Just thinking about how much I love you."

I can't say more, even though sometimes I feel like he deserves more. Scratch that. I *know* he deserves more, but I don't need to be a blubbering mess, more so than I'll already be later tonight.

Caleb's never been a guy who's backed down at my tears; can you blame him? In his own way, he lets me know that I'll be okay. First, he kisses my forehead. Not just one kiss but several. Next, he moves to my left cheek and then shows the same love to the right one. When his mouth finally lands on mine, his tongue darts out, licking my bottom lip. A moan falls out of my mouth involuntarily. Knowing that it will make us even later, he places a hasty kiss on my lips and pulls away.

"Later, Nat."

My eyes have drifted closed but slowly open at his words.

"Okay."

He chuckles and shakes his head. The word has taken on an entirely new meaning over the past several months and every time one of us catches the other using it, all we can do is laugh.

To change the subject and distract myself from the sexiness in front of me, I ask, "You ready for your speech tonight?"

No surprise, he clams up.

As best man, it's only right that he gives a speech at the rehearsal dinner, but when he volunteered to do it, he was in the middle of the open waters and had a few beers in him. But since it was Ainsley who asked him, he couldn't say no. Not that he would have said no to Grayson either. She hasn't asked for much and knew how much it would mean to Grayson for Caleb to speak. So he agreed. And then I swear he forgot about it until earlier this week when the realization of how soon he would have to do it began to creep in. We've been practicing all week, but it's not the same as being up in front of all the people. At least the dinner is just close friends and family, so I've focused his attention on that. It's worked up until now.

I find his face and grab his chin in my hands. His worried expression is nothing compared to the uneasiness hiding in his eyes. "You'll be fine, BG. You've got this."

He grunts in response. So I let it go.

He finishes helping me get dressed, and I have to hand it to the girls. Taking in my appearance in the mirror, I don't look half bad. From behind me, I see Caleb's reflection in the mirror and know he agrees.

Walking up behind me, he snakes his arms around my waist, laying his hands palm-down against my belly. He nudges my hair off my neck with his nose and nuzzles into my neck. Reveling in the moment for a quick minute, I place my hands on top of his and whisper, "Thanks. Nugget and I love you." His teeth nip at my collarbone in response.

"I love you, Storm."

"We have to go..." I start, but when he makes no move to let me out of his grip and his hands are still caressing my belly and his lips, well, yeah. They are doing more than just caressing my neck.

As swiftly and ungracefully as I can, I pull out of his grasp. It's not easy. Have I mentioned he's much bigger than me?

Finally, he relents and lets me go.

"Later, BG."

Again, he grunts his response, and the awkward shift to his pants doesn't go unnoticed. At least he plays it off like he's only just changing his clothes. *Yeah, okay, Big Guy. Keep telling yourself that.*

He quickly changes into his dress pants and a blue button-down. I literally have to tear my eyes away because between leaving the top two buttons open and the rolling of his sleeves, the man wears the shirt like it was made solely for him. When I start fanning myself, he parrots back the word, "Later" with a smirk.

Touché.

I manage to slip my feet into my flats even though I can barely see them past my protruding belly. I give myself a final once over and start walking toward the hall. Caleb follows behind, doing up the strap of his dressy watch.

Once downstairs, I grab my clutch, apply a coat of lip gloss, and I'm ready to get going. Even though I'm a little winded, I know if I take a seat, I won't get up again. Luckily it's actually time to leave.

From the corner of my eye, I watch as Caleb grabs a duffle bag from the closet. When I question him with my eyes and a nod of my head to the bag, he answers, "I didn't think either of us were going to feel like coming back here tonight, so I booked a room at the inn. Consider it our babymoon."

Cue the tears. Again.

"Aww, BG. Thanks."

He drops the bag and hurries over to me. With the pads of his thumbs, he tenderly wipes my tears that have slipped down my face, the ones I have no control over lately.

Knowing we have to leave, he just pecks my lips. "See why I said later?" He cracks a sly smile.

I giggle. "Promises, promises."

He turns away, grabs the bag, my dress and his tux, and heads for the truck.

Yep, let the accepting of the love continue.

* * *

*A*insley absolutely refused to have a rehearsal for the ceremony. She wanted nothing to do with having to practice getting married. She withheld sex from Gray for over a week until he finally saw things her way. That was her only "bridezilla" moment. Man, that girl has gusto sometimes.

The rehearsal dinner is at the boat club, which wasn't a surprise until I learned Ainsley was the one who suggested it. I guess when she has a strong opinion about something, she voices it. Like wanting Caleb to give the speech tonight.

She asked me to make sure Bella didn't get too wasted. I about laughed in her face at that one. It's *Bella*. The girl does what she wants, when she wants. Which Ainsley knows, but she told me I had to try. For Grayson. So that's my main goal tonight.

Dinner is a buffet with an open bar. The club is decked out in navy blue and grays. They aren't the colors of the wedding; Grayson wanted tonight to be separate from the wedding colors so it's more of a nautical theme. I'm not sure what they finally decided on for the theme of the wedding. Like I said, I'm just showing up where and when they tell me to.

There are only like twenty or so guests here tonight, family and close friends. It's interesting to watch Ainsley interact with her family, especially her mother and brother. Her usual glow dims with each interaction. I can certainly empathize with her; I know that feeling all too well.

I've kept Bella away from the bar as much as I can. I'm kind of feeling exhausted, and it's too much for me to keep getting up out of my chair to watch her. She still seems pretty sober for now. Plus, my attention needs to stay on Caleb.

I figured tonight would go one of two ways for him: either he wouldn't drink anything until after his speech or he'd be all over the beer for the courage to make the speech. Surprisingly, he chose the former. He's nervous as all hell, not that I expected anything different. I haven't seen him smile since we stepped foot in the door, and whenever we are sitting, his legs are bouncing non-stop.

"Are you sure you don't want just one beer, Caleb? It might be enough to just take the edge off." He shakes his head. "Okay, help me up."

I push my chair back and start to get up. His questioning eyes watch my movements. I throw my arm out to him and that sends him into action. He helps me stand up, and before I can stand all the way, I find myself tilting into him for support.

"Whoa, Nat. You okay?"

Well, that's one way to get his attention off his speech.

"Yeah. Just got up too fast, I guess."

"Fast" is subjective, but in this case, it applies. My heartbeat starts to elevate and a wave of exhaustion hits me again. I drop my head and take a couple of deep breaths. Once I've steadied myself —with Caleb's help—I motion for him to follow me.

As I make my way to the exit, I see Ainsley rushing over from across the room. She must have seen my reaction. "Natalie, are you okay?"

"Fine. Just more tired than I realized. I just need to take Caleb outside for a minute. We'll be right back." I observe Ainsley's face turning to Caleb who just shrugs his shoulders because he doesn't know what's going on. "Can you grab me another water and maybe another plate of chicken? Clearly this baby needs more food." I laugh to lighten the mood a little.

"Um, sure thing. I'll have it at your table when you get back."

"Thanks."

She turns around to head back to the party.

"Come on. I need some fresh air."

I've gotten my strength back so now I'm kind of dragging Caleb outside. This seemed like a good plan in my head before I stood up, but once outside, I slow down. Which Caleb notices right away.

"Storm, where are we going? Are you sure you're okay?" My actions have sent him into hyper-protective mode.

I nod, brushing him off for a minute as I slowly lead us to Grayson's boat. Once we are in front of it, I motion for him to climb on. His face bears a questioning, almost disbelieving, look, and he doesn't move.

Catching my breath, I start to talk. "You need to step on the boat, Caleb. I'll stay here, unless you need me up there too." He's about to say something in protest, since he's holding up his hand, but I push it aside and continue. "Your speech. You know how just stepping on the boat calms you. Go."

As if a light bulb goes off in his mind, he cracks a slow smile. "Oh, Storm." It's all he says, but it's the way he says it that I know he gets it. And that I'm right.

He takes a few steps and climbs the ladder to get on board. Once he's on board, it's like his worries fade away and a serene look replaces the worry. I watch as he makes his way to the front of the boat and grabs hold of the railing and then hear the footsteps behind me. I don't have to turn around to know it's Grayson.

"Natalie, are you okay? Ainsley said something was wrong and here you are out here, and where is Caleb..." He stops talking as I motion to the front of the boat. And then *he* gets it too. He puts his arms on my shoulders and gently massages them.

"He just needed a minute to be calm. He'll get through it."

"He never would have thought of this."

"I know. That's why I had to make sure to get him out here." I turn my face up to him. He's looking down at me, that "big brother" look of love in his eyes. "After all these years, did you ever think we'd be here? You marrying the girl who stole your heart with one kiss, me pregnant, engaged to a guy like Caleb?" I can't help but laugh at the way life has played out for us.

"Never in my wildest dreams did I ever think I'd find Ainsley. And you! Truth be told, I figured you would have been knocked up way before now." Now it's his turn to laugh.

"That's actually not far from the truth," I tell him. "But I'm glad things worked out this way. For both of us. I don't have to tell you that Ainsley's a fucking catch, Gray. Don't let her go." I can feel the tears prickling my eyes so I turn my head away from Grayson and quickly dab at them. He doesn't question my actions; he just spins me around and wraps his arms around me, pulling me in tighter.

"I love you, Natalie."

I manage to bring my arms around his waist, despite the basketball that is my stomach in between us. "I love you too, Grayson. And I'm so happy for you." We stand there a few more minutes, until we hear Caleb's throat clearing from above us.

"Trying to steal my girl, Gray?" Caleb bellows from above, climbing down the ladder.

Grayson's hold on me slowly loosens. Before he lets go completely, he pops a kiss on the top of my head.

"Never, man. Just couldn't get married without one more hug from Natalie."

Once Caleb is back on the pier with us, he puts his hand out to shake Grayson's. Grayson grabs it and pulls Caleb into him for a hug. Once they are done hugging, he looks Caleb over and asks, "You good, man?"

He nods. Pointing his head in my direction, he replies, "Thank goodness for this one. I needed the calm that I only get on the boat."

"Come on. Let's get back to the party before Bella sends out a search party for us."

My comment elicits a deep laugh from the guys. As I could have hoped, all of Caleb's nervousness has slipped away and been replaced by calm.

Caleb and I walk hand in hand up the pier, Gray a few steps ahead of us. As we walk, Caleb brings his face down to my level.

"Thanks, Storm."

"Anytime, BG." He leaves me with a kiss on my forehead before pulling his face away.

Looking toward the end of the dock, I notice Ainsley has made it outside, waiting for us. Her concerned look melts away the closer Grayson gets to her. Instead of the jealousy I felt several months ago, I look up at Caleb. And I see it: the look of unwavering love for another person. I squeeze his hand and because he's mine, he gets it.

"Everything okay?" Ainsley asks once she's wormed her way into Grayson's arms.

Caleb is the first to respond. "All good. Is it time for the speeches yet?"

I don't miss the inquisitive look that passes between Grayson and Ainsley. I also don't miss the kick from the nugget into my side. Hard. I wince, the pain enough for me to drop Caleb's hand and even stop walking. Caleb doesn't miss any of it and as I'm bending over, he tips up my face.

"Nat, you okay?"

Even though I'm slightly keeled over, I see the worry on his face. There goes my "calming" plan from earlier.

"Just got kicked by your future soccer player, a little too hard. I'm fine." I try to wave it off, but that sucker hurt. And I can't hide it from Caleb.

I hear him tell Grayson and Ainsley we'll be right in. I can't be certain, but I'm sure their looks match Caleb's to some degree.

Caleb walks me over to a bench and forces me to sit before I can put up a fight. He sits down next to me and starts to rub my belly. I lean back against his broad chest, taking any comfort I can.

Apparently, I'm a wimp lately. This doesn't bode well for labor and delivery.

After he's rubbed my abdomen for a few minutes, he leans his head down to meet my forehead. "Better?" he asks.

"Yes," I reply weakly.

What the heck?

"You ready to go back inside? We don't have to stay too much longer. Then we can head to the inn or home, whatever you want."

I take a deep breath, inhaling the warmish spring air into my lungs. "Ready."

He helps me up, making sure I'm completely steady before grabbing my hand and leading me back inside. When we get to our table, he makes me sit and then forces a cup of water into my hand.

"Drink. And then eat." He scoots the plate of chicken in front of me.

Realizing I'm parched and downright starving despite the food I ate earlier, I don't argue and just dig in.

Kylie and Bella are seated across the table from me, giving me the stare down. "What?" I ask as I stuff my face with food.

"You're okay?" It's Kylie who asks, despite Bella's concerned look. I watch as she gets out of her seat and comes to sit next to me. Without permission, she lays her hand on my thigh. When I question her gesture, she sighs.

"Just making sure you're really okay. You had me worried." I hear Kylie grunt and Bella whips her head around. "What? She did."

Kylie half smiles and just shakes her head. "How about another drink, babe?"

I drop my fork as I remember Ainsley's one request she had of me. Shit. I did a piss-poor job of keeping Bella sober tonight. But as I look her over, I realize she's not even tipsy. And she sees right through me.

"I've only had one drink. I know Ainsley didn't want me drunk and gosh darn it if I don't love that girl. Could she be any more perfect for my brother?"

"Not even if she tried," I confirm.

We turn our attention to the happy couple. She's sitting in his lap, laughing at something he's said, a look of pure bliss on their faces. Grayson has a hand on the small of her back, and the other one twists through her hair.

Ah, that's why she left it down tonight.

"They make me sick," Bella whispers on a groan. She's not quite quiet enough because I hear Kylie snort. Without even turning around, Bella gives her wife the finger to which Kylie hisses, "Behave, Bella."

I can't help the chortle releasing from my mouth. They truly are the perfect match.

As I continue to watch Ainsley and Grayson, Caleb appears in front of me. He kneels to my level. "If you're sure you're okay, I'm going to make my speech now."

I nod my agreement. "I'm fine, I promise." It's not the total truth, but he needs to get his speech over and done with. I'll be fine. "Go. Make me proud." I pull his face into mine, surprising him a bit if the wild look in his eyes is any indication, and smack a kiss on his lips. "The warm-up for later," I whisper in his ear. He nods as a smile creeps onto his face. Standing up, he grabs Bella by the hand and drags her over to Ainsley and Grayson's table.

From behind me, I hear Kylie shout, "Good luck, babe. Not that you'll need it." Bella turns around and blows a kiss in her direction.

As the pair make their way across the room, the nugget kicks me again.

"Ky, come sit next to me, please."

I can't even turn to look at her because not only am I still wincing from the kick, but there's a searing pain in my esophagus. The stupid heartburn is back. And of course, my Tums are in my bag in Caleb's truck.

I do my best to hide my pain from Kylie, and either I do a good job, or she can see through it and knows I just need someone's comfort right now. She sits in the chair that Bella vacated, sliding it closer to me so she can grab my hand.

"Just breathe," she whispers. I nod my understanding.

Caleb speaks first. His speech is short but to the point. His eyes stay trained on a point in the back of the room, but his voice is steady. I find myself mouthing the words along with him. Once he's done, he finally finds my eyes. I plaster a smile on my face so he knows he did a great job but also to mask the pain in my chest.

Bella's up next, and she has the entire crowd laughing along with her. Her speech is short too because she's going to speak at the wedding tomorrow. In her words, "I'll save the good stuff for tomorrow."

She ends with this: "Grayson, when we met Ainsley at the bar that night, I knew you were done for. I'm so happy you didn't let this one go; she's *the* prize. And Ainsley, thanks for taking my brother off my hands. I would say I'll miss being the center of his universe, but I'm happy to give it up to you. You truly are one of a kind. I'm fortunate to call you my sister."

I watch Ainsley wipe at the tears that slip down her cheeks. She pops out of her seat and embraces Bella in a hug. Following behind, Grayson wraps his arms around and pulls both women into him. So of course, I start crying too. More like bawling. Until I realize that my not being able to breathe through my tears is making the heartburn in my chest way worse.

As best as I can, I try to calm myself down and let the tears subside, all the while willing the burning ache in my chest to stop. I try drinking water but that doesn't seem to help. In fact, it might make it worse.

"Shit." I try to mumble it, but Kylie catches sight of me. I can only imagine the grimace of pain etched on my face.

"Natalie, you are not okay. What do you need?"

"Caleb," I manage to squeak out, voicing the words around the acidic fluid at the back of my throat.

As if he already knows, he's suddenly standing in front of me. I meet his gaze. The worry lines around his eyes are practically popping off his face with concern; the one in between his eyebrows is deeply creased.

"I need the Tums from the bag. Please. And hurry." Another blast of burning pain shoots down my chest. I start to swear in my head and then I realize that some of it's actually coming out of my mouth. I can't even care about the scene I'm making; I just want the pain to stop.

It feels like hours, but I'm sure it's just minutes that he's gone. He's got the bottle open and shoves the pills into my hands. I toss them in my mouth and start to chew feverishly. By the time I'm sticking my hand out for two more, the pain has slightly subsided. Enough for me to ask for a glass of milk.

Trust me on this one; it works.

Grayson comes over with the milk in his hand, his jaw set and face wrecked with concern too. Once I've gulped down some milk and swallowed more Tums, the pain eases. I look over at Grayson and then to Ainsley.

"I'm sorry. Didn't mean to steal the show. That's more of a Bella thing to do."

Everyone laughs. Well except for Caleb. Because he's still too concerned to joke.

I grab his hand and pull him in toward me. He kneels next to me. "I'm okay." His expression is unchanged. So I try again. "I'm okay." This time I draw out the end of the word, and ever so slightly, the corner of his lips tick up. "Hear me again. I'm O-K-A-Y." That does it. His face softens and he buries his chest into my non-existent lap. When his hands find my belly, he lets out a sigh of relief. Leaning over to get as close to his ear as I can, I whisper, "Your speech was great, by the way. You totally nailed it."

He mumbles something I don't understand, but I let him have his moment. I grab the milk and finish it off. With the heartburn mostly subsided, I look over to Grayson.

"Dessert?" I ask with a wink.

He laughs. "The cake will be out shortly."

I lose the amusement for a moment. "Cake? There aren't any cupcakes?"

I'm seriously disappointed in them. But again, it's their party and who would want to make cupcakes for their own rehearsal dinner?

Ainsley comes over behind my chair. "Are you really okay?"

I nod. "It's one of the worst feelings in the world, the burning. I keep telling myself that I need to suck it up because in a few short months, labor pain will be way worse." And the nugget takes that as his or her cue to kick me again. This one hits down where Caleb's head is.

And then because I clearly haven't cried enough today, I hear Caleb whispering to the nugget.

"Kid, please take it easy on your mother. She's been a good host to you so far. She loves you, more than you will ever know." It's not so much the words as how tenderly he says it. Because I know he means every word.

"Hey, BG. Can we go now? They don't even have cupcakes at this shindig!"

I'm hoping it comes out as the joke I meant it to be, and when I hear Ainsley's giggles behind me, I know it hits the mark.

I feel someone come up behind me. When I turn slightly, I find Grayson leaning down next to me. "I baked cupcakes for tomorrow's reception. If you tell her, consider yourself unfriended."

"Seriously?" I shriek, trying to hide my surprise. He smiles and nods and then puts his finger over his lips. Yep, that Ainsley is seriously one lucky woman.

It takes me all of about two seconds to register my man still whispering to our child and realize she's not the only one.

Leaning back down to Caleb, I whisper, "I love you, more than you will ever know."

13

CALEB

*a*fter the debacle at the rehearsal dinner, Natalie decides to call it an early night. She can barely keep her eyes open on the drive to the inn, even though it isn't far. When we get there, she is already asleep so I go inside to check us in. I reserved the room for three nights, two for the wedding and then one more as a bonus surprise for Nat. Even though we live one town over, it's sometimes nice to break up the monotony of our routine and day-to-day life.

Once I have the key in my hand, I walk back to the truck and climb inside. I gently tap her shoulders. "Nat, we are here. Let's go inside and get you changed."

She mumbles something I don't understand, but she starts to move. I'll take that as a good sign. I grab the bag and our clothes for tomorrow from the backseat and make my way over to her door. She's got it opened but hasn't really attempted to slide out.

"Can you climb down, Storm? My hands are kind of full."

Instead of answering, she awkwardly contorts her body as she very slowly slides herself down to the ground. "Not sure how much longer I'm going to be able to do that in this condition," she prattles when her feet hit solid ground.

"Yeah, I hear ya. I'll see what I can do."

I grab her hand in mine. She interlaces our fingers together and then brings the back of my hand up to her mouth for a kiss.

"Remember when we talked about 'later' earlier today?" she asks as we walk inside the inn.

I don't want to answer her; I know where this is heading. And I'm not going to like her answer.

"Yeah?" It's the best I can manage.

"You meant later as in tomorrow, right?"

And there it is. But I really can't blame the woman. Eight months pregnant, heartburn like nobody's business, and being the nugget's punching bag, all take their toll on her. I'm convinced this is why morning sex was invented. For pregnant people who are just too tired at the end of the day.

"Of course, Storm. Later as in tomorrow morning. Before the wedding. I'm not going all day ogling you in that gorgeous dress without fucking you first. Even if it makes us late for the ceremony."

She halts but because it takes me a minute to realize she's stopped, I keep going, dragging her arm with me a little.

"Caleb, we can't be late to the ceremony. Did you not see how your kid already stole the show today? Not happening. She takes a breath then quickly adds, "The being late to the ceremony. Not the sex. The sex will be happening." She shakes her head and mutters to herself, "Late to the ceremony. Ha. Funny man."

I can't help but chuckle.

"Thank you for clarifying that. Can we continue inside now?"

Without answering, she starts waddling again. Yep, I said it. There's no other way to describe the way she's walking except as a waddle. But damn does she do it well.

Nat's always been beautiful in my book, but she wears that pregnancy glow like a rock star. And that second trimester? My dick has never seen so much action. Pretty sure if I could keep her knocked up just for months four through six, I would do it in a heartbeat.

Once we've made it inside the inn, I lead her to our room. The front desk wanted to give me a room near the honeymoon suite, which I hastily passed on. I don't even want to imagine the use that room's going to get when Ainsley and Grayson get here. I'll gladly take a room at the other end of the inn to avoid hearing their shenanigans.

When we come to our door, I hand Natalie the key so she can open it up. She opens it up quickly and darts to the bathroom. I drop the bag and hang up our wedding clothes in the closet.

"Much better," she exclaims as she walks out. "Unzip me please." She turns and puts her back to me. Slowly, I slide the zipper down her back, then push her sleeves off her shoulders. I'm about to move her bra straps out of my way when she turns her body around to face me, a scowl on her face. "If you stop the moans, I'll take the help in getting undressed and redressed. If the moans continue, you're SOL in helping me."

Fuck if her brazen attitude isn't turning me on more. And I was moaning? That I don't believe.

I bite down on my bottom lip to keep from moaning and continue to help her undress. I keep telling my dick it's purely in kindness to Natalie; clearly he's got plans of his own.

Once she's undressed, she stands in front of me. "Too. Tired. Caleb." Her eyes fall to my erection.

"It's not his fault he can't hear you," I retort.

She shakes her head and stifles a laugh as she grabs her PJs from the bag. Well, it's just one of my old shirts she manages to shimmy into without my help.

I settle down on the bed and turn on the TV while she finishes getting ready for bed. After washing up and brushing her teeth, she climbs into the bed next to me. With a quick peck on my cheek and an "I love you" in my direction, she settles herself on her side to attempt sleep. Even though she's tired, she's not at all comfortable. It's only a matter of time before she's tossing and turning and up to pee again.

It's barely morning, but since I've been awake pretty much all night long, I decide to go and grab us some coffee down in the front lobby.

I'm met with Ainsley, who clearly had a similar idea. Once I grab my cup, I take a seat across from her at the table.

"Hey. You're up early."

She seems startled to see me but quickly catches herself. "Oh, Caleb. Wasn't expecting you." She takes a sip of her coffee. "Yeah, I couldn't sleep. Not sure if it's the wedding today or the fact that Gray wasn't in bed with me. Probably both."

I chuckle, the sound echoing around the otherwise quiet room. "Where'd he sleep?"

"Back at our house. I didn't think he'd be so traditional about the whole 'can't see the bride before the wedding thing,' but here we are. Oh, how's Natalie?"

"She'll be okay. She's still sleeping, but it was a somewhat restless night. Most nights are these days."

Ainsley's face softens. "I can only imagine. And I can't think it will get any better any time soon."

I shake my head. "I'd like to say I think she knows what she's in for, but I don't truly think she does."

"How do you mean?"

I think a minute before answering. "Just the changes to her body, having to go through labor, adjusting to motherhood. Truthfully, I'm not sure she's processed it all."

There's something about this girl that gets me to spill things I wouldn't dare tell anyone else. In the year I've known her, she's gotten more out of me than almost anyone else, aside from Natalie.

"You know her better than I do, but my guess is that she's scared. It's the fear of the unknown for her." She places her hand on top of mine. "However, I feel like there's more to Natalie than she lets me see, so I can't say anything for certain."

Even though I know she's not looking for me to confirm what she's said, I nod. "You'd be correct in your thinking."

She sighs. And because I don't do heavy well with others, I quickly change the subject. "Excited for today?"

She pulls her hand away and smiles. "Very. Nervous too. Not about marrying Grayson; just about how today will go. I can't wait to be Ainsley Abbott; I just would have been happy to do it on a smaller scale. But Grayson had different plans, and clearly I let him have his way."

Her expression doesn't change one bit throughout her answer. The girl is ridiculously happy, even if Grayson's demands were a little more than over the top for the wedding. It actually surprised me every time I would hear what he wanted or Nat would tell me something he said. Didn't think the guy really would have too many thoughts about his wedding day, but I guess you never truly know everything about a person. If she's taught me anything, Nat's taught me that.

"He's lucky to have you. You know that right?" Sheepishly, she nods. "I saw it on the boat that first weekend. He fell hard."

"Sometimes it's still so odd to me that we came together so fast, but he's the most real thing I've ever had in my life. And I fell hard too." She goes quiet, and I know not to pry anymore, so we sit in comfortable silence, enjoying our coffee.

After a few minutes, she gets a text. I can only assume it's Grayson the way her face flushes after reading it and then furiously typing out her response. I'm glad that he's so ridiculously happy too. The guy deserves it like no other.

When my phone dings, I figure it's from Natalie, so I'm surprised to see Grayson's name.

Enjoying your coffee with my girl? *wink emoji*

Very much so

She good?

Very much so

Thanks, bro. See you soon

I slip my phone back into my pocket and finish up my coffee. "What time do you need Natalie wherever she needs to be?"

Ainsley picks her head up from her phone to answer me. "Hair is in my suite at ten. Tell her to bring everything so we can get dressed there."

I look at my watch. It's only 7:30 which gives me plenty of time to wake her up to cash in on my "later" promise.

"She'll be there, showered and ready." From Ainsley's expression, I can tell she knows what I'm up to.

"Thanks, Caleb. Tell Nat I'll see her soon. I've already got some Tums stashed for her in my room, the ceremony and the reception. Think she'll need anything else?"

Her kind gesture catches me off guard. Talk about a true friend.

"That should be good. I'll make sure I have anything else she might need."

She stands up and throws herself into me for a hug. Impulsively my arms wrap around her body and squeeze her.

"You truly are one of a kind, Ainsley. Grayson's extremely fortunate."

She shrugs me off. "I'm the fortunate one. See you later." With that, she grabs her empty cup, tosses it in the garbage can, wiggles her fingers in a wave, and heads back to her suite.

I quickly make a cup of coffee for Nat and walk back to my room to see what kind of storm is brewing there.

She's still asleep when I creep in. Not really wanting to wake her (she needs her rest and all) but knowing we don't have the luxury of time on our hands, I climb back into bed next to her and lay behind her, wrenching her into my hold. I nuzzle her cheeks with my nose and wait for her to stir.

Without opening her eyes, she asks, "How much more time can I sleep before I absolutely have to get up?"

I wrap my arms around her belly and try to find my nugget. Knowing what I'm doing, she positions her hand down near her thigh and yep, there's my kid. A foot or something at least.

"If I say ten minutes, is that long enough?"

"Have you taken into account how many times I'm going to have to pee? And how long it takes me to pee?"

"Absolutely."

"Rouse me in ten minutes," comes her reply.

I take the time to enjoy the peace and quiet of the room, Nat resting in my arms, my baby lolling around in his or her cocoon. She doesn't last even five minutes when she's uncomfortably pushing up from the bed mumbling, "So much for that time. Gotta pee again."

She huffs and waddles to the bathroom, and I make quick work of disrobing. I lay back down on the bed to wait for her. On her way back, if she's surprised I'm naked, she doesn't let on. She spies the cup of coffee and questions me with her eyes. "Yours." Her lips turn up into a smile, she takes a long sip, then continues back to the bed.

Before climbing back in, she sheds her undies. She climbs onto the bed but doesn't slip under the covers. She's not yet close enough for me to reach her so I grab the hem of the shirt and yank her closer. She falters slightly, and her hands fall to the bed to catch her.

"Lose the shirt, Storm." I try to remove it, but she pulls out of my grasp.

"No." Her tone is adamant even though her face has a playful look.

"No?"

"No. You have access to what you need." When I continue to stare at her and question her second 'no,' she continues.

"We don't have much time. Are we doing this or what?"

She almost sounds irritated, put off that we are having sex. So I call her bluff.

I look over to the clock on the nightstand. "Oh crap. You're right. We don't have time." She follows my gaze to the nightstand and when she turns back to me, she's not only got a smirk, but she's suddenly maneuvering her way out of her T-shirt.

Point one to me.

Since she seems to be struggling a bit, I help her out, gentleman that I am. Moving on top of me, she straddles my legs and huffs out, "Thanks." She reaches behind her to unclasp her bra and when she does, her heavy breasts topple out.

Nat's been blessed with a good amount of breast, but damn, pregnancy has done wondrous things to them. Like make them more supple and ample. And even though they are *way* more sensitive now, I've found in the last few months that when Nat's totally in the mood, I can touch, lick, nip, all to my heart's desire. It's only when she's not in the mood do I need to stay far away. Yep, learned that lesson the hard way.

Before I reach out and make any sort of contact with them, I assess her facial expression. As if she knows exactly what I want, she looks down at her breasts and makes a motion, granting permission. She actually takes my hands in hers and tries to guide them to her breasts, but I've got other plans. I cautiously tug her by the ankles, dragging her body down a bit so that I don't have to sit up too much, then I put my arms around her waist, dragging her even a little closer. She's a little hunched over me, but one look at her face tells me she's not complaining or uncomfortable.

Once I get my mouth on one of the already pert nipples, I swirl my tongue around it and then suck it into my mouth. On a moan and an exhale, Nat's head falls back. I quickly make my way to pay the other breast the same attention since we are short on time. Nat's moans escalate while I massage my way around her breasts with just my tongue.

When Nat's had enough, she pushes my head away, maneuvers off my lap in somewhat of a jerky fashion, lays down on her side, facing me.

I've let her make the decisions regarding how this whole "pregnancy sex" works, like what positions are most comfortable for her. It's made my life easier without having to guess how uncomfortable she will be, and it's made Natalie even that much hornier and receptive to sex.

Before I can even move into a position, she's thinking better of her decision, and suddenly pushing herself onto all fours. "Stand up behind me. I think this bed's a little higher than ours and this position will work."

Ah yes, The Edge of the Bed.

Did I mention that Nat researched positions for sex during pregnancy? While I told her we could just experiment, she's now determined to try them all. At least once. Look, I'm not going to argue with her. She's pregnant. And horny. Honestly, I don't care where she wants me as long as my dick ends up inside her, I'll make it work. So when she says "stand up," that's what I do.

I watch her as she manages to line herself up at the corner of the bed. Then she sticks her ass up in the air and lays her head on the bed, resting her body on her arms. The scrunched-up expression on her face leads me to believe that she's not quite as comfortable as her research led her to believe she would be. But again, I'm not arguing.

Just to make sure it's what she wants, once I'm in position, I ask, "You good?"

In response, she mumbles something but reaches out her hand with a thumbs-up in my direction. I take my dick in one hand and start to stroke myself; with the other hand, I find her clit and begin to circle my thumb around the tiny nub. Every so often, I drag my fingers a little lower so I can make sure it's good for her. Yep, it is.

As I continue to stroke myself and warm Nat up, her moans from before echo around the room. They spur my hands to work faster, and while I'd like to be able to make sure Natalie is thoroughly satisfied more than once, unfortunately we don't have the time. So I have to settle for being inside her when she comes. That doesn't stop me from teasing my fingers inside.

It's on the fourth time I've worked them inside, curled them to her favorite spot, and then removed them that she growls out, "Caleb. Don't make me beg."

I withdraw my fingers from both her clit and her slit and move closer to the bed. "Scoot back just a little." She follows my orders and wiggles her way closer to the edge of the bed. Putting both hands on her waist and lowering her body just a tad, I line up and enter her in one thrust. This time her moan is a scream, one that reverberates around the small room and has me thrusting faster.

I keep my hands on her hips, holding her body level with my erection. Thrust in and out, I attempt to bring my hands around to grab her breasts. My hands cup her breasts, tweaking each nipple with a gentle tug as I continue to move my hips.

Pulling out for a minute, I drive back inside when I hear Nat's labored breathing escalating. She's close, so close. And if I just angle myself a little more to the left, she'll get there. I grab a hold of her nipples again, give a gentle squeeze, and she explodes.

I watch as her fingers fist the sheets. Her vagina clamps around my dick like a vise, and the "fuckkkk" that comes out of her mouth, spurs me to move faster. My breathing increases with each thrust I make. And then my balls pull up with my release.

I don't stop pumping until I've completely emptied inside her, and while my fingers are still massaging her breasts, her hips are rocking on their own accord now.

I pull out, once my breathing starts to return to normal and pat her on the ass. I quickly walk to the bathroom to grab a towel. By the time I'm back, Nat's laying on her side, her hands rubbing circles on both sides of her belly. I settle down next to her, raise her top leg in the air and start to wipe her down. When I'm done, I lay down behind her and wrap my arms around her in a spoon. I place my hands on her belly just slightly in front of where hers are. She places hers on top and then starts rubbing both hands over her abdomen.

"So?" I ask.

She pretends to think for a minute, but it gives me time to nuzzle my face into the side of her neck soon after feathering a few kisses right on her hairline.

"Ah, it was okay. Maybe a six. Not sure it would work at home. Our bed might not be the right height."

Like I said, she's determined to try each position once. And then she rates them. Anything that earns a seven or higher gets added into the rotation when we don't have the time to try something new or she just needs to get off.

She sighs heavily, a sound I've come to know well the past few weeks.

"You okay?" My hands stop their movements waiting for her answer."

"Yeah, just tired still. And it's going to be a long day. On my feet."

"You'll have to make sure you sit when you need to. Ainsley will understand."

She stops the movement of our hands and twists her head back to look up at me. "We better start getting moving right? Like, I don't have time for a quick nap?"

I take in her facial expression. There are some bags under her eyes, but nothing that wasn't there yesterday. She's a little pale, and her eyes do look more tired than usual.

"Why are you so tired all of a sudden? Is there something else going on?"

As if her other pregnancy ailments weren't enough, now I have to worry about her being more than exhausted too?

She shakes her head. "I toss and turn too much at night, and I'm up at least twice to pee. And my breasts are heavy. And I'm eight months pregnant. And your kid isn't tiny. Does that about sum it up?" There's an edge to her tone, almost as if she's challenging me to something. What that something is I have no clue.

So I reply with, "Right." And then because I really have nothing else to add, I kiss the top of her head and leave one on her belly. "I'm going to shower. You want to join me?"

"Nope. Going to rest here until it's my turn to shower."

Glancing at her, she's already got her eyes closed. Before I head to the bathroom, I cover her up with the blanket.

I'm glad we got the sex out of the way already. She'll be lucky if she doesn't fall asleep at the reception. The thought makes me chuckle a little, imagining her sleeping at the table or on the chairs. Guess I better do my best to make sure that doesn't happen.

* * *

$\mathcal{T}$he ceremony is flawless. Nat looks like a beauty standing beside Ainsley. Her hair is pulled off her face in some sort of small braid, but the majority of it hangs loosely down her back in waves. Whoever did her makeup worked magic because the tired girl that graced my bed less than a few hours ago is long gone. The light blue strapless dress practically molds to her body, pregnancy bump included. It hugs her curves in all the right places. She stands out next to Bella and Kylie mostly because of the baby bump, but she plays the part of a bridesmaid well. Every once in a while she shifts to one foot so she can stretch the other one. Even though it's not a long ceremony, standing in one place is certainly taking its toll on her. Not that anyone else would notice the strain on her face; her "genuine" smile is plastered in place, and I've noticed a tear slipping from her eye at least twice.

Ainsley looks gorgeous in her floor-length wedding gown. It's also strapless but that's about all I can say about it. Oh, it's white. Pretty sure Grayson hasn't taken his eyes off his soon-to-be-wife since she walked through the doors on the arm of her father. His reaction when he first saw her had him gulping for breath; he was *that* enamored. As he should be. Like I said, she's gorgeous.

As the ceremony continues, I watch Nat from my position next to Grayson. I can tell she's getting more tired as the minutes pass. When she catches my eye, she mouths, "You and me soon" and then she smirks. I smile back in return, knowing that once the baby's born, it will be our turn.

I don't pay too much attention to the vows, as evidenced by the fact that Grayson has to shake my shoulder for the ring. As I dig it out of my pocket, I mumble, "Sorry," but he's clearly not too worried about it; he's still sporting that huge-ass grin as he takes the rings from my hand. Glancing back over at Natalie, she "tsks" me with a shake of her head. And then a wink. I roll my eyes in return and then pretend to focus back on the wedding. Yet again, I'm not paying any attention to the exchanging of rings; I've only got eyes for Natalie. I watch as she stifles back a yawn and then she's clapping her hands, in turn with everyone else, as Ainsley and Grayson share their first kiss. Throwing my hands together, I catch the tail end of it and snap out of the trance that Nat has on me. Not that she knows I'm watching her. I'm stealthy like that.

Once Grayson and Ainsley are pronounced husband and wife, they head down the aisle, hand in hand. Bella and Kylie file out behind them, Bella making Kylie laugh about something she's going on and on about. I wait my turn and for Nat to slide in next to me. I lock elbows with her as we walk back down the aisle.

"You holding up okay?" I ask her. Taking in her appearance, she doesn't look too tired.

"Ah, I'm okay. I need to sit and need some water."

I dig into my pocket and grab out the small bottle of water I stashed in there earlier. Handing it over to her, she beams up at me. Once it's opened, she practically downs the entire bottle in one gulp.

"Thanks, BG. That will hold me over until we get into the reception." She pauses for a minute, then adds, "You missed Grayson's mistake, didn't you?"

I look at her, questioning what she's asking me. She looks at me funny, like she knows I missed out on something. How she knows is beyond me.

"Um, what?"

"Yeah, I thought so." She giggles.

"Are you going to fill me in?" I ask, impatiently waiting for her response.

We are nearing the end of the aisle, almost to the back of the room. She's got her head focused on the ground, but her shoulders move up and down, shaking with laughter.

When she looks up at me, she flashes me a Cheshire cat-style smile. She motions to bring my head down closer to her and lowers her voice before she begins to speak.

"When he was repeating the vows after the officiant, he said he takes 'Ainsley Grace Abbott' to be his wife. Everyone cracked up and when he realized his mistake, he laughed it off saying that it's finally about time she's an Abbott." She continues to laugh, like it's the funniest thing in the world. I love her amusement, even if it is at my expense.

We get to the back of the room and head off to the hallway and soon after, she's finally controlled her giggles. I quickly scan the hallway for a chair, spotting one in the corner. I quicken our pace to get to it, making her sit. She doesn't fight me and just sits, letting out a deep exhale as she does so. And then she continues with her story.

"When I looked over at you, it didn't even faze you he had said anything wrong. What were you so mesmerized by anyway?"

I kneel in front of her, placing my hands on her thighs. "You." It's all I say.

I take in her expression as my word hits her. The smile she gives me in response to my answer reaches her eyes and radiates off of her. Then she giggles again.

"Don't worry. Your secret is safe with me. I won't tell Ainsley or Grayson."

"Gee, thanks, Storm."

I give her thighs a gentle squeeze then stand back up. Looking around, I notice people starting to spill out into the hallway. "How much time do we have until we have to take pictures or be at the reception or whatever it is we need to do?" I turn back around to face Nat.

Her head rests on the back of the chair, her eyes half closed. When she doesn't respond, I ask again. This time at the sound of my voice, her head jerks up.

"Huh?"

I can't help but laugh. It's going to be a long night.

* * *

$\mathcal{N}$atalie holds up well through pictures and during the rest of the reception. She even drags me out onto the dance floor, for both fast and slow songs.

Not that I would have expected anything different from Grayson, but the wedding is a fun time. The guy knows how to entertain and throw a party, even when it comes to a wedding. I'm not sure where he gets it from, but he makes it work well. There wasn't even one time when the shit-eating grin slipped off his face. Or his new bride's face for that matter.

I've made Natalie sit for most of the reception, but it doesn't take much encouragement from me. People keep coming over to her, rather than her having to go to them. The entire night, I've sat back and watched her expressions. She almost seems content; for the first time since I've known her, she's finally at peace with herself. It's taken a long road to get her to this place, but I wouldn't change anything in our past to get here.

Over the past several months, I've learned this baby was the best thing that could have happened for her. For us. And while I know the last months of pregnancy, and adjusting to motherhood, are not going to be smooth sailing, knowing where she is right now, especially from where she's come, I've got the confidence she'll be okay. That we'll be okay. More than okay, actually. Dare I say, great?

When dessert comes out, Ainsley's squeals catch me off guard for a moment. Me and the other hundred guests.

"Grayson! I don't know whether I should be ecstatic or hate you for the aggravation you put me through." She stomps over to where he is, next to the cart of cupcakes someone just wheeled in. Personally made by Grayson himself. For his bride because it's what she really wanted. If it were anyone else, I'd be sticking my finger down my throat, but for Grayson, I wouldn't have expected anything different. The guy is great people.

He goes to start talking, but she shushes him with a finger over his mouth. There's much chatter going on, and I realize the music has stopped and everyone turns to watch her every move.

I find Natalie sitting at our table and slowly amble my way over to her. Once behind her chair, I drape my hands over her shoulders and give her ear a nibble. She reacts with a small gasp and sinks back into the chair, bringing her face closer to me, craning to look back at me.

"He fucking made her cupcakes," she states as a smile creeps onto her face, the one that actually reaches her eyes. And while I'm glad that it's there, I recognize it was *Grayson* who put it there. So, I'm going to have to up my game. I can't even make a boxed cupcake, let alone a few dozen from scratch, but I'll figure something else out.

"Yeah, the bastard did," I agree and then turn my attention to Ainsley.

Her hands on his chest push him slightly back. "One question. When? When did you decide to make the cupcakes?"

"The night you suggested them." He keeps a stoic look on his face, not giving anything away.

Ainsley shakes her head. "For months, I've been begging you for this. Months! Months you let me argue with you about it. And you had already decided that you were going to do it?" He sheepishly nods his head. "Why?" Her question is barely audible and for the first time this evening, her smile fades.

"My reason is not appropriate for all of our family and friends to hear."

With his answer, the bastard smirks. But either his answer or his actions have the desired effect on his bride.

She sidles up closer to him and in a not-so-subtle voice declares, "You're damn lucky I love you, Grayson Abbott."

With that, she slides a cupcake off the table and smashes it to his face, rubbing it all over his nose and mouth. The crowd erupts in cheers and laughter while we wait for Grayson to react. I hear Natalie whisper, "Oh shit," but my attention stays focused on my friend. Without even hesitating, he grabs Ainsley by the waist with one hand and tugs her into him. The other hand reaches around to the cupcakes on the table, but at the last minute, he bypasses the cupcakes and throws his hand in her hair, crashing his face into hers. As if she anticipated it, the girl doesn't even falter as she kisses the shit out of him.

I glance down at Natalie and wonder what she'd do to me if I pulled a stunt like that.

"I wouldn't even think about it, BG," she warns, reading my mind without even a glance in my direction.

14

NATALIE

*S*omehow the last of my pregnancy flies by. It's like I blinked and the finish line is in sight. Work has been crazy so I've put a lot of my energy into that. Ainsley and the girls threw me the best baby shower. Despite my pleading, Caleb wanted no part in a "Jack and Jill" shower. Can't say I really blame the guy. He hates the spotlight so he was none too happy to drop me off at the boat club before it began and come pick me up when it was over. And of course, lug home all the goodies for the nugget as well as the leftover cupcakes that we served for dessert.

My due date is two and a half weeks away, but for some reason, there's something I can't shake today. I can't put my finger on what it is exactly, but something's off. Not in a bad way; Nugget is fine. He/she is happily growing inside me, moving around, kicking like a sports player. They tell me he/she's not going to be as big as first expected, which I couldn't be more thrilled about.

It's not the baby that's nagging at me. And after I unloaded ALL of my fears on Caleb last month, it's not that. Nor is it Caleb. The guy has been nothing but doting my entire pregnancy. If I said jump, he asked how high? I wanted food? He was out the door on the way to pick it up before I had called it in.

Every day I let him know how much I love him and at least

weekly he makes me check in with how I'm doing emotional-wise. It may be the pregnancy and all the hormones, but even I can admit how much talking about my issues is totally helping. It makes me regret not talking to him for all those years, but I can't change the past. All I can do is move forward to the future and not look back.

But I just can't shake the nagging sensation.

I spend the morning at work. I'm trying to cut my hours back slowly before I go on maternity leave. After lunch, I head out. I'm not sleeping well at all, and I feel like I've been exhausted for the last several months. I take naps whenever I can. My bed has never seen so much action. And well, that's saying something for as much as Caleb and I use the bed for things other than sleeping. Today will be just another day I nap.

At home, I find a note from Caleb stuck to the refrigerator door.

Storm-

   Rich and I had to go out of town to Portland for the day. Call me for anything big, otherwise Ainsley and Gray are around if you need anything immediately. I love you. Keep the Nugget safe another day. Be back later tonight.

                                             BG

   As if the Nugget can sense his or her Daddy's note, there's a huge kick to my side. *Fuck, that hurts.* The one to the other side has me doubling over in pain. My left hand grabs onto the counter to steady myself. When I'm accosted from the other side yet again, I somehow manage to lower myself onto the ground. As I lay myself down, I realize I don't have my phone, just in case I need it. Guess it doesn't matter all that much since the kitchen floor is as good as any place to curl up and take a nap.

   I don't know how long I sleep; I just know the sheer amount of pain in my abdomen ruing me awake. It radiates down my right side and it takes me all of a few seconds to realize it's not the baby.

"No, no no no NO!" I scream out into the kitchen. This cannot be happening. Not today. Of all days for Caleb to go out of town.

All I can think to do is rationalize with Nugget. *Yep, I'm going there.*

"Nugget, Daddy is way too far away from home for you to come right now. I know they said I'd be in labor for hours, but it's still too soon. Be a good baby and do whatever you need to do to come in a few days. Tomorrow even. Just not right now."

I don't notice the tears falling from my eyes until one lands on my lips. I wipe it away with the back of my hand, but it doesn't stop others from falling. *Stupid hormones.*

I maneuver myself to my back, not at all gracefully, but since I can feel my anxiety heightening and my blood pressure on the rise, I don't care. I just need to get more comfortable and calm myself. Easier said than done at this point, but I'm convincing myself that this will all be okay.

Under my breath, I plead for this to stop. For that one contraction to be an anomaly and not the start of anything. Maybe I'm just overreacting. It's easy to convince myself of this for a few minutes. I rub my hands over my belly. The baby reacts to my touch, a foot here, a butt over there. I smile knowing that I'll finally get to meet this tiny little person soon. Just not today, I beg silently.

After a few minutes, everything returns to normal. Still exhausted, even more so now, I slowly push myself up on my hands and knees, take a few breaths to rest here, and then make myself stand up. I grab my phone off the counter as I waddle to the couch. Once I settle into a somewhat comfortable position, I shoot Ainsley a text.

> Please come over. It may be nothing, but I need someone. And hurry if you can.

I rest the phone on the top of my belly. I watch as it rises and falls as I breathe in and out. My eyes get heavy and start to close.

After a short time, they spring open with another shooting pain in my abdomen.

"Fuckkkkkkkk!" I yell to the empty room.

As if I can rub the pain away, I start to massage where it's concentrated the most, knocking my phone to the ground in the process. It's of no use. The pain continues, my breathing intensifies, and I wince in pain. I try to focus on my breathing. That's what they said to do, right? Yeah, way easier said than done. All I can focus on is the pain splitting my insides in half. I grit my teeth, preparing for the worst of it, when it stops. On an exhale, I moan out in discomfort.

I'm not naive to think this is nothing. I just hope that hours of labor are long enough to get Caleb home. Speaking of, I should probably call him.

I slide myself down the couch a bit, dangling my arm over the side, trying to locate my phone by feel, not able to really move my body. When my fingers finally close around it, I hear the door open.

"Natalie, where are you? I'm here."

Oh thank goodness.

"I'm in the living room."

I watch as she comes into view, panic schooling her features. "What's going on? Your message was a little cryptic."

Because I'm completely overwhelmed with my situation, I focus on her. Flour prints decorate her yoga pants and hoodie. There's some smudged on her face and her hair is falling out of the messy bun. Her cheeks are slightly pink as if she ran here. Hands on her hips, she's expectantly waiting for an answer.

"I think I had a few contractions. Two at least." I'm surprised at how even and calm my tone is.

I expect her to get even more panicked. I'm pretty sure I just told her I was in labor. But what does she do? She comes over to where I lie on the couch, lays her hand on my belly, and asks, "What do you need me to do?" I love how she's so direct and to the point. And so much the calm I need right now.

"I need to call Caleb. But I don't want to worry him. I mean, it could be Braxton hicks, right?"

She shrugs as if she would really have the answer to that question.

And as if to answer my own question, another contraction hits.

"CALL HIM!" I grit out through clenched teeth, as the pain overtakes my abdomen yet again. This one seems to be a bit stronger, almost like a "Yep, it's real!" confirmation.

I huff out and breathe through the pain. Okay, I *try* to breathe through it. Cause this pain? Yeah, no fun. I thought period cramps were painful? A walk in the park compared to this pounding and beating my abdomen is taking.

When I've ridden it out, pretty much thanks to Ainsley's soft hands massaging my back, I can focus on something other than the pain. Like the fact that she's sticking her phone in my face.

"It's on speaker," she whispers.

"Nat!" comes Caleb's strangled cry.

Hearing the worry in his voice does nothing to make this any better. So I say the only thing I can as an attempt to try: "Need you." No truer words have ever been said. I need his touch, his embrace, his calming demeanor. I need the guy like I've never needed him in my life. And I've been in a dark and stormy place, and I still need him more in this moment. "Please hurry." It's a whisper, but I'm begging.

"On my way." The confirmation is there in his voice.

The relief I feel causes a small smile on my lips, but it's short-lived knowing he'll be at least a few hours. And this pain? Could last way longer than that.

I hear Ainsley continue the conversation with Caleb but exactly what they discuss doesn't register. The next thing I know, she places a warm compress on my forehead.

"I don't know what I'm doing here, but Caleb said this might help. But if you don't want me to do something or you need something different, just ask."

"Ok. Thanks. I'll just lay low for a while until Caleb gets home. Did he say how long he'd be?"

She sits in Caleb's recliner. I crank my head over to look at her but don't like the way she's nervously fiddling with her fingers and avoiding my stare. She hesitates, then blows out a breath.

"He said there's some kind of accident on the highway."

I gasp because really? It's the universe again. Telling me it hates me.

She quickly continues. "Grayson's home and he can be here if we need him. You need him," she quickly corrects. "This is a you thing, not we."

At the thought of her thinking I don't want or need her, I say, "We. Tell him *we* need him. Please."

At my words, some of the hesitancy drains from her. She starts furiously typing away at her phone. I close my eyes, attempting to relax before the next bout of pain hits. Relax is clearly not a word in my vocabulary today.

As soon as I let go of some of the tension in my shoulders and other places, Nugget kicks me. While the pain is not nearly as bad as the contraction pain, it catches me off guard and causes me to tense up again.

I can't help the swears that come out of my mouth. "Fuck, shit, damn that hurt." My face scrunches up with pain. Breathing through it does nothing. When I feel a light touch on my leg, it causes me to pause. I momentarily forgot Ainsley was here. I curb my swearing, for the time being at least. "Sorry. Didn't mean to go all Janet Blair."

"You know I've never been in labor before, right?"

Her eyes find mine. There's something telling in her eyes but don't quite know what. I'm not sure where she's going with her line of thinking.

"Um, yeah. I know."

"So I have no idea the pain you are in. Do whatever you need to do, yell whatever you need to yell, to get through it. Heck, feel free to yell at me if you need to. All I can do is offer you my support."

Damn her! Because I need something else to add to my plate right now, cue the waterworks.

"Oh Natalie. I'm sorry. I'm not any good at this. Don't cry."

"It's not you. It's me," I blubber out. "You're too sweet. And I'm just so glad you're here right now." I interlock her fingers then squeeze them gently. Well, my goal is gentle, but when the next contraction hits, my grip on her tightens. She starts muttering under her breath, but my focus is less on her and more on the pain. The searing pain ripping through my abdomen.

"How the fuck do women do this? Screw natural labor. I'm getting all the drugs! All of them. The minute I get to the hospital. They can give them to me that quick, right?"

Ainsley glares back at me. Her "are you kidding me" look has me easing up slightly on my grip. Through clenched teeth, I grin. It's more like a grimace but it has her glare softening.

As the pain continues, I do my best to just get through it. Without breaking Ainsley's fingers.

When it finally ends, in what feels like a year later but is most likely only minutes, she doesn't move her hand right away. Even though my eyes are closed, I sense her watching me. Her hand stays put in my tight grasp.

I'm not sure how long we stay like that, her hand in mine, me lying there like I've got this labor thing handled in any way. All I do know is Grayson eventually shows up. He ignores Ainsley altogether and comes and sits on the floor next to the couch by my head.

"Hey, Nat, how's it going?"

I want to be my sarcastic self, the one side of me he knows best, but I'm kind of a little vulnerable right now. And as it appears, honest as shit.

"I've been better. Pretty sure I just mangled your wife's hand and I'd apologize for it, but I can't say I'm all that sorry. But on another note, thanks for coming. Stay at your own risk."

He looks to Ainsley who just shrugs and holds up our intertwined hands. "It could be worse," she tells him with a smile. I don't miss his mouthed, *Love you,* or the air kiss she gives him.

"So what do we do now?" he asks.

"Now, we wait for Caleb to get his ass back to town and get me to the hospital." It's subtle, but I don't miss the look they give each other. "He'll be back to drive me there, right?"

Any confidence I had in thinking that he'd be back soon flies out the window right then. I'm overcome with a new emotion: helplessness. There's no way I can do this without him. Not a fucking chance in hell! Nor do I even want to. And so I wallow for a few minutes. While I do, I convince myself that getting to meet Nugget sooner rather than later is worth it. And as a "ha ha who are you kidding" move, my body says otherwise.

"Fuckkkkkkkkkkk!"

It's drawn out and yelled at the top of my lungs. When I try to ball my hand into a fist, I realize I can't because Ainsley's still got hers in mine. On instinct, I squeeze it. Hard. It lessens the fact that my abdomen currently has a knife cutting through it. No that's a lie. It does nothing to lessen the pain of the contraction.

Fuck. This. Shit.

It lasts a while again, and while I'm glad Grayson's managed to sit me up and rub my back and I'm still squeezing the shit out of Ainsley's hand, it doesn't go unnoticed that neither one of them are Caleb.

"I need him," I squeak out. "Gray, go get him." I'm begging, pleading for him to follow my wishes. "Please." The tears slide down my face. I don't bother wiping them. They aren't going to stop. Closing my eyes, I sigh.

Grayson lays me back down, totally avoiding my request.

"Natalie." He tries to get my attention. My eyes don't open, but I turn my face in his direction. "Nat, we need to keep track of your contractions. Do you know when they said to call?"

I shake my head. "Can you call now and ask? Just pretend

you're Caleb. No one will mind." I'd giggle because in any other context, that would be comical. But while in labor? Not much is funny.

"Ok. We'll figure it out. Are you okay for a few minutes if we leave you here and go make a phone call?"

I wave him away and let go of Ainsley's hand. Pretty sure she may need that back.

"Be quick please."

While they are gone, I think about a plan of action. Once Caleb gets here, he'll take me to the hospital as long as the doctor says it's time. Otherwise, I'll just let him hold me and take away my pain. I know it's crazy, but let's not argue with the woman in labor.

Ainsley and Grayson take care of calling the doctor. I can't go anywhere until the contractions are like five minutes apart. I guess thank goodness for small miracles they aren't that close yet.

I ride out a few more hours at home. Barely. I managed to vomit all over Grayson during a particularly strong contraction. To his credit, he's not even slightly fazed. While Grayson runs home to change, Ainsley cleans me up. I cave and really break down.

"I can't do this. I don't know why I thought I could. I can't handle this pain, especially without Caleb. Where the fuck is he? Please give me something."

They placated me every time I asked, changed the subject, distracted me with stupid ice. I know something's going on, but they don't think I can handle it. And while I don't disagree, I don't think I *can't* handle it either. The not knowing.

Ainsley places a new compress on my forehead. I grab her wrist and make her see my begging. "Please. Where is he?"

"He's on his way," she starts, but I interrupt her.

"I know that! Why isn't he here yet? He's been on his way for hours. It doesn't take this long to get back here, especially when he knows I'm hurting."

The tears come again. At this point, I'm beyond caring. I'm also sure Ainsley doesn't deserve my ire but she's here and he's not.

And the pain is overwhelming me to beyond something I can't handle.

Out of nowhere, my mother's words come flooding back: *You always were weak against pain, Natalie.* Right about now, I'd have to agree with her. Because *this* pain? Totally making me weak and wondering how I can handle the rest of it, however long it lasts.

At my wit's end, I grit out, "Get him on the phone. I need to talk to him. FaceTime him. Call him on the tom-toms for all I care. Just let me talk to him."

Surprisingly, Ainsley reacts only by grabbing my phone off the side table. She hands it to me after she's set it up for FaceTime with Caleb.

"Thank you." Her return smile isn't big, but it's a smile none-theless.

It takes forever to connect, but when it finally does, I can't contain my disappointment when Rich's face fills the screen. "Where's Caleb?" It comes out as a growl.

Rich seems flustered before he answers. "He's taking a leak."

"When will you be home?" My tone is clipped. I'm sure Rich notices it but chooses to ignore it.

"We are about an hour away. As soon as the highway opens up, I'll drive him straight home."

"Yeah, you better." Then his words sink in. "Wait, what? What do you mean once the highway opens up?" I hope to heck he's kidding with me. As I watch his face get more flustered, I can tell he's not.

"There's a major accident. The highway's been shut down for hours." This comes from Grayson, who has just entered the room again.

Oh my god! Could this day get any worse? And then for shits and giggles, it does. Another contraction pummels me, knocking the phone off my lap. I open my mouth, but my voice is silent. The pain is just too much. And when I think it won't ever get better, I hear it.

"I'm here, Storm. Breathe, baby. You got this. You can do it."

I block out the pain for just a moment. So I can yell at Nugget's father.

"BG! Get the fuck home now. I don't care if the highway is closed. Figure it out. I NEED you. Like six hours ago." After a breath, and for good measure, I add, "Please, Caleb. I can't do this without you." I don't need to go into details about why I need him, especially with Ainsley and Grayson here. In a whisper, I say, "I'm fucking scared."

I hear him yell, "Grayson, get her face on the phone. Now!"

And the good guy that he is, he scrambles to pick it up off the floor and shoves it in my face. Since the contraction has passed, I grab it from him. And I get the first look at my guy. One look at his frazzled self, and the tears cascade down my cheeks.

Before I can get a word in, Caleb begins to speak. "Fuck, baby. I'm so sorry I'm not there. But you need to listen to me. Can you do that?" I nod. "Need the words, Storm." He runs his hand down his face, the concern evident.

"Yes."

"You can do this. Don't doubt yourself. You know Nugget needs you to be strong. You do this for Nugget until I get there, and then I'll fucking do whatever you need me to."

His eyes don't ever leave mine. Despite the fact he's miles away and I'm in the throes of labor, I don't miss the love reflected in them. The love that's always there in his eyes. Since the day I met him.

"Please hurry. Please," I implore.

"I'm doing my best. Trust me."

And I give him the only word that applies: "Okay."

I watch as one side of his lips turns up in a smile. "That's my girl. I'll see you sooner rather than later." He blows me a kiss. Put Grayson on, please."

"I'm here, bro. What do you need?" He grabs the phone from me and exits my view.

While Grayson and Caleb discuss the situation, Ainsley comes back over to the couch. "What can I do? I feel helpless."

"You want to have this baby for me?" I amaze myself that it comes out so serious-sounding.

She giggles. "Yeah, no thanks. I'm good for a while."

"Oh, what did you decide?" We had a discussion a while back about kids and how she wasn't quite ready yet.

She shrugs. "I'm still taking birth control if that's any indication."

"So, you haven't decided anything yet?" Typical Ainsley.

"Nope. But he's okay with it for now. He hasn't said much at least." She cracks a slow smile.

It's crazy how Grayson has so many opinions about certain things. Like his wedding and the fact he's ready for kids. But in his awesome way, he lets her have her own time on things. Just one way he's perfect for her. And she for him.

"Wise choice. This could be you." I wave my arms over my abdomen.

"You'll forget all this pain once you hold that baby in your arms."

"I highly doubt that. How's your hand by the way?" I take a quick peek at the fingers. They are red, with a few nail marks along them.

She rubs them on instinct. "Fairly certain not anywhere near as bad as your contractions. I'm all good."

Grayson interrupts our chat. "Okay, the highway appears to be getting cleared soon so with any luck, they'll be here in about an hour or so. Rich knows what's at stake."

"Thank you. For everything. In case I forget later when my life gets even more overwhelming. I truly would not have survived today without the two of you." I look between the two of them. "I love you both."

"Nat, anything. You know that." That's Grayson with a squeeze to my shoulder.

"No place I would have rather been." That's Ainsley, with a rub to my belly. "You got this."

"I sure as hell hope so, because it don't feel that way right now."

Forty-two minutes and six contractions later—I timed and counted—Caleb rushes through the front door, Rich on his heels.

"Natalie!" The sound is pure joy to my ears, the sight of him better than a mirage in the desert. And he looks like hell. I guess sitting in the car on a closed highway will do that to you.

He squats down next to me on the couch. Turning my head, I put my hands on his cheeks. "Of all days to have to go to Portland."

He shakes his head and laughs. "No, Storm. Of all days to go into labor." For the first time in hours, the tears running down my face are ones of happiness.

"I'm not sure if we are allowed, but please take me to the hospital."

"Sure thing. Let me just go grab the bag. It's all set, right?"

I nod. I packed the hospital bag weeks ago, just in case. I've never been so grateful for being so organized in my life.

Another contraction hits. Caleb senses my pain, grabs my hand, and whispers in my ear, "Breathe, baby. You got this." His voice soothes me, something that's been lacking all day, and for some reason, this contraction doesn't feel as bad. A resurgence of hope flows through me that with this guy by my side, maybe I can do this.

Once the contraction has passed, he quickly dashes upstairs. When he comes back down, he's changed his clothes into something more comfortable and has the bag. With Grayson's help, I've managed to sit up on the couch.

"You ready to have this baby?" Caleb asks as he tugs me up by the arms. I land in his embrace. Knowing this will be the last time it's just him and me, I take comfort in him holding me. After the day I've had, I need it more than ever.

"More ready than you know," I mutter against his chest. "Just have to pee one last time before we go."

I waddle myself to the bathroom. As I'm washing my hands, it feels like I'm going again when I feel wetness trickle down my legs.

"Oh shit! Caleb. Come quick. And bring a towel or two!" As much as I try to move out of my own way, I can't. All I can do is laugh at how not funny this situation is.

Caleb practically busts down the door. His eyes dart from the floor to the toilet to my wet legs, questioning what's going on. "You missed the toilet?"

"Pretty sure my water just broke." That's when his gaze settles on mine, the wildness in his eyes like something I've never seen.

"Oh." And there's my man of few words. But he sets into motion getting me cleaned up and delegating the rest to Grayson and Ainsley.

"We owe them big time for today," I inform Caleb as he's helping me change my pants. I don't bother with undies; less to remember at the hospital for when we come home.

"We'll make it up to them."

Back downstairs, we say our goodbyes and thank yous to the Abbotts. They assured us they would clean up and lock up after they leave. And let the girls know we were on the way to the hospital.

"I'll let you know when we want visitors. Although I'm pretty sure I've got no shame left after today."

Grayson hugs me with a smile. "Nat, it's not the first time I've cleaned up your puke, but I won't be disappointed if it's the last."

My hand flies to my mouth. "Oh my god! I forgot about that night. Yeah, that was not my finest moment." I shudder at the memory of that night.

"No, it certainly was not." He chuckles as I pull out of his embrace.

Ainsley's hugging me next. "Do I even want to know?" I shake my head. She leans in and whispers in my ear, "You got this. I love you. Be strong. That baby is one lucky kiddo."

"Thank you. For all of today. But I can't say more. I'm done crying for now."

She laughs. "Okay. Text us soon with an update."

"Oh, we will."

Caleb drags me by my arm out to my car. I can't even get up into his anymore so I stopped trying weeks ago. Considering he can't really lift me anymore, he had to relent.

The drive to the hospital should take no longer than ten minutes. With three stops for my contractions, each one stronger than the rest, we finally arrive after forty.

Caleb called my doctor on the way over and let them know we were coming so that helped speed things along. Before I knew it, I was in a hospital gown, in the bed, and monitors strapped to my belly.

Four more contractions later—Caleb thought it was fun to watch them on the monitor and tell me just how strong they really are, as if I didn't know—the doctor finally comes in to check me.

"Okay, so your water broke at home and contractions are about three to four minutes apart. Let's see how far along you are." Again, no shame. I don't even care who's in the room at this point while she checks me. "Wow. You're about six cm and progressing nicely."

Once her hands are out of me, I ask for the drugs. Again. I've asked everyone who's entered my room. It's like my prayers are finally answered with her response.

"I'll send the anesthesiologist right up. Try to relax as much as you can. You've still got some hard work ahead of you."

I breathe through a few more contractions before the epidural takes effect. But then once it does, my body finally relaxes. I'm pretty sure I fall asleep in the middle of a conversation with Caleb.

I'm not sure exactly how long I sleep for, but when I finally wake up, it's pitch black outside. Looking over to Caleb, the poor guy is all crammed on a tiny cot. They must have brought it in when I was passed out.

"BG." I start whispering. "Hey, Caleb." I try a little louder when he doesn't stir. "Yo, daddio." That's what gets him.

He springs up, only to crash back down with an ache in his back. His attention turns to me. "You okay?"

In all honesty, nope. Not one bit. I know I'm more relaxed now, but the pain isn't completely gone. But on top of that? There's still the issue of not thinking I can do this. Like, what if I'm too tired to push? What if I suck at it? And the biggest question that's been weighing on my mind since I got pregnant: what if I'm just as bad as my mom?

Caleb and I discussed the last question ad nauseam. It's his mission in life never to let me feel like I'm becoming her. And I know he'll succeed, if only for Nugget's sake. But deep down, I already know I'm better than she is. The nugget may know he/she was unplanned but "mistake" will never be in our vocabulary.

"Storm? You want to enlighten me. I hear you thinking over there."

Closing my eyes and releasing a long sigh, I admit, "Just reassure me I can do this."

He's quiet for a few minutes. I kinda feel a few contractions, and there's some pain in my back. Opening my eyes, I find his face right in front of mine. And I see it. His love for me.

"Stop it. I've told you, you've got this. It's not going to be easy, but it will be more than worth it." He takes my hand and places it on my belly then lays his hand on top. "You, me, and Nugget against the world, Nat."

His assurance is everything I need and then some.

"Okay. I've got this. I just needed to hear it one more time." He places a long, drawn-out kiss on my forehead.

"I love you, Natalie Pressman. Keep that in mind as our baby comes into the world soon. Don't ever doubt it."

I don't have a chance to respond when the doctor walks into the room. "How are you feeling, mom?"

It's about the fifth time she's called me "mom". It's odd to think in a little while I'll actually be someone's mom.

Caleb grabs my hand when I start to speak. "Better after my nap. My back is starting to ache more, and I feel so much pressure in my abdomen."

"Well, let's get you checked. Sounds like you are getting there."

She does her thing and after removing her hands, she's got a smile on her face. "Ten. Let's get you set up to start pushing."

And that's when I lose it. For real this time.

"For real?"

My breath quickens to the point where I almost can't breathe, tears fall down my face, and if it weren't for Caleb, I would have gone into full-on panic mode. He anticipated it.

He leans down and whispers in my ear. I don't even know what he's saying; it's the fact that it's his voice in my ear that calms me.

And then all that worrying I did earlier about not knowing how to push or sucking at it? Out the window.

Five hard pushes and the baby practically slides out. The world stops and all sound vanishes until I hear two things I'll never forget: "it's a girl" and the sound of a newborn crying. I've got tears running down my face, Caleb's tears joining them as he leans over me, kissing every inch of my face.

He readily accepts when they ask him to cut the cord, and then for the first time in her life, they lay my daughter on my chest. The strangest thing happens: not only does she instantly calm, but her eyes find mine. I don't know if she can even see me and I don't care. It's then that I know without a doubt, that this tiny creature just changed my life. Because now, it's all about her.

It's true what they say about having a piece of your heart on the outside of your body. It's the most terrifying and wonderful feeling all wrapped into one incredible being.

"Haley Elise," I whisper. "Welcome to our world, Nugget. Mommy loves you so much already." She's a gooey mess but none of that matters. I lift her to kiss the top of her head and with the most confidence I can muster, I exclaim, "Thank you for choosing me."

Caleb doesn't even hesitate to take her off my chest and snuggle her into him. She's tiny, only a little over six pounds— doctors were so off base with their estimates—but she's dwarfed by her daddy's arms. If I didn't feel it before, seeing the two of them fit together so perfectly, so right, it hits me again.

It's amazing how one tiny creature can change your entire life in the blink of an eye. For me, that tiny creature came in the form of a six pounds, two ounces baby girl on May sixteenth at 3:53 a.m. My life will never be the same. And as terrifying as that is, I'm so ready for the challenge.

15

CALEB

*I*t's very early in the morning, just my girls and me in the room, and I'm the only one awake. *My girls*. It has a nice ring to it. Despite a rocky start, Nat held up like a champ when it mattered the most. And to show for it, we have this gorgeous baby girl.

It's too soon to tell who she looks like, but I'm going to go with Natalie. She's completely bald with just a tiny smattering of peach fuzz on her head. Her eyes are the same shape as Natalie's, but she's got my nose for sure. She's so tiny and practically fits in the crook of one of my arms. Simply perfect.

Since she was born at like four in the morning, we decided to wait and text everyone. I'm sure we will get some backlash for it, but it's kind of been nice, just the three of us. All of that will change once the texts go out and visitors flock to see the baby.

From over in her bassinet, I hear tiny whimpers. I get up from my "bed" and find Haley squirming around, trying to fight her way out of the swaddle. Picking her up, I prop her up on my chest and sink back down on the bed. I'm sure she's hungry; the nurse said to feed her every couple of hours. But Nat is sleeping so peacefully, and I hate to wake her. It's only been about forty-five minutes since she conked out. I think the epidural is finally wearing off.

Today might be an even longer day than yesterday, but I'll do whatever I need to do to let her get as much rest as she can and won't hesitate to kick people out of the room to accomplish that.

Haley is almost back to sleep when I hear Natalie start to stir.

"Hey, she's awake? I'll feed her."

Glancing over at her, she pushes herself up to a more seated position, wincing only slightly with leftover pain. I climb up from where I'm sitting and walk the baby over to her mother. Nat's already got her left breast out of the gown, in position to feed her. The nurse said that the lactation consultant would be in later this morning but to just keep putting the baby to the breast as much as possible to get her used to it. Granted, this will only be the second time, but she seems to be a natural. At least Nat says she's latched; like I'd know any better.

"What time should we text everyone? You know they are all going to show up as soon as they possibly can."

She's right. Especially since most work from home and/or have flexible jobs. But if we wait too long, they'll hound us.

"I'm thinking like eight would be best. Maybe. I'm going to rest my eyes while she eats."

"Do you have to go to work today?" Her voice is hesitant, one I'm glad I can quell with my answer.

I shake my head and hope she can see it. I'm not stupid to think that she isn't more tired than I am, but it was a long day and night. Not that this "bed" is comfortable.

"Ok, good."

The next thing I know, she's whispering my name. "Caleb. Can you take her? I gotta pee."

I rub the sleep out of my eyes. It was a quick nap so not much sleep going on. Peering over at Natalie, she's got the baby in between her legs, resting her head back. My eyes go wide at the clock behind her alerting me that it's after 8:30.

I jump out of bed. "You let me sleep that long?" I scoop Haley up into my arms. It's only been a little while, but I miss holding her already.

"Dude, you were passed out. Not that I can blame you."
Looking over at me, she motions for the baby. "Put her down. I
need help getting out of bed."

And so begins having to split my time between my daughter
and my woman.

The day is a blur of activity. Natalie, she fucking rocked it. You
wouldn't know that she was up almost all night. She pulled herself
together for every visitor. I guess I'm not really surprised too
much; it's not like this is a foreign concept to her—presenting a
different face to the world. I'm just in awe of how she handles
everyone, including our daughter.

Kylie, Bella, Ainsley, and Grayson all end up visiting at the
same time, all four of them arguing about who gets to hold her the
longest. I hate to admit it, but Grayson definitely hogs her the
most. I've learned so much about my friend this past year he's
been with Ainsley.

Inside, Natalie's an emotional wreck. I see her little tells
when any visitor holds the baby. How she takes a deep breath
before handing her over. How her fingers fidget every so
often. How the smile doesn't quite reach her eyes. Like always,
she hides it well from everyone. Except apparently Kate. I
notice how Kate sees through her act and even though she
takes the baby as soon as she walks in, she makes sure to let
Natalie know the baby's okay. And Natalie visibly relaxes
more. I'm guessing it has something to do with Kate being
a mom.

About fifteen minutes into their visit, Kate literally kicks
me out.

"Go home and shower, brother. Then stop and bring us food
and coffee. Natalie, what are you craving that you haven't had in
about nine months?"

"A caramel macchiato from Joe's. And a cheeseburger from
Murray's." She hums it as it comes out, licking her lips when she's
done. "Oh, and a piece of cheesecake from Trephines. Please, BG.
You're the best." She flashes that smile in my direction. She's still

exhausted, but damn she's beautiful. Even more so knowing how she suffered and delivered our daughter.

"Got it. Kate, what can I get you?"

"Double espresso, grilled cheese with bacon, and a slice of the pecan cheesecake. And a Coke." She looks over to Natalie. "Aren't you forgetting the most important thing?"

Natalie's face gets a puzzled look as she glances over to Kate.

"A beverage of the adult variety?" Kate winks at her.

"Oh. Oh!!" She perks up at that. "Can I?" She looks from Kate to me. I shrug, having no clue about this stuff.

"Is she due to eat soon?" Kate asks. Natalie checks the paper she's been recording her food on and nods eagerly. "If she eats while he's gone, you can drink it first when he gets back and it will be fine. I did it the day all my kids were born; they are fine." A fit of giggles accompany her comment.

Natalie smiles at her then turns to me. "Thanks, I love you. I don't even care what it is. Just get me something."

I grab some stuff that has to go home, give my girls a goodbye kiss, and start toward the door. "Wait, we are allowed to drink at the hospital?" I direct it to Kate.

"I wouldn't go announcing it that you're bringing us wine, but one bottle is fine."

"Wasn't thinking about yours." With one more kiss to Haley, I'm out the door with an, "I'll be back soon."

I take my time showering and getting the food and drinks. Heck, I even stop in at the bar for a celebratory beer. I only get one text from Nat the entire time.

> ETA? Kate wants her dinner. And I need my macchiato.

> 10 mins out. Picking up the dinner now so it's the hottest.

A wink face emoji is all I get in return.

Kate stays late and even though she's tired, I can tell Natalie enjoys her company. They've always gotten along well enough; they just never really get to hang out because Kate always has the kids and Nat really thought they didn't have much in common. I'm glad to see them both laughing and happy. It looks great on both of them, something I've missed lately on Kate especially.

"Let me know when I can bring the kiddos by to your house. They are dying to meet her, especially Quinn. Just a forewarning."

"Of course. Once we get home and settled into somewhat of a routine, we'd love to have them visit."

Kate scoffs at Natalie's use of "routine," having some experience with newborns.

"Keep me posted. She's a beauty." She hugs me, stops off at Nat's bed for a hug, and then squeezes Haley's fingers. "Love you, Haley. You're a lucky little one." Then she's out the door with a wave.

Nat's eyes are already closed. "Wake me when she needs to eat. Thanks for the food and drinks. I needed them after these last two days." Her mouth opens so wide with her yawn, it about swallows her face.

"You're welcome. Try to get some sleep. I'm here."

I can't guarantee she even hears me; she's already asleep, the poor girl. So I place a kiss on her forehead, grab my baby and settle in to watch them sleep. It's been a long day for me too, but I'm not the least bit tired.

I have a feeling this is going to be my new normal.

* * *

The first three weeks of Haley's life are rough, to say the least. Two visits to the pediatrician because she's not gaining enough weight, seven sleepless nights and one emotionally-charged Natalie keep me on my toes. I haven't seen *my* Nat in three weeks, since that night at the hospital with Kate. And I know she's struggling with everything. The one thing I can say is she's talking to me. When she's not retreating inside herself. Which she's doing a lot, more than normal. She refuses to give Haley formula which I'm on board with as long as Natalie eats herself. She's been lacking in that area. I don't want to get to the point where I'm nagging her, because I can't have her going someplace dark.

On one particularly difficult night, she's crying. It's a usual occurrence lately so it doesn't tip me off to anything. The baby's in her cradle next to Nat's side of the bed. She's sleeping for now; I checked. Nat's lying on her side, facing the baby. Her face is flushed, her eyes red from crying. Her hair's in the braid that Kate put in yesterday when she was here.

Kate has been nothing but a godsend to all of us. It's been so good for Natalie to have a "mom" friend. Ainsley and the girls have been great, but Kate gets it. She's been there and can relate. She even couches some of her advice in a way so it doesn't seem like we are doing anything "wrong," but she offers a different way to try.

Lying down behind Nat, she doesn't react when I draw her to me, wrapping my arms around to rest on her disappearing belly.

"I need to tell you something." It's spoken in such a low voice I can barely make out the words. "You can't judge me."

Instantly I tense up, but again, there's no reaction from her.

"Anything, Storm. You know that." Her nickname slips out, but she needs to hear it, as much as I need to give it.

"I fell in love the minute she was put on my chest. And I know it's only been three weeks or so, but my love for her has only grown, so much so that it's bigger than me."

She stops then. I hold my breath, waiting for the but, the shoe to drop.

"I love her more than life itself, more than I've ever loved myself, but now she's here, my biggest fear is that I'm going to repeat the mistakes of my past."

Her voice is so small, almost as if she doesn't want to admit it aloud. The fact that she has voiced it is huge; she's come a long way, to be able to admit it even just to me.

I have to tread lightly with my response.

"Nat, you admitting this to me means you're not going to repeat your mistakes. And you know I'm always here to talk about anything; you can let me in. Which you're doing right now." How I phrase my next question is crucial. "She needs you, you know that, right? Like, I can't even feed her, unless it's formula."

She sighs. "My heart gets that. Rationally, my head gets it too. It's not that I'm planning to leave her, even though I know she'd still be in the best care with you. It's just this...." she hesitates. "This urge I can't explain. But I promise to talk to you about how I'm feeling, and I know you'll be there for me. And I love that. So much. And if you aren't around and I felt I had to run, I'd just drop her to Kate."

The fact that she's so nonchalant in her speaking, the fact that she's thought this through, worries me. Not enough to keep me up at night, but that this fear will always be there, just out of reach.

"We can work something out so that you have the time you need when you need it."

"Thank you for understanding. I know I can be better for her. It helps having an escape plan if need be. And I get as a mom there's no such thing as quitting, but knowing she's in great hands with you gives me comfort. I'm highly certain I would miss the shit out of her if I actually did leave." She goes quiet for a minute. Then adds this: "It's this kind of thinking that makes me feel I'm already a horrible mother."

And that comment pretty much breaks me. I sit up so quickly it catches us both off guard. I grab her face in my hands and force her to look at me.

"Do not do this, Natalie. DO. NOT. That girl knows only love from you; she knows how much you love her. For the past three weeks, you have only focused on her. You have put her first in every aspect of your life. You are an awesome mother. I'll make you believe that until I'm blue in the face if that's what it takes."

Her eyes well up with tears, and one escapes. It's not the tears that get me; it's the look of devastation on her face. The look that conveys she's not good enough.

"Enough, Natalie. Enough beating yourself up. She's three weeks old. We will revisit this when she's older and you aren't sleep deprived, have raging hormones and are still adjusting to motherhood. Until then, just stop. Haley is lucky to have you. If you can't see that, then maybe you should follow whatever it is your head is telling you to do."

Her eyes open in shock at my last statement with an "I can't believe you just said that" look. It's harsh. I get that. But I can't fight her demons for all three of us. And if she's the girl I think she is, she'll hear my words as they are intended: she needs to stay and fight because she's Haley's mother and right now, it's all about Haley's needs.

I'm torn between keeping her in my arms and walking away to let her process what I said on her own.

"Okay."

It's all she says. As for the meaning behind it? Yeah, I'm clueless.

Haley starts whimpering in her bassinet. I go to get up, but Natalie gets up first. She wipes the tears with her sleeve and grabs Haley out and into her arms. She whispers something in her ear; what it is, I can't hear. With Haley in her arms, she settles herself back on the bed. I move over to give her more space, but she grabs my wrist before I can get too far.

Her expression conveys it all: she's sorry. I know that look even though it's one I haven't seen in a while. She hasn't needed it in a while. And truthfully, I don't know what she thinks she needs to apologize for.

"Stay, please." Her voice is so small, almost helpless.

And so I do. I keep one of my hands connected to her the entire time she feeds and burps Haley, and still as she changes her diaper. Haley's not quite asleep, so Natalie lays her in between the two of us.

While she fed Haley, Natalie's tears stopped. I feel like some of the heaviness of our conversation not ten minutes ago has been lifted, but I can't confirm for sure.

"My boss called me today. He implied like he was checking to see how the baby was doing, but I know he was looking for me to tell him when I am going back to work."

Now, some of her emotional outbursts from earlier make more sense. The one thing Natalie hasn't really discussed is her going back to work. It's more a question of *when* rather than *if*. Each time it came up, she told me we'd talk about it once the baby was born. In her own way, she couldn't deal with being forced into making a decision for so far in the future, not knowing what the future held. We toured a few daycare places and interviewed a few nannies, but nothing was set in stone. I told her I'd support any decision she made, whether that be going back full-time, part-time, in six weeks, in six months, and once I even joked about her not going back at all. She laughed at me like that was the craziest idea of them all. But when she went quiet after it, I knew it was a possibility.

"So what did you tell him?" I'm curious as to where her mind is at.

"I told him that Haley is the sweetest baby ever and avoided his question about when I'd be returning. Because honestly, I don't have an answer for him. I'd like to think I'll go back eventually, but I don't know for sure if I really want to."

This woman drives me crazy. Not fifteen minutes ago she's talking about up and leaving her kid with me, and now she doesn't know if she even wants to go back to work. To her credit, that could have more to do with the actual job rather than being with the baby, but I don't probe any further into the matter.

Rather than start what would be a heated argument, which wouldn't even end up in any type of makeup sex, I blame the stupid hormones for her indecisiveness. I'll be thankful for the day she's back to being somewhat less emotional. Except, knowing my girl, that's really not going to happen. And damn it if I don't love that about her. So I placate her with, "Your decision. I'm here to listen and talk and be supportive. Just let me know what you need."

"And if I need to stay home with her for the time being?" She uses that tone she usually saves for goading me, but I don't think she's challenging me in this case.

"Then stay home with her. We'll be good."

She breathes a sigh of relief. "I feel a little like Ainsley when she ignores decisions she has to make." With a giggle, she turns to face me. The laughter fades, and she questions, "You're sure it's okay?"

I don't bother to answer her in words; I just give her my look. The one that lets her know she shouldn't question my judgment.

"Ah, never mind. Let's go with decision evaded for now."

"Good plan."

My Nat isn't quite back, but I'll take the girl who's here now until mine finds her way back to me. I know she's still in there and when the time is right, she'll come out of hiding. I'm a patient man. Less than twenty days to go until Nat's six-week checkup, not that I'm counting or anything. Like I said, I'm a patient man. And she's more than worth the wait.

16

NATALIE

"Caleb, grab me another outfit for the baby, please. She just vomited again!" I call up the stairs to him. I hate to use the word vomit, especially since it's just breast milk, but this girl vomits like there's no tomorrow. It's been two months, and she's miserable. Poor baby.

There's nothing worse as a mom than seeing your tiny baby in pain, knowing there's nothing you can do to ease it. And I've tried. I've changed my diet, cutting out the usual allergens: gluten, milk, eggs, nuts, but nothing seems to be helping. Her doctor's appointment is today, and I know what they are going to say: reflux meds. If it's going to make her better, we are willing to try.

Other than when her belly hurts, she's the most easygoing baby. She's quite the sleeper, even at only two months, and she's got such a calm demeanor. That's all Caleb.

I undress her as I wait for Caleb to bring down her new clothes. Not that I'm at all surprised, but the guy is a great dad. I wasn't around when all his niece and nephews were babies, but I've heard stories about how he never shied away from anything. The guy was meant to be a dad. And every time I see our daughter in his arms, my heart melts, and if it's possible, I fall more in love with him.

He comes waltzing down the stairs, dressed casually in loose-fitting track pants and a black T-shirt that fits snugly over his torso and upper arms. Between recovering from Haley's birth, dealing with the emotions and hormones after, and Haley's reflux, sex has been nonexistent. Despite Caleb's many advances, I've pushed him away every time. Good man that he is, he's been so patient, no matter how frustrated he is. But I can tell his patience is running thin lately, as much as he tries not to let me see it. I feel like I'm finally at a place that I can get back on board with it. Like soon if the heat I feel in my core is any indication.

He pecks my cheek and hands me her new clothes. "Hope this is okay. Not sure what we have going on today."

He picked out the onesie Grayson and Ainsley bought her. Not surprisingly, it's got a cupcake on it and says "Sweet as a cupcake."

"This works. I think we are just going to lay low today after her appointment. She didn't sleep well."

He glances down at me, a look of confusion covering his face, almost questioning what I said. "Yeah, I heard her whimpering. I told you I'm happy to get up with her, even if it's a work night."

Because I've been breastfeeding, I've taken all the night feedings and let him sleep. At first, it was just easier because it wasn't like he could help feed her, and then we kind of just fell into that routine. Selfishly, as tired as I am the next day, having her in my arms allows me to relax the tiniest bit, knowing even if she's not sleeping or when she's in pain, at least she's still breathing.

I have to wonder if the worry of her not breathing will ever fully go away. We tried one of those sleep monitors, but it went off way too much since she's such a wiggler when she sleeps. Caleb had enough of that nonsense on day two. Can't say I blame him; it was rather annoying and since neither one of us was getting any sleep, it didn't do any good.

"Yeah, I know. It's just..." I trail off. I talk to him, I do. I tell him my fears. And he knows when to just let me have my silent freak-outs. Or as the case may be, not so silent ones. I love that he's so hands-on, for all of it.

"We need to leave in about ten minutes. Finish getting her ready. Let's just stop for burgers or something on the way back."

"Sounds good."

I finish my task of getting Haley ready and quickly feed her. She only has time to eat on one side, but she seems satisfied. Even though she doesn't love her car seat, she tolerates it most days. Unless she's in severe distress. Today seems to be okay. For now at least.

The pediatrician gives us a few more things to try before she will prescribe medicine. She needs to be burped more often and after eating, she wants Haley to be positioned upright rather than laying down. The kid falls asleep halfway through her feedings so that one's going to be tougher. The good news is that she's gaining weight, slowly, on her own time, but even a few ounces is progress at this point. Yay for small miracles.

Caleb drives through our favorite burger joint as well as Joe's Coffee, before heading home. As he hands me my macchiato, I ask, "Is the coffee so I'm not exhausted later?" I return his questioning glance in my direction with a wink.

"Don't tease me, Storm. Don't. Tease." Oh, he's worked up all right. Poor guy.

"What if I said I wasn't teasing?" His eyes study my face, looking for confirmation of my comment. I reach my hand over to his thigh, rubbing it tenderly, making sure I hit close enough to where he aches the most. "After her last feeding, I'm all yours," I rasp. "All. Yours."

His eyes go wide, his brows shooting straight up to his hairline. I can only chuckle at his next move: he speeds out of the parking lot to get home. Why he's rushing I have no clue. It's only lunchtime.

He pulls the car into the driveway, and as soon as it's in park, he gazes over at me. His look has morphed into something more calculating, like he's plotting something. He leans over the console, his breathing hot on my neck, and whispers gravelly in my ear, "I'll feed her a bottle for her last feeding, give her a bath, and put her down. That will give you time to do whatever you need to do, even if that just means getting naked and waiting for me. And no, no arguments. I need to feed her too." He pulls away and he's out of the car before I can even respond.

Well, okay then.

Even more turned on, I grab the baby out of the backseat. "Looks like Daddy's finally getting what he wants." Even though she's sleeping, my daughter smiles at my comment.

About an hour later, as I'm just finishing up feeding Haley, the doorbell rings. Not having the slightest idea of who it could be, I cover myself up, prop the baby up on my shoulder and push up off the couch. Without looking, I fling open the door, instantly regretting it.

"Mom! What are you doing here?" I'm sure she detects the feigned enthusiasm. She's lucky I was able to keep all of my surprise and contempt out of my voice.

"Hello to you, too, dear." Her voice is resigned, but I don't miss the sarcasm it's laced with. "Aren't you going to invite me in?"

Against my better judgment, I move out of the way. She slinks in and takes in her surroundings with disapproving eyes. She's been here a total of two times and has something to say every time. As if on cue, she comments, "So this is her?"

I really shouldn't have higher expectations for their meeting. But I did. Which is why I haven't invited her to see Haley yet. Seeing as she's here on her own accord, I thought maybe she would be a little more enthusiastic about meeting her granddaughter. Clearly I'm wrong.

I turn my body so my mom can get a better look at Haley. She hasn't yet burped so I'm hesitant to turn her around just yet. "Haley, meet your grandmother. Mom, this is Haley."

My mother awkwardly reaches out her hand and touches Haley's arm. "She doesn't look like you."

She's right. She's the spitting image of Caleb, but she's got my eyes.

"Right? I do all this work for ten months, and her father gets all the credit." I laugh, my attempt to lighten up the mood.

My mother scowls. "Speaking of, where is her father?" She glances around again.

I can't imagine what thoughts must be floating through her head. Our house isn't large by any means, but it suits us. The decorated style reflects who Caleb and I are as a couple. It's bigger than the trailer I grew up in, yet she still manages to find fault with it.

"Working. His company has a big development in the works."

"And he leaves you here with her alone?" Her tone is laced with malice, her indication clear as day.

I don't mean to, but I gasp. Is she serious right now? She has no idea about my past.

"Wow, Mom. Thanks for the vote of confidence." I don't know how else to respond to that comment, and this time, I don't keep the ire out of my tone. I let out a long sigh. "Why are you even here?"

"I wanted to meet Haley. She's over two months and there's been no invitation yet. So I figured I would just invite myself."

"Yeah well, you're always busy. I figured you'd be too busy to come for a visit now. Clearly I was wrong."

We stare each other down. In the time it takes her to respond, I silently vow to do better with Haley. For like the thousandth time since I first discovered her growing inside me.

My mother ignores my jabs, one of her better qualities. She was always fond of saying, "If you don't have anything nice to say, don't say anything." Of course, she ignored her own advice, constantly jabbing and picking on me.

She interrupts my thoughts with, "Can I hold her?"

Is it bad that I want to say no? I want to deny Haley's grandmother the chance to hold her. But instead, I take Caleb's high road he's always touting about.

"Sure, but she hasn't burped yet. She's quite the spitter."

"Oh." It's the way she says it, not what she says. I'm shocked when she actually puts her arms out and practically rips her off my shoulder. "Gee, she's so tiny. I don't think you were ever this little. But then again, you always did like to eat."

I crack a smile. It's the best I can do.

"Have a seat on the couch."

I grab the nearest burp cloth and hand it over. They are literally scattered in every room of our house. God love Grayson who bought them by the caseload soon after she was born. I'm highly certain Ainsley has a few at her house too for when we visit.

My mother tentatively sits down on the couch then proceeds to "hold" Haley. She's awkward with her, not like a grandmother should be at all. My mom's arms are outstretched, and Haley's at a funny angle. Luckily her head is strong and she can hold it up on her own for the most part, for a little while anyway. My mom's lips upturn in a small smile, but as quickly as it appears, it's gone.

I sit and watch them interact. I feel like I should be asking my mother a bazillion questions, everything from newborns to being a new mother. But I don't have any. I've pretty much asked them all to Kate but also, I don't want my mother's advice nor her opinion on how to raise a daughter. Ironic, huh?

Before long, Haley spits up, all over my mother's lap. I swear, Haley smirks, almost as if she's laughing at what she did.

"Oh!" my mom complains. "Well, I guess she is a spitter." She holds Haley out in her arms, her face filled with disgust. "Take her." As I grab her from my mother, I offer her a towel, which she accepts all too readily and begins to scrub the vomit off her. "She does this often?"

I nod to confirm. "At least five times a day. Usually more."

"What's wrong with her?"

I'm momentarily stopped by her question. I tilt my head toward her, not quite understanding the meaning behind it. "What do you mean?"

She shakes her head as she looks up at me, the disgust changed to confusion now. "It's not normal for a two-month-old to spit up *that* much."

"Her pediatrician thinks it's reflux. I'm working on changing my diet and a few other changes to help alleviate some of the pain and vomiting."

"You're breastfeeding her?" she questions, her tone chiding me.

Again, is she serious? I can't handle this today. She's too much, even more than usual.

"Yep. Why, is there a problem with that?"

My comment catches her off guard. "N-no. Just surprised is all. I didn't think you'd be this, this motherly."

And that's about all I can tolerate. I'm pissed and rightly so.

"It's not like I had the best example."

Oops. The words tumble out of my mouth. Sometimes it's that no-filter thing Caleb's always on me about.

I'm about halfway up the stairs to change Haley's outfit again and I call out, "I'll be right back." Hugging Haley tightly into my chest, I whisper to her, "I swear your grandmother. What the heck is wrong with her?" Haley smiles up at me, my anger draining away, at least temporarily.

My mother's parents died when I was like three. I don't remember them at all. All I have to go on about them is what my mother's told me over the years, which hasn't been much. She didn't get along with them well. No surprise there.

Back downstairs, I find Caleb home, even more irritated than before. "Hey." When he turns to me, I question why he's home with just my look.

His answer doesn't surprise me. "I can't. I'll be upstairs." He practically rips the baby out of my arms and with that, his anger ebbs slightly. He drops a kiss to my forehead before he stomps up the stairs, cradling and snuggling her into his chest.

I slump back into the recliner. My mother's sigh pulls my attention back to her.

"He doesn't seem happy?" Her tone oozes contempt. He's never done anything to earn her dislike of him, but she's always held a grudge when it comes to him.

"Must have been a hard day."

"He good to her?"

I whip my head around to her, my glare meeting her scowl.

"He's. The. Best. Haley's one lucky girl."

"Well, at least he's a good dad."

I stare, open-mouthed at her. What she's insinuating, I have no idea, but I don't like it. And I'm just done for the day.

"That man upstairs is the best man I'll ever know. He's cleaned up messes in my life that you created. You, Mom, who was never around. He's never left me, when he should have walked away. He never has and he never will. He's not going anywhere, and I thank my lucky stars every day that somewhere along the way, I did something right in my life to find a guy who puts up with any bullshit I throw his way. And I've got so much baggage, it would probably sink a cruise ship. So, whatever it is you think he's done to make you never like him, that's your problem." I push out of my chair, fueled by my anger at her, but more so by the way the truth of my own words hit me. "But honestly, you should make it your problem somewhere else. I'd like for you to leave now." I walk over and open the door, not even caring about the shocked look on her face.

I don't watch as she does what she needs to do, but I hear her moving around. When she reaches me at the door, all she says is, "I did the best I could."

I bite my tongue, holding back the words I really want to say. Instead, I leave her with this: "If I've learned anything from you, it's that sometimes the best is still not good enough. Goodbye, Mother." Slamming the door behind her, the shock even more prominent with my words, I don't feel any bit of guilt. "Good riddance," I whisper as I walk upstairs.

In our bedroom, Caleb's got a sleeping Haley cradled into his side, one arm wrapped protectively around her. When he sees me standing in the doorway, he goes to speak, but I cut him off.

"Not today. Please." My eyes implore him to understand, to let me have this.

He doesn't say anything, just watches me for a few minutes.

Then when he does speak, it's not at all what I'm expecting. "How many more hours until her last feed?"

I'm about to answer him when his lips turn up into a smirk and he waggles his eyebrows at me. I saunter over to the bed. Reaching my arms out, he questions my actions. "Give her to me." He doesn't move except to snuggle her up closer to him and then starts to protest. "Caleb, give me the baby." My tone is demanding and with a confused look on his face, he gently hands her over to me. She doesn't stir as I cradle her in my arms and walk out of the bedroom, calling over my shoulder, "Clothes off now, BG. I'm making good on my promise early tonight." It takes only moments for my words to sink in before I hear the rustling of the sheets.

I lay Haley down in the crib in her bedroom, the one we've only used for naps so far. I'm still not ready for her to sleep anywhere for the night but my bedroom. Thankfully, she stays asleep, and on my way back to our bedroom, I start stripping out of my clothes.

Pushing the crappy visit from my mother out of my mind, I go and love on the man who has my heart. Three times.

17

CALEB

*N*at's text came in while I was doing a walk-through at the latest model home we're building. I didn't see it right away. By the time I had finished meeting with the realtor and all the necessary paperwork had been completed and signed, it was nearly five p.m. I told her I'd be home by three but the inspection went longer than I thought, and of course I left my phone in the truck.

The phone rings in my ear before I can finish reading her text. After ten rings, it goes to voicemail. I toss the phone onto the passenger seat and peal out of the driveway. I'm on the highway before I even know where I'm going.

Her text was short but the meaning was huge.

I dropped Haley off to Kate.

That was it. The rational side of my brain thinks back to this morning's conversation. She said she had to do something, but for the life of me, I can't remember what it was. Can I help it Haley's got me wrapped around her pinky finger? She's just started giggling and damn, it melts me every time. If I thought Nat made me a sap, I was wrong. So wrong. My baby girl's got nothing on her mamma when it comes to knowing how to make me come unhinged. The fact that she's only three months old doesn't bode well for me.

Coming upon Kate's exit, my emotional side kicks in. She just needs a break; she's only with Kate for a few hours. I told her I would be home earlier and clearly I wasn't around and she had something to do. Why she wouldn't bring her to Ainsley or the girls baffles me for a moment. Then my brain whispers the reason: Kate's a mom. She gets the need to get away. And that's what has me racing down Kate's road at a speed way above the legal limit for this neighborhood.

Once in the driveway, in which Natalie's car is noticeably absent, I throw the truck in park, not even concerned with my haphazard parking job. I sprint up the stairs and push open the door. I'm met with squeals of laughter from my nephews and my niece, coming from the back of the house.

"Hey," I call out. To alert them I'm here but also to find out where they are.

Kate comes down the stairs as I listen for more clues.

"Hey." My eyes find hers, and the smile she wears slips off her lips as she takes in my haggard appearance. "What's wrong? Are you alright?"

She reaches the bottom step and as if she senses the tension I'm feeling, wraps her arms around me in a hug of comfort. I feel my body stiffen slightly at her touch, but soon I can't contain the anxiety running through me, and I take comfort in her hug. She lets me just wallow in the hug for a few minutes, as I allow my breathing to come back to normal. I'm not even aware when it became so fast-paced, but all I can process at the moment is Kate's arms running up and down my back. She's not saying anything, which is so unlike her, but at the moment, she seems to know exactly what I need.

After a few minutes, her curiosity gets the best of her. She lets me out of the embrace and instructs me to sit. I let out a sigh, run my hands through my hair, and take a seat on the stairs. Still trying to control my breathing, I hang my head in between my legs. Taking a seat next to me, she waits for me to speak. When I don't, she starts. "You want to tell me what's going on?"

I pick my head up and find her worried expression sizing me up and down. I get it; even though I may be her little brother, I've always been her protector, the one she could count on to have her back. I don't do soft, especially with my sister. Well, I didn't until now.

"She's coming back?" My voice is low and I'm not even sure she heard me. Her face registers the shock she feels. I can't be certain if it's from what I asked or how I asked it. Probably both.

"Who?" A bewildered look clouds her expression.

"Natalie. How long did she say she'd be gone for?"

"Oh, she didn't say. She just asked if she could drop Haley off. Of course I said yes. We love her."

I don't like her answer nor the nonchalant way she says it.

"And when she dropped her off, how was she?"

"The baby was fine. She's always so chill. Can't imagine where she gets that from." She lets out a small giggle.

"Not the baby. Natalie. How was Natalie?" My voice is stronger now, almost to the point of anger, even though I'm not angry. I can't be.

Kate stares at me. In some ways, I get it. Not only am I acting so out of character, she wouldn't understand why I'm asking what I'm asking. What the true implications are behind Natalie's actions.

Rather than address my question, she asks one of her own. "What is going on? Did you not talk to her? I figured you knew the baby was here and why."

Slowly, I shake my head. "My meeting ran late and I knew Nat had something to do today, but I don't know what it was. She just sent me a text she had dropped the baby off here. She didn't answer when I called her." My blood pressure is on the rise again. This time, I feel when my breath starts to quicken. I jump up off the stairs and start to pace.

Before we can do anything else, Quinn comes bouncing in.

"Uncle Caleb, you're here. Haley is here. Mommy said she can't have chicken nuggets. Can she?"

I'm momentarily caught off guard by her question. Once it registers, I shake my head. "No, she's too little for chicken nuggets." And then like a lightning bolt, it hits me. "Bottles?" I squeak out. "How many bottles did she leave?" I look to Kate and wait for her answer. When Kate doesn't answer fast enough, I take off for the fridge, Quinn and Kate on my heels.

"I don't know how many she left. She just put them in the fridge and told me they were in there. She may have mentioned something about you coming and knowing when she was hungry. That's why I thought you talked to her."

Her words don't sink in. To my ears, I know she's talking but I can't put any meaning to her words, especially since they are laced with confusion. In the kitchen, I bolt to the fridge and tear open the door. Sitting on the top shelf are two bottles of pumped milk. Upon closer inspection, there's a sticky note stuck to one of them.

BG,

If you need more, there's a stash in the freezer at home. I may be late but please don't give her formula. Back later.

Love you!

Storm

PS Breathe

I can't help but cackle, after a huge sigh of relief. Even though it takes a few more minutes to come down off my high and for my breathing to return to normal, the smile never leaves my face.

Before I go in search of my baby, I take a seat at the table, grab my phone out of my pocket, and send a text.

Not funny. In no way was that funny.

I don't wait for a response from her. I don't even want to know how she's going to respond. But knowing her so well, she won't.

After a few minutes of sitting, I go in search of my daughter. This time, I do follow the squeals, leading me to the playroom. Haley lays on the floor on her playmat, surrounded by her cousins. Owen pulls on the toy so it drops down close to Haley's face. She cocks her head to look up to the noise and giggles. Beside her, Owen giggles too. I get it; the sound is infectious and before I can even walk close to where they are playing, I'm already laughing.

At the sound of my laughter, both Owen and Aiden turn to face me. Their smiles get bigger at the sight of me. Let's face it. Haley's cool and all, but Uncle Caleb? I take the cake in that department. My arms are outstretched as they hightail it over to me. Even at eight, Aiden still practically jumps in my arms. His dad doesn't know what he's missing.

"Hey guys. How's my baby?"

"Well, she doesn't smell anymore," Owen says, pinching his nose with his fingers.

Questioning his comment, I turn my attention to Aiden.

"She puked all over herself and Mommy before. So Mommy had to clean her up and change her clothes. I didn't think it was all that bad, but Owen here was gagging."

I can't help but chuckle. Haley spits up. A lot. Her reflux is getting better, but she's still got a long way to go. Which is why Natalie won't give her formula. While it seems Natalie has made it so she can't leave, unless she wants the baby to either starve or be given formula, the what-if is always in the back of my mind. As much as I can't consciously think about it, it's there. It's because we've discussed it. She promised me she'd talk to me if she was feeling anything even remotely related to her not being able to handle anything. And she has. I've never been more thankful for the flexibility in my job the last few months.

Thank fuck Natalie doesn't have postpartum depression. She's a hell of a strong woman, but there are just some demons you can't fight. That's a battle Natalie would never win.

Shaking off my deep thoughts, I carefully scoop my daughter off the floor. Holding her high above my head, I smile at her, making sure to keep my mouth closed. I learned the hard way to always keep it shut. Her face erupts into a grin, her little lips turning up the slightest bit. It's when she giggles as I tickle under her arms that finally erases any bit of worry I had earlier.

Seriously? This face? No way anyone could walk away from this face.

"Hey, Hales." Natalie hates that nickname, but the first time she giggled was when I called her that so she's stuck with it. Her mamma be damned. "How's my girl?"

I bring her back down and cuddle her against my shoulder. She's still so tiny and fits cradled in my one arm, especially when she crunches up her legs. Placing a kiss on the top of her head, I can't help but inhale her scent. The baby soap scent still lingers from her bath last night. I told Natalie to buy stock in that shit; its smell is addictive.

Still cradled against my shoulder, Haley starts to squirm. Kate comes into the room, followed by Quinn.

"What time did Natalie drop Haley off? Like when's the last time she ate?"

Kate looks at her wrist. "She dropped her off about three maybe, and she fed her right before she left. Nat's got the breast-feeding down to a science already with this one."

"It was tough the first month or so. There were many tears, mom and baby. But when Natalie sets her mind to something, she doesn't back down. Especially with the reflux. She hates seeing her in such pain when there's nothing she can do about it."

"You're preaching to the choir. I've got two rambunctious boys who've each broken a bone. I get it. And Haley's just so little." She literally grabs her from my arms. "Can I feed her? You always get to."

I'm about to argue I don't really, but something tells me to stop. "Sure thing. I'll warm it up for you." The smile on my sister's face confirms I made the right decision.

After Kate feeds Haley, most of which ends up all down my back since I burped her, Kate feeds her kids chicken nuggets. "I have leftover chicken marsala if you want some," she says to me once her kids are happily gorging on their food.

"Yeah, sure. Thanks."

Natalie might be a hot mess in many areas of her life, but as a mom? She's got it all handled. Not only does she have extra clothes for the baby in the diaper bag, but somehow she manages to stash an extra shirt for her and me. For Nat, this is huge. And I know it's only been three months but the way she's stepped up to the plate to stare down her biggest fear is no small feat. Of course, the inclination to run might never go away for her.

Back in the kitchen, after I'm all cleaned up—new shirt and all —Kate's got Haley all changed and snoozing on her shoulder. We carefully make the baby exchange, and I put her in her car seat to nap. As I'm taking in the beauty of my daughter, I'm totally caught in a daze. I don't realize Kate's behind me until she starts to speak.

"She's not going anywhere. She loves that little girl."

Her words are shocking, to say the least and when I whip my head around to face her, her expression is etched with concern. "How? When? What?" I shake my head back and forth to try to comprehend what she's telling me. I can't though. I can't understand how she could know. Unless... "She told you?"

Kate sheepishly nods. "She told me all of it." Her voice is barely above a whisper. "I always knew you had a heart of gold, but my god, Caleb. You're like a freaking saint. To stay? After all that? I don't know how you did it. How you *do* it."

I slouch down against the cabinets and slink down to the floor, running my hands through my hair. It so needs a trim but with the baby's arrival, I haven't had much time.

"I've loved her since the minute I saw her. That's all there is to it. She keeps life interesting." That earns me a snort from Kate who's sitting directly in front of me, mimicking my position. "Every time I had even an inkling to walk away, my future looked bleak. The weeks she was gone were torture. Pure. Torture." As I talk, quick glances at my sister let me know she's listening intently. I stop to catch my breath and gather my thoughts and she takes it as her opening.

"Why didn't you ever say anything? I always knew there was something off about your relationship, but I couldn't tell exactly what it was. And selfishly I had my own stuff going on."

I shrug. "Exactly. You had your own shit to deal with; my stuff pales in comparison."

"Why do you always do that?" There's an edginess in her tone.

"Do what?" I don't know what she's talking about.

"Downplay your things. Your girlfriend running out on you, multiple times, is not nothing, Caleb. It's huge. Especially because of how you reacted. How you never left. Do you know how many guys would have walked away the first time, let alone times after that?"

"I would have been one of those guys. In college and even after." I give her my truth, the one thing I've only ever told Nat.

She shakes her head. "No. You can think it's her, but it's not. You have never been one of those guys. Why you even think that is beyond me."

For the second time tonight, I go to argue with my sister, and yet again, something holds me back.

Although Kate's older by a few years, she's always treated me like her equal. I was never her "younger" brother. While I'm sure it had something to do with being bigger than her for most of my life, it's also Kate. Age means nothing to her; it's literally just a number. I never understood why she treated me that way; it was all I ever knew so I just accepted it as such. And that's why I'll just accept her words now. While Kate is the more social one of us, her words always hold power and meaning. When she says something, it means something. I always have to remind myself of this fact when dealing with her.

"I'm not sure I can ever think she's truly done running. That makes me a horrible person, right?"

My eyes are trained down on the floor. I don't even want to

know how she's going to react to that comment. But I feel like I needed to get it out, and since Kate knows the truth now, who better to confess it to?

Her answer catches me off guard again, straight and to the point.

"It makes you human."

Eyes still cast downward, I hear her getting up. Before I know it, she's squatting down next to me. "Natalie's a very lucky woman. You better believe I made sure to make that clear when we talked." With a kiss to my cheek, she leaves me there, speechless.

I'm not sure how long I sit on the floor of Kate's kitchen. Truthfully, I'm not even sure why I'm somewhat paralyzed and not able to move. It's not until I hear Haley starting to stir that I'm brought out of my funk. With a glance at the clock, I figure it's about time to make my exit and head home.

I pack up all of Haley's things and strap her in her seat. She's not quite awake, but she smiles at me in her sleep. "Come on, cutie pie. Let's go home and wait for Mamma."

I find my sister and her kids on the way upstairs.

"You're leaving?" It's Aiden asking the question.

"Yeah. I have to get Haley home, fed, and in bed before Aunt Natalie comes home." All four of them rush back down to give kisses to Haley and hugs to me. My sister's is the longest one.

"I know we talked a lot about her love for your daughter, but don't ever doubt her love for you. It's there, sometimes so much she can't contain it. Just continue to be there to catch her. It may not seem like it now, but she needs you more than ever. And when you both need a break, drop off that munchkin here and just be a couple. She needs that and you deserve that. Take her on a date or better yet, make her take you on a date." She chuckles at her own words. "I love you. After Dad, you are the best man I know."

My only response is to squeeze her tighter. I swallow the lump that has managed to form in my throat. Pulling away, I whisper, "I love you, Kate. Thank you."

Without another word, and before the tears start to fall, I pick up Haley's car seat and her bag, and I'm out the door.

On the ride home, I reflect on the evening. I still haven't heard from Nat, which is somewhat unusual, but I have to believe if she were really in trouble, she'd let me in. I'll let her have it if she doesn't.

I'm surprised to find Natalie's car in the driveway when we get home. After unloading all the gear and the baby, I find the house empty. Guess she's out with someone else. I flip on all the lights in the kitchen and living room. From the corner of the kitchen where I placed her car seat, I hear Haley's whimpers. She's not much of a crier, except when she's hungry or when her stomach is upset. Those poor wails are forever engrained in my mind.

I scoop her out and send a text to Natalie asking about her ETA. The last feeding of the day is her absolute favorite time to bond with Haley. If she'll be home soon, I'll comfort the baby so she can feed her rather than give her a bottle.

> I'll be home in 5. She's good?

> We'll be on the couch waiting for you.

Kicking off my shoes on the way, I lie down on the couch, carefully maneuvering the baby to lay on my stomach. She's a little restless, hungry, and slightly irritated, but nothing I can't handle until Nat gets home.

I hear the back door open just as Haley lets out a scream. She's waited long enough.

"I'm coming, baby. Just have to pee." Natalie pokes her head into the room, flashes me a smile, and disappears.

Despite the tiny ball of fury on my chest, I'm quite comfortable. Even as her hands ball into fists and flail about, I know there's not much I can do until Nat gets her and sticks her boob in her mouth.

Nat comes rushing in. "Okay, okay baby girl, I'm here. She takes a few seconds to pop a chaste kiss on my lips with a "hi" in my direction, then she grabs the screamer and cuddles her into her. Haley calms slightly just with her touch; just being in her mother's arms soothes her. I'd be jealous except I know the feeling; moms just make everything better.

"Bedroom," Natalie calls out to me as she climbs the stairs. I push myself up off the couch and follow her. By the time I get to our bedroom, Haley is sucking away, her body totally calm.

I settle down next to them on the bed, careful to avoid bumping Haley's head. Before I can say anything, Natalie's asking me, "How was she?"

"The best. The kids loved entertaining her and being entertained by her. Kate fed her around 6:30 I think and then she slept pretty much the rest of the time we were there."

She takes in my appearance, the fact I'm wearing the T-shirt from the diaper bag not lost on her. "She got you?" The creases around her eyes begin to show as her lips turn up into a smile.

"All down my back. Almost her whole bottle."

"Poor kiddo." She laughs with a quick peek down to a guzzling baby. "No wonder she's practically starving."

I hesitate with asking my next question. "I know you told me this morning, but where were you tonight?" There's a sense of pleading in my tone. I know she won't miss it.

"I had to meet a client for dinner. Then Ainsley, the girls and I went for dessert." Haley pops off her breast. Like the expert she's becoming, Nat props her up on her shoulder and rubs her back. When she's satisfied with her burp, she switches her to the other side. "I'm sorry."

For a minute, I think she's talking to Haley since she's so quiet with her words. Not that she has anything to apologize for to Haley. But then she nudges my foot with her leg and I realize it was meant for me.

I look over at her. Her furrowed brow conveys the unease she's feeling. "For what?"

"Making you think I ran. It wasn't meant to be funny or to make you upset. I thought you would have been home earlier, and

I needed to go. Kate told me to drop her off anytime I needed to, so I took her up on the offer. It wasn't until I was writing the note that I realized what I did and how you'd react. It was a total mom fail moment on my part."

I'm glad she's told me the truth. The fact she knew how I would react tells me we are on the same page. And I'm glad it wasn't intentional. Oh how far she's come, how far *we've* come. In light of her communicative mood, I decide to ask the question that's been weighing heavily on my mind since earlier. "When did you tell Kate?" I don't even bother to clarify what my question means.

She sighs. Not in an "oh crap" kind of way, but one that lets me know she'll answer. "The night after Haley was born. I was still a little loopy from the pain meds, and I'm pretty sure she thought I was making it all up at first, high on the meds. She knew I was serious when I told her how you reacted each time.

"She didn't ask any questions, offer me any advice, or seem to even judge me. She was holding Haley and when she woke up to eat, she handed her to me, gave me a careful hug, and told me I was a lucky woman. The next time she came to visit, she unleashed a slew of questions on me. She didn't yell, but I could tell from her tone she wasn't happy with my past actions, or at least some of them. I answered them as honestly as I could, including about the night I cheated. She didn't react much and her expression remained stoic throughout the entire conversation. Before she left, she again told me I was a lucky woman. And she offered me two pieces of advice: if I ever got the urge to run, I had to take Haley with me. I didn't realize it at the time but it's because by taking the baby with me, I'd still have to be a mom. I couldn't be selfish and walk away from her. She still needs me, and despite thinking walking away from her might be in the best interest for me, it never would be for her. And it's only been three months, but I can't imagine walking away from her, especially when she needs me the most. Even if I left her in the care of the best father. She needs her mother."

Her words have a profound effect on me. Like a light bulb goes off: things happen for a reason. For Storm, Haley is that reason. The reason she has to stay. Because even though she could take her with her if she ran, she knows it would destroy the only other person who loves her more than life itself: her father.

"Oh, Storm." It's all I can manage. And then I have to know. "What was the other piece of advice she gave you?"

"To take you on a date."

The chuckle is out of my mouth before I can stop it. "I bet she said she'd watch Nugget too, right?"

She whips her head around to mine. "Yep. We should totally take her up on her offer. I'm thinking an overnight might even be good." She waggles her eyebrows at me.

I'm sure the shock must register on my face but if it doesn't, the gasp I let out gets her attention. "You're going to leave her overnight?"

I think today was the longest she's been away from the baby. And it might seem like she handled it okay, but I know her. On the inside, she was flipping out. It's why, twenty minutes after the baby has fallen asleep on her breast, she won't give her up. Even to me. I've tried to take her more than once and every time, she pushes me away.

"Yeah, maybe that's taking it too far. But I could certainly handle a date night with my soon-to-be-husband."

"Make the plans and tell me when to show up, and I'm there."

"Deal." She yawns. "Okay, I'm officially exhausted. She's all yours. Her PJs are on the changing table in her room. Flip on the monitor too, please. And remind me what you have in the morning?"

I think ahead to the morning as I gently lift a sated and sleeping Haley into my arms. "I'm free until the afternoon."

"Cool." Her eyes slip shut. "Love you, BG."

I take my time changing Haley into her pajamas. She hardly stirs as I change her diaper and clothes. I pop a binky into her mouth before laying her down in her crib. It pretty much swallows her whole, a tiny bump against the backdrop of the teddy bears and blocks that cover her sheets. With one last kiss to her head, I turn on the monitor and leave the room, closing the door behind me.

Walking back to my bedroom, a jumble of thoughts speed through my mind. It's been quite the day for information. The one constant I take solace in is Natalie isn't going anywhere. I'll do anything in my power to make sure she doesn't change that.

First up on the list...finally make her my wife.

18

NATALIE

I stayed true to my word; I talked to Caleb when things got rough, when I had even an inkling to run, when my thoughts drowned me, thoughts that I wasn't a good enough mother to Haley. Except, deep down, I know I am.

The girl is thriving. Eight months old, starting to crawl around the house, always smiling. She's Caleb's mini-me in personality, a fact that I'm ever so grateful for, for a variety of reasons. She's got him wrapped further around her finger, and every time I see her in those muscular arms of his, my heart melts, and a piece of the wall that's hardened around my heart crumbles.

Even on my worst days, the days when work is rough, when she's more interested in her surroundings than feeding, the middle of the night wake-ups because she's teething, even on those days, there's no inclination to run. Sure, I sometimes hand her off the minute Caleb comes through the door at night, taking an hour or so to myself, but I'm always back in time for her bath and bedtime. It's my favorite time of the day, especially when we both do it.

Every Friday, we have date night. Sometimes it's the three of us, but at least twice a month, it's a true "date," just the adults. We do different activities each week, and even if we end up at Target, it's the fact we are together. It's also the one night a week sex is a guarantee. Sure, a few times we literally go through the motions, but I promised myself this is what we needed as a couple, and I would uphold that promise. Unknowingly, Caleb's always on board with it.

His latest thing is the wedding, except I'm not quite there yet. I'm definitely more there than I was the first time he asked me, and more than when I finally said yes. For the first time in our entire relationship history, we are at a great place, and I don't want to rock the boat. Not that having a wedding, marrying the man I love, changing my last name, would upset the dynamic of our relationship, but I can't take that chance. Not with everything we've gone through in the last year. Call me a coward, but when you live in a constant state of feeling like you aren't enough, it's hard to break away from that thinking, even when things are good. One huge life change could tip the scales too far one way and send me into a tailspin, a storm of epic proportions. I think Caleb knows I'm not ready to face all my fears yet, so he's not pressuring me.

Speaking of, I hear the kitchen door open, his heavy footsteps trekking through the house. "Hey, I'm gonna shower quick, then we can drop Haley off to Kate for the night. You packed everything she needs?"

This week's date consists of our first overnight away from Haley. I've been on edge all week, vacillating back and forth between knowing she's in Kate's very capable hands, she'll be fine, and the worry that she needs her mother. Irrational? Yes, but seeing as my period is due any day now, I'm even more of an emotional mess.

Caleb has made it very clear I am not allowed to change my mind—she's staying with Kate no matter what. The guy doesn't ask for much, so when he feels strongly about something, I try to go along with it.

Putting aside my mother's guilt and the urge to be in control over the situation, I've had a week dealing with my emotions. Caleb did baths and bedtime every night this week because he knew I needed to decompress, deal with my shit. And after he put the baby to bed, he held me all night long, making sure I was truly okay with what was happening Friday. Because if he really thought I'd struggle with it, he wouldn't let her stay with Kate.

I love him more for knowing exactly what I need, for pushing me outside my comfort zone knowing I have him as a safety net if I fall.

"Yep, her bag's all set." I don't need him to know that I fed her a few extra times today, selfishly needed the comfort only Haley can give me. She somehow knew it was more of a comfort thing rather than for nutritional benefit. Caleb's kid if there ever was one.

"Awesome. You need to shower or get ready?" He takes in my wardrobe of lounge clothes, eyeing me suspiciously.

"Kate's going to pick her up, so I figured we could start the night in bed and then head out later. The movie's playing at midnight at the multiplex."

He ponders my thoughts a moment, then walks over to the couch. "So, I shouldn't shower?" I shake my head. "But I'll definitely need to later?" I nod. "And we can get popcorn at the movies?"

"Duh." I roll my eyes at him, even letting him take Haley off my chest where she's been dozing for a little while. As much as I'm going to miss the heck out of her, he will too. He just hides it better.

"Great plan, Storm," he mutters, laying a kiss to the top of my head, and vacating the living room.

"Where are you taking our kid?" I query reservedly.

"Her bedroom. I'll bring her back before Kate gets here. Just need a few minutes alone with her."

He totes her upstairs, and when I know he's made it to her room, I quickly turn on the monitor, knowing full well he knows it's on.

"Hey, kiddo. Missed you today. It was a rough day at work, so I'm glad your mommy decided we could stay in for a bit. I wasn't ready to go back out immediately. This way, we can work on a brother or sister for you."

The audible gasp tumbles out of my mouth, the fact I can't tell if he's serious or not making my heart race.

"Caleb!" I yell up the stairs. "Bite your damn tongue."

"You always said your kids would never be only children. I'm just helping her out."

Oh, he's crazy if he thinks we are seriously getting to work on a sibling for her. Sure, we've adjusted to parenthood, but she's eight months old for crying out loud. She needs to be an only child for a little longer.

"Talk to me when she's two or three," I call back upstairs. "Heck, when she's out of diapers, even."

Those fuckers are expensive. And even though we can totally "afford" them now, old habits are hard to break. Sticker shock is real when you grew up poor. I've given the job of purchasing diapers to Caleb. He Amazon Primes them, on a somewhat accurate delivery schedule so we never run out nor have an abundance. And here I thought construction was his area of expertise.

I view him on the video monitor. He's settled in the rocking chair, cuddling her close into his chest. As if his words had a direct line to my ovaries, I can feel the pull in them, low in my belly. The ache to give her a sibling. Thank goodness for IUDs.

He leans into her ear, whispering something I'm not privy to. She rewards him with that smile that melts my heart. I watch for a few more minutes, until there's a knock at our door, followed by a, "We're here!" Kate rushes in, followed quickly by her three minions.

"Aunt Nat, is she ready?" Quinn asks, barely able to contain her excitement at seeing my girl. She runs over to me on the couch, bouncing on her toes in front of where I sit.

"Uncle Caleb's finishing up getting her ready now," I respond, matching her smile with one of my own.

I definitely love how even if Haley grows up as an only child, she'll have her cousins, even if they are older than her. I missed out on both siblings and cousins, so she's got one aspect covered.

"Mom says she can sleep in my room," Quinn continues.

"I said maybe," Kate chides.

Quinn rolls her eyes. "That means yes."

"Glad to know she's got you pegged," Caleb comments, coming into the room with Haley.

"Just wait, dear brother. Just wait. Let me go on record now and say *no* won't be a word in your vocabulary once Haley starts talking."

She knows her brother well. He's going to be such a sucker for whatever Haley wants, and he'll have a hard time saying no to her. The man hardly denies me anything, but his daughter? Yeah, sucker, big time.

Kate wastes no time in grabbing Haley from him. Haley lights up in her aunt's arms, confirmation she's going to be just fine tonight. But, it's not her I'm worried about; it's me.

Like she can sense I'm flipping out inside, my daughter reaches her hands out to me, and I take her from her aunt for one last, long hug goodbye. Everyone gives me the time I need, the time I take to say goodbye to my girl, if only for one night. I hold her tightly, cradling her to my chest, whispering messages of love in her ear, trying to keep my emotions at bay, not allowing my own insecurities to be transferred to my daughter.

"Okay, Storm. The kids are getting restless." Caleb's voice breaks through my haze of saying goodbye to Haley.

Zeroing back into my surroundings, I give Haley one last kiss before handing her to Kate. "Have fun, sweet girl," I coo, my voice catching in my throat.

"I'll text you hourly updates," Kate appeases my anxiety. "And feel free to come get her as soon as your keeper allows it." She laughs in Caleb's direction, and brother and sister share some sort of nonverbal communication, a message not meant for me.

I address Kate's kids. "Make sure she's happy, and fed, and laughs, and..."

Caleb cuts me off, pushing them all out the door.

"Have a great night. And don't text us in the middle of the night if she wakes up unless it's an emergency."

Slamming the door after their exit, he opens his arms wide for me, knowing exactly what I need. I wrap myself up in him, allowing his physical and emotional strength to surround me, protect me, take away my worries.

After a few minutes, he silently asks me if I'm okay. With a nod of my head as my answer, he declares, "Now that the kids are gone, the adults can play."

His attempt at levity hits the mark, just what I need to snap out of this dark place I was heading. Rather than focus on the negatives, how much I'm going to miss her, I choose to focus on the fact I have people in my life who love my girl almost as much as I do, allowing me to put aside my mom hat for the night and be a woman. A woman with a hot man ready to cater to my every whim, to indulge all my fantasies, to get me to scream his name several times, without having to censor how loud we are.

It's these thoughts that have me smiling, admitting, "Race you to our bedroom."

I start up for the bedroom but Caleb's arms grab me, halting my progress. I question his motives, wondering why he's stopping me. He gestures his head over to the couch. "Remember when?" he asks wistfully.

"You wanna?" I ask, wagging my eyebrows, slipping my yoga pants off as I walk toward the couch.

Caleb rushes past, beating me to the couch, his entire body already completely naked, his erection staring me in the face. The sight of it causes me to stop walking the last few steps I need to reach him, my shirt pushed up my arms, stuck in mid-air.

Dragging my tongue slowly along my lips, the sight of his cock shouldn't have this effect on me. We have sex at least once a week, sometimes more. For some reason tonight, my hormones, like my emotions, are on overload. I'll chalk it up to the first time we've had sex without any chance of being interrupted by Haley.

I stare at his dick until I hear his throat clearing. "It looks the same as it always does, Storm. Take off the rest of your clothes."

Once upon a time, I'd argue for the sake of arguing. In this moment, I obey his orders, his husky voice sending goose bumps up and down my entire body. And once I've shed all my clothes, I step closer to him, awaiting more direction. This may have been my idea, but I'm turning over all control to him for the evening, knowing he'll not only take care of me but make it worth my while.

He wastes no time pushing my body down on the couch, assuring my head hits the pillow and not the arm of the couch. Adjusting the pillow so it's more comfortable, I focus my attention on his nakedness again. His abs seem even more pronounced lately, as if he's been working out harder at the limited time he gets at the gym. The short hairs on his chest have been cleaned up recently and before I can stop them, my fingers reach up to touch. Soft, as always, like my man's heart, especially now with Haley in the picture.

He swats my hand away playfully, a smirk toying on the edge of his lips. "I think," he starts, "we should do this without hands. Like old times."

"Fuck yeah," I breathe out, totally on board with his plan.

He steps away from the couch, disappearing for a short while. In anticipation of what's to come, my body starts to throb, wetness starting at the juncture of my thighs. If I didn't think he'd punish me for starting without him, I'd use my fingers to rub my clit. It's only a matter of time before he takes away my ability to do exactly that.

I sneak my right hand down my abdomen, yet before it can touch where I ache the most, he's back, yelling at me.

"I said no hands, Natalie," Caleb reminds me, his insistence raspier than before.

I don't stop the giggle that breaks free as it riles him up more. He stalks over to me, determination set on his face, a look I love, one I live for.

Gently, he bounds my hands together with a tie from his closet. It's not tight; he leaves enough room for me to wiggle out if necessary. As much as he enjoys the whole "no hands" approach, he doesn't need complete dominance over me. It also comes in handy—no pun intended—on those rare occurrences I need a little assistance to get me over the edge. Based on what I'm already feeling and the resolve in his eyes, I'm not going to need it tonight.

"Arms up, legs wider," he instructs after a careful perusal of my body.

I comply, my pulse quickening with the devotion clouding his eyes.

He hasn't laid a finger on me, except to tie up my hands, yet I ache more, extra wetness leaking out, eliminating the need for lubricant. I wish I could say it's like this every time since giving birth. Again, just something special in the air tonight.

My eyes land on Caleb's chest again. Without the ability to feel him, I train my focus on the up and down of his chest, the steadiness of his breath, the calm before the storm so to speak. I know from experience his chest won't stay so rhythmic, so relaxed. I take it all in now, using the visual to turn me on further. Even if he doesn't make any moves soon, it won't take much for me to be ready.

His body moves, his position changes, until his arm snakes in between my legs.

"Hey," I blurt to get his attention. "You said no hands."

His brow furrows in confusion as he looks between my face and where his hand is at. "Me too?" he questions. Biting my bottom lip into my mouth to keep my thoughts inside, I give him a nod. "No hands?" His mind can't wrap around what I'm suggesting.

And really, I'm not sure exactly how this will work. I just know I want to start with his dick inside me, not his fingers. And in my usual fashion, rather than tell him this, I use a different tactic. One I hope will work in my favor today.

"You don't have to tie them up," I begin, "but only use them if you can't hold back."

My challenge issued, he scratches his head, trying to come up with a way to meet my crazy demands. He assesses the situation for a minute or two, driving me even more insane. Now that he's not doing anything to me, I crave him more. And wonder if I made a mistake in my proposal.

I shouldn't doubt the man.

Resourceful as ever, he climbs up onto the couch. When we got a new one a while back, we went with one with a deeper cushion, giving us more space. Not that he needs it right now as he hovers over me, his arms settling down near my shoulders, holding up the entire weight of his body.

Since my thighs were already pretty wide, one hanging off, he aligns the head of his cock—without the use of his hands—at my entrance. A warning lacking, he pushes inside, and again, I'm thankful for the extra lubrication my body provides. A fact he no doubt noticed on his perusal earlier.

My eyes close upon his intrusion, my teeth biting down on my bottom lip.

"Fuck, Caleb. Why does it feel so much better tonight?" My voice is already panty.

"It does, doesn't it?" His question bounces around the otherwise quiet room. The sounds of our breathing adding the only other noise.

Without another word, he pushes in, pulls out, setting the rhythm to our lovemaking. My arms writhe above me, my hands itching to break free, but I'll keep them tied up, giving him the only thing he's asked for.

With each thrust, my hips rise to meet his, the slapping of our bodies joining in on the soundtrack, warring to take control of the song.

My mind stays on the couch, and even though I can't see him through my closed eyes, I imagine the way Caleb's jaw tightens as he climbs closer to release, right along with me.

It's been a while since I've let myself focus on just Caleb and me, relish our coming together as man and woman, without any other context. I find it freeing, so much so, I feel the minute my breath catches, the start of my orgasm unlocking, emotions flooding my abdomen and my heart.

My eyes shoot open, not wanting him to miss my reaction.

"Thank you, Caleb," I cry as I topple over the edge, the muscles in my legs tightening as I free fall toward ecstasy.

He doesn't let up, not having found his release yet, continuing to pound into me, his pace steady, not in a race to compete with me, just needing to eventually finish.

Locking his eyes with mine, he holds my gaze, the faintest smile ghosting his lips. He pulls out slowly, and one last time, he shoves back in, grunting as he empties inside me.

True to his word, his hands never once touched me. Not my breasts, not my face, not my clit. As I come down from the high, I take stock of how the fact makes me feel.

Sated.

This time, I didn't miss his hands nor having the ability to touch him. Next time, my mind might change.

Pulling out, he shimmies me over, taking full advantage of the extra space to cuddle me beside him for a few moments to catch our breath. Slipping the loose tie off my hands, I meld into him, needing the extra closeness even after sex.

After a little while of snuggling, Caleb practically carries me up the stairs to our room, seeing as how I'm spent from the first round of orgasms. He whispers promises of more after the movie, if I'm up for it. Thing is, I am, but I'm also not. Because as much as I'd like him to get me off, maybe use his tongue this time, I could really use the uninterrupted sleep. Especially after a late-night movie. Decisions, decisions. Maybe I'll let Haley stay at Kate's a little longer in the a.m.

"As much as I want to get you all clean in the shower, in the spirit of saving time, I think we should shower separately."

"But then, we'd actually be wasting more time. If we shower

together, it will be one shower; separately, it's two, ergo, more time." I try to reason with him; secretly, I love when we shower together without the sex. "It's been so long since we hopped in together. What do you say, for old times' sakes?" I appeal to nostalgia, just like with sex on the couch. And once again, with a deep sigh, Caleb relents and gives in.

"No shenanigans, Storm. None. Not a one," he advises, a serious expression taking hold of his features.

"Sir, yes, sir."

I salute him, making sure he knows I mean business. I'll play by his rules for the short time we are in the shower. And I stick to my word, equating to us just getting washed before we get dressed and ready for dinner and the movie.

On the way to dinner, I send a quick text to Kate for an update. As I figured she'd be, Haley's fine, enjoying the time with her cousins, not really missing me. I find I'm really okay with this news, happy she's happy, cherishing the alone time I have with Caleb, the most time we've had together since she entered this world.

Over dinner at Trephines, conversation centers around our jobs. It's not that we don't talk about the daily, but it's the usual "work was good" or "can you believe this happened today?" Being able to sit, uninterrupted, and discuss work is something we don't get to do often. It's refreshing.

While I was pregnant with Haley, we talked a lot about when I would return to work, and in what capacity. I'm only back to part-time, but I kinda love it. For me, it's the best of both worlds: being with adults part of the day and spending the rest of the day with Haley. She only has to go to day care for half the day, but it's perfect for her socialization skills. At some point, I may return full-time, but for now, since Caleb assures me a full-time income isn't necessary, I'll keep the status quo. When there are more kids, I know we will reassess.

"Hey, babe? What time of year do you want to get married?" Caleb's not so smooth segue into the "wedding" debacle.

"Sometime warm, by the beach, in Maine," I reply, my answer at the ready since I knew he'd ask sooner rather than later. "Preferably when Haley can walk herself down the aisle."

"So, April, May, June?"

"Not April since that's Gray and Ainsley's month and May is Haley's. June could work, although that's kind of soon for this year."

I swear, sometimes Ainsley and I are so much alike, not wanting to make these decisions regarding our wedding. For different reasons, of course.

"June next year is kinda far off," he admits, "but if that's what you want, we'll do it."

I beam at him. He's itching to get us married sooner rather than later. I'm beyond grateful he'll agree to wait another year so I can have the wedding the time of year I want it. This way, it gives us more than enough time to get to a place where I'm totally on board with marrying him.

As much fun as being as the "midnight" showing is, Caleb and I both agree we've had enough and leave halfway through. It's not like we haven't seen it before and don't own at least one copy somewhere.

Tucked into bed next to Caleb, the darkness surrounding us, he whispers, "I'm proud of you, Storm. Just want you to know. Haley's lucky to have you for a mom."

His words bring moisture to my eyes, because yeah. I'm proud of myself too, and it's taken me a lot to admit to myself this very truth. I'll never be a perfect mother or wife, once I finally earn that title, but every day I come a little closer to perfection than the day before. I know I will continuously mess up, but one thing I can say with one hundred percent certainty is Haley will grow up knowing the unconditional love of two parents, and I hope she never once has to question our love for her. If I accomplish that, I've done my job as a mother.

As for my relationship with Caleb, I know it won't ever hit the breaking point, the point of no return, mostly because he won't let it. He won't let me give up on me, and neither will he. With him by my side, I'll always know I am enough, just the way I am.

And it's this fact that has me curling up closer to him, cradling myself into his strong arms, knowing he'll protect not only me, but our daughter as well.

We'll always be *his* enough.

EPILOGUE
CALEB

*I*t was supposed to be our month to get married, but there's yet another obstacle in my path of making Natalie my wife: my son. We weren't trying, at least not actively; Nat still had an IUD for goodness' sake. Apparently, someone else had other plans for us. Nothing was stopping this kid from choosing us to be his parents.

Nat's due any day now. She's quite miserable, chasing after a toddler all day, working a few hours part-time on one last marketing campaign, not to mention the diabetes this pregnancy brought with it. She's handled every step like a rock star; from finding out to being diagnosed with diabetes to even finding out it was a boy—he needed us to know, despite every safeguard we took to ensure we wouldn't find out. There was no mistaking his penis on the ultrasound. It took about five minutes for Nat, the ultrasound tech and me to calm down from the fit of giggles that ensued.

Since we found out, Nat's been a little better prepared, setting up his nursery a little more masculine than we did for Haley's. He already has an entire wardrobe of clothes, hand-me-downs from Bella's and Ainsley's kids. The only thing he needs is a name.

Nat and I can't agree on any name we like, not a one. Whatever I say, she's quick to turn her nose up at, and vice versa. We've already decided Caleb's out, but she's willing to use it as his middle name, as long as we can come up with a first name that goes with it. I've started throwing names at her I can't stand, just to rile her up, make her see reason. She doesn't find it humorous.

Haley comes barreling into the living room, throwing herself at my legs to stop her movements.

"Dadda, me uppy."

I waste no time obliging her, something I've found works against me almost every day. At just over two, she's not only got me wrapped around her finger, but I cannot say no to her. The girl is spoiled rotten, and in a few days, it will be exacerbated with the birth of her brother. It's the running joke in our house as much as our son has made his presence known from day one, he's got a rude awakening coming.

"Where's Mamma?" I question her, knowing Nat won't be too far behind her, just slow as molasses.

When she finally waddles in, her hand on her lower back, her abdomen protruding and swollen with life, I soak in the essence of my fiancée. She's swollen everywhere; her engagement ring had to come off around month five because her fingers were so big. She has informed me that we are not getting married until she can slip it back on without any type of struggle. I'd argue with her, but I learned to keep my mouth shut a long time ago. Well, about nine months ago when she yelled for two days about knocking her up. Again. Without any regard for if she was ready or not, which she was *not* ready for. Except deep down, there was no question she wasn't ready. She just likes to give me a hard time.

She's also made it abundantly clear I was not to leave the city starting two weeks before her due date. In her words, "I will not labor without you this time, wondering where the hell you are." It isn't an issue for me, since I don't plan to put her in that situation again.

"I'm quitting my job. I'm over this working shit." Nat awkwardly throws her body down, collapsing into the recliner. It takes her a minute or two to settle in, get as comfortable as she can, which involves heavy breathing and lots of shifting around. I stifle my laughter but can't help the smile that appears on my face. Talking directly to her abdomen, she says, "Little dude, please come sooner rather than later. Tonight, even. Tonight would be perfect."

"Don't you have a presentation on Friday?" I remind her, tickling my daughter, eliciting a bout of giggles from my mini-me.

Natalie huffs, exhaling on a huge sigh. "If you want to be technical about it, yes. But something has to give and since I can't quit being pregnant, being in labor, fighting contractions, giving birth seems to be a better option. At least that's temporary."

So glad she sees bringing our son into the world as the better option here. I'd be a little worried if she chose her job. The one she loved yesterday and apparently hates today. I'll give her a pass, but won't let her quit until after the baby's born. Just in case.

"Dinner?" I ask, hopeful she has a suggestion because I'm out of ideas.

"Barrett," she answers.

"Not a f-ing chance. Good try though."

Exasperated again, this time with me, she lies back, appearing to become one with the recliner. "This poor kid is never going to have a name. Why can't we just do the whole 'Junior' thing?"

That earns a cackle from me. "No. We already have a 'Junior' in our lives. And I don't think Ainsley and Grayson would take too kindly to that." And Nat would be pissed if one of our friends named their kid the same as one of ours. "Besides, we already vetoed Caleb as a first name."

"I hate when you are the voice of reason." Her playful tone doesn't quite match her words. "I think we should wait to meet him and then decide."

"Fine. Back to dinner."

"Pizza. With black olives and onions." Letting out a large burp, she adds, "No onions. Just olives."

"Sounds good, Storm."

Depositing Haley onto the ground and putting on a movie for her, I order the food and then go pick it up, assuring Natalie I'll be back in ten minutes and ordering my son not to get anything started while I'm gone.

* * *

*A*fter a dinner of pizza, of which Natalie eats exactly one slice, removing all the olives because they are "upsetting her stomach," I bathe Haley. As I'm brushing her hair, I ask her, "Are you ready to meet your brother soon?"

"No."

I laugh at the truth of the statement. Her two-year-old mind can't process what's changing for her, that soon she'll have a sibling, even though we've tried to explain it to her. We aren't exactly sure what she thinks is going to happen when Natalie gives birth, but I guess we will have to cross that bridge when we get to it. For now, I'll allow her to live in her only child bubble before her world gets turned upside down.

Nat's lying down in our room, so I bring Haley in to say goodnight. She's got her eyes closed, a pained grimace sitting tightly on her features.

"Storm, you okay?"

With Natalie, it could be anything, but seeing as how we are this close to her giving birth, it most likely relates to that.

"I think you should ask your parents to come stay the night. Just in case," comes her reply, her expression tightening.

I dart into action, instructing Haley to keep Mamma company while I call my parents and pack the last-minute additions to our hospital bag. In less than the five minutes it takes me to make the call and pack the bag, Natalie manages to sit up in the bed, fully awake and alert, her hands rubbing her abdomen.

Not to scare Haley, I grab her from our bed, depositing her in the crib.

"Mamma will be in a bit to say goodnight. I love you, baby girl."

Fortunately, the girl's exhausted and settles right down, her eyes closing instantly. She won't know if Nat doesn't come in to say goodnight, but that won't stop Nat from actually doing it. Especially if tonight is the night.

Back in my room, I focus on Natalie, watching for any clues, winces, telltale signs she's in pain or labor.

"My parents are on their way. What can I do for you?"

She's hunched over the side of the bed, so I kneel below. When she picks up her head, her eyes glisten with tears. "I really just want Craig," she moans.

My adrenaline running higher than usual, it takes me a while for her request to process. "Nice try. No."

"Andrew?"

"Nope."

"Mike? Stephen? Tyler?" Each name she spits out, her optimism grows, hoping I'll give in to her this one time.

"Oh, I like Stephen Tyler. He'll be a big star for sure. Let's go with that one."

She's on to me, shaking her head before I've finished speaking. "Funny one, BG."

"Hey, it was your idea." I help settle her back onto the bed, propped up on a bunch of pillows. "What do you need for real? That has nothing to do with names."

"A seltzer. The black cherry one. Not the regular cherry one. In a cup with three ice cubes." Her eyes have closed again, but she smiles at me.

"Be right back."

I make quick work of getting her drink to her specifics. Before I can head back upstairs, I hear the front door open.

"Hey, we're here," my mother calls out from the living room.

She makes her way to the kitchen, demanding a hug as soon as she enters. "Baby coming soon?"

"So Natalie thinks. Maybe. She just said it would be good for you to be here just in case. Spare bedroom is all made up for you guys. Haley's already asleep. Now we wait."

And wait we do. Nothing happens that night. Or the next day nor the one following that. Natalie makes her presentation at work on Friday, then tells her boss she's done for a while. She doesn't outright quit, listening to my words of wisdom, but she tells him she won't be back for a while.

My parents decide to just stay, which I thought for sure would send Nat into labor, if only to get away from them for a bit, but our son has other plans.

Finally, early Sunday morning, Natalie wakes up in pain. Pain from contractions.

Another waiting game begins—this time the countdown to when we can go to the hospital.

Unlike with Haley, Natalie's contractions come on faster and stronger, and within an hour of their onset, we are off to the hospital. The whole ride to the hospital is a blur, Natalie screaming, alternating between obscenities and names for our son. I don't know which is worse.

Upon arrival, we are set up in a birthing suite, and within ten minutes, she's in a gown, hooked up to a monitor, and begging for an epidural. She's already at six centimeters, and the doctors warn her the epidural might stall the labor. She looks to me, as if I have some kind of power to decide for her.

"Storm, do what you need to do," I advise her, already knowing she's going to take the meds. She nods once, then asks for the epidural, right before another contraction hits.

"Thatcher," she grits out, trying to breathe through the pain.

As I rub her back, I politely decline her. "Not the 1950s, babe."

She mumbles some more obscenities under her breath, directed at me, no doubt.

While we wait for the epidural, Natalie's a mess, the pain not letting up. She has yet to make any real progress because her body's so worked up and stressed. Nothing I say or do seems to be helping, including shooting daggers at any medical professional who walks in the door.

Her forehead's covered in sweat, her water broke about twenty minutes after we got into the room, and she hasn't stopped crying. Trying to keep myself calm is a major problem, and if I could trade places with her, or take even half of her pain away, I would. Since that's not possible, I've rubbed every part of her body she'll let me touch, hoping it brings an ounce of relief.

An hour of pure hell later, the anesthesiologist finally makes his appearance. He takes one look at Natalie, apologizes profusely for the tardiness, and sets to work. The relief isn't instant, but I know when the meds kick in by the way her face softens along the edges, the mask of pure pain slowly fading away.

Ten minutes later, she's asleep. I take a few moments to breathe, not having sent enough oxygen to my lungs while she was miserable. The nurse encourages me to sleep, but I'm too hyped up on adrenaline and worry to even attempt it. So, I sit around and wait for Nat to wake up, checking on Haley and sending a few other texts letting our friends know the baby's coming today.

AINSLEY

Ah, sweet. Junior can't wait to meet his new buddy.

KATE

Good luck to Natalie. Love you guys! Can't wait to hear the news.

GRAYSON

Rest up!

I smile at that one. *As if.*

"BG," I hear whispered from Natalie's bed. Giving her my full attention, she's awake and calm, the effects the combination of the epidural and the nap. "Jared."

I don't know if it's the way she smiles when she says it, or because I'll give her anything after the hell she went through, but I return her smile.

"Yes. Definitely, yes."

"Okay." She winces slightly, breathing through the small amount of pain the contraction brings. "He's coming now."

I leap out of my chair, expecting more of a reaction than her shifting in her bed, settling herself into a more comfortable position. I push the button for the nurse. While we wait, I feather kisses on Nat's forehead and cheeks, cherishing her for going through this pain for our kids.

"I love you, Natalie. As soon as we can, I'm going to finally make your last name match the one our children and I share."

Prepared for her reaction, I anticipate the worst. Instead, she surprises me. "I'm gonna hold you to that, BG. But right now, let's meet our son." Her eyes open, tears pooling at the corners, the love she has for me, for our son, shining through.

"Yeah, let's do that," I agree just as the doctor and nurse come barreling in.

* * *

*J*ared's actual birth is mostly a haze. Two hours of pushing, talk of a vacuum birth, an emergency C-section, as well as forceps are all tossed out as Natalie struggles. Doctors forewarned us that he'd most likely be big, bigger than Haley, and this time, he proved them correct. But my girl is determined to do this naturally, despite her exhaustion. Since no one's in any danger, the doctor lets her continue. Until she gives that final push, the one that pushes his head out, giving her a burst of energy to continue when they allow her to.

His cries fill the small room, and once it hits my ears, I breathe a little easier knowing that the hard part is done. Physically, at least. I have no reason to believe that Jared's going to go easy on us.

"Nine pounds on the dot," the nurse excitedly exclaims. "Well done, Mom."

Tears stream down Nat's cheeks, some from pure exertion, others from pure joy. After the cord is cut, and Jared's "cleaned" up, the nurse places him in her arms. I snap a picture for me, the first mother-son bonding moment I know she'll want for herself, even though she won't want to share it with anyone.

Cuddling him close, whispering words into his ears, she turns to me. "He's got your eyes and nose." Dragging her finger along his cheeks, she looks to our son then back at me. "Caleb Washington, I swear to god if you get me pregnant again before this kid turns two, you will not want to see what kind of havoc this Storm can make."

A loud chortle rumbles out of me, the sound echoing around the room. "Message received loud and clear. Besides, two is kind of a nice number anyway, and we've got one of each."

"Ah, we'll see. Let's take some time to get used to two, have a wedding, take a honeymoon. No rash decisions should be made in the delivery room."

"I love you, Natalie Pressman."

"Don't make me cry."

"Too late, Storm."

We have a lot to get used to, we'll be overwhelmed with two, but as Natalie snuggles our newborn son into her, there's not a doubt in my mind she isn't overcome with love for him. Even if he was unplanned, just like his sister, sometimes the things in life we don't plan for our life's biggest blessings. For me, I've got three now.

I never "planned" for Natalie, but my life would be devastatingly dull and thoroughly incomplete without her.

And hey, I've always loved a good storm.

* * *

*C*urious about when Caleb and Natalie first met? A bonus scene can be found here.

Continue reading for a peek at Grayson and Ainsley's story, *Defining Us.*

DEFINING US

I was never a girl who believed in love. And love at first sight? Surely that didn't truly exist. So imagine my surprise when, after one kiss from Grayson Abbott, I asked him to marry me! I was kidding of course, but there was something special about the guy that even I couldn't deny.

Our connection was instant; he felt it, too. The only problem was he didn't know the secret of my past that I buried years ago. The closer we became, the further down I buried that secret.

I know he deserves my truth, but when I finally come clean, will there still be an "us"?

Defining Us is Ainsley and Grayson's story.

AUTHOR'S NOTE

If you've made it this far, THANK YOU from the bottom of my heart. I'm always amazed when people choose to read the books I've written. It's sometimes still hard to believe I've got nine books under my belt, with so many more to come. I hope you'll stick around for what's in store for 2020!

Out of all my books, *The Breaking Point* is a true labor of love, no pun intended. I started writing it back in 2017, shortly after finishing *Defining Us*, knowing there was more to Natalie's story than she let us "see." However, I didn't quite foresee how troubled she was until I started writing her and Caleb's story. And boy does she have her issues!

From the very beginning, it's always been very much *her* book. I heard Caleb's voice in my head, but his was just much quieter. As you well know, he's got this way about him, a man of a few words, protective of those he loves—aka Natalie. I questioned his actions at many points: why would he stay after *all* she put him through? And every time I came back to the same conclusion: because he LOVES her. He never wanted her to be alone, and it's my hope his unconditional love for Natalie shines through.

I struggled to write this book. A lot. There's a part of me that, like Caleb, is protective of Natalie, fearful of what people are going to think about her. That part wants to protect her, keep her to myself and my beta readers. However, just like every other story I've written, hers deserves to be told, to be out in the world.

Another reason I struggled is because Nat and Caleb's story deviates from my "normal" type of book. I pushed myself out of my comfort zone with this one. Their book is full of a type of angst I'm not used to writing. Natalie is a strong character, who may be hard to like at times, but like everyone, we are shaped by our experiences, and she's no different. And I know there are women out there who will relate to her, at least on some level.

As I debated how to make Nat more "likable" from the beginning, a friend said something that really resonated with me: *It's like characters in a movie you don't like. In the end, it's the actor who portrayed the character so well to be unlikable. Same goes for your writing.* The more I thought about it, the more I realized she was right. But honestly, not everyone has to "like" everything about everyone; it's what makes us unique. And when it came down to it, this is *her* story: the good, the bad, and the behavior that comes along with it.

Denise, your notes, thoughts, and comments are invaluable, as always. And your additions to the playlist were spot on! I am so proud to have finished the draft way before the imposed deadline. Of course, it still took several months to edit, revise, and edit again. Seriously, the duet and the author event this summer did me in, and we both needed a break after those! And it still may not be "perfect," but perfection is highly overrated. Here's your "thank you to my editor" comment. Every day, I'm so thankful to have you in my corner supporting and encouraging me, making me evaluate my own writing so it can be that much better.

Krista, where to even begin? Thank you for talking me down off the ledge I had climbed on, ready to toss most of the story out the window. Thank you for your suggestions for teasers. Most importantly, thank you for understanding Nat and the "you've made her perfectly flawed" comment. Because that day, I needed to hear it. I really appreciate every share, every shout-out, every *everything* you do to help more people know about my books. Can't wait for your thoughts on the "baseball" story!

Missy, thank you for carving time out of your busy schedule to read Nat and Caleb's story. I'm so glad you loved it, even though Natalie isn't one of your favorite characters I've written. Lee Brice says it best: she's "hard to love." Hopefully you know this song, but if not, please make sure you look it up and give it a listen.

Jen and Tanya, thanks for your unwavering support for all things author-related. More importantly, thanks for your real-life friendship. I love our text thread, even if messages get lost and misconstrued because "apple and androids don't play nice." Can't wait for our next Chick-fil-A lunch. Next time, we'll make sure to confirm the location, ha!

Kelly, thanks for your support at the author event. Hopefully you'll join me again for another one. And if not, we can at least plan another day in the city!

Megan, for the gorgeous new cover! It's so fitting for Natalie and Caleb. I love the logo for the series name. I adore working with you, seeing what magic you come up with for each new book. Thanks for making it such a nice working relationship. I can't wait to see what you create for future characters.

ARC readers and bloggers, thank you for taking a chance on this book. I know how many great books are available to read and how valuable your time is. I hope you've enjoyed Nat and Caleb's story.

Members of Taylor Delong's Tribe, thank you for being on this journey with me. Whether you've been here from the start, way before there even was a tribe, or are new, having a group of people I can share/vent/talk "shop" with every day warms my heart.

Author friends, thanks for the camaraderie. There are too many people to list, and rather than leave anyone out, I'll just say a blanket thank you to anyone and everyone I've had the pleasure of interacting with lately. How's that for vagueness? But for real, it's so great to have a community of such awesome people to "work" with.

Mom and Dad, thanks for encouraging my love of reading and writing. I wouldn't be where I am, publishing my ninth book, without your never-ending support. I love you.

Lastly, **E and A**, as you get a little older, I love being able to discuss certain aspects of my writing with you, those that are "G and PG" rated, of course. Funny things characters say, choosing character names, tidbits of what my characters do, those kinds of things. E, I love how we've become "sprinting" partners on occasion. Every time I see you working on your own story, I smile. A, you've got quite the author's voice too. I can't wait to see what both of you have in store as you develop your own voices as writers. I love you, more than you will ever know.

ABOUT THE AUTHOR

Taylor Delong writes small-town, contemporary romances full of heart and heat. Her cinnamon roll heroes protect the ones they love and will leave you swooning. She has been reading and writing for as long as she can remember. It's always been her dream to be a published author. She spends her days chasing after toddlers and her nights scribbling down stories and ideas the characters in her head dictate to her. She lives in CT with her two children.

Check out her website for more.

SCAN ME

Printed in Great Britain
by Amazon